I0633328

The Pirate Who Loved Me

Anthony Fox

chipmunkapublishing
the mental health publisher

Published by
Chipmunkapublishing
United Kingdom

http://www.chipmunkapublishing.com

ISBN   978-1-78382-556-1

Also by this author: Anthony Fox

Author of How to Pass a Degree with Confidence

It's Never Too Late

A Space Time Apocalypse

Babylon: The Gateway to the Gods

Artist on: Fine Art America Visit My Gallery Here

I thank family and friends for their encouragement during this project.

Anthony Fox

Chapter 1

The year was 1667 and the previous year England had just suffered from the great fire of London. And England was also at war with Holland. England was a successful seafaring nation at this time, and so was Holland. It was a war between two great nations over the riches of the colonies and the trade routes that they controlled. At the same time, pirates were the scourge of the seas around the world.

***

A young boy called Nathaniel had just finished his early morning chores on the farm where he helps his parents. He had decided to walk the short distance into the nearby village. He was hoping to see some of his friends from school who lived in the local village of Trethowan on the southern coast of Cornwall, England. The village of Trethowan was named after Lord Trethowan. He first made the village a port for shipping, which traded in the export of tin ore. It once was one of the busiest ports for the export of tin ingots to places as far afield as the Middle East.

Nathaniel Curnow was born in April, 1652 in the parish of Truro, to loving parents who had prayed for a son to eventually help them run the farm of beef and dairy cattle. Nathaniel, by the age of fifteen had taken over most of the chores on the farm from his father. In the mornings, he would milk the cows, and in the afternoons he would feed the cattle. Nathaniel, who was called 'Nat' by his friends and family liked to listen to the sailors' tales whenever he could find the time to wander down to the village. He would sit outside the local Inn where the sailors would meet to drink ale and tell their tales. With his blond hair, blue eyes and a pinkish complexion, he had the typical features of the local Cornish people. He enjoyed listening to the sailors' yarns from the ships that visited the port and hoped that one day he would visit some of the distant places the sailors had talked about.

The village of Trethowan had seen better times early in the seventeenth century when tin ore was mined locally and smelted into ingots and then exported all around the world. At the time, the port of Trethowan was said to have been busier, at times, than the port of Bideford. In the seventeenth century Bideford was a major port in England on the northern coast in the county of Devon, and it was only a three day ride on a fast horse from Trethowan to Bideford.

On top of the cliff looking down into the bay, Nathaniel saw a ship approaching the port. It had been several weeks since the last ship had sailed from Trethowan loaded with tin ingots, Nathaniel had remembered. Nathaniel had watched as the sailors had loaded the tin ingots onto their ship. Where that ship was bound for, Nathaniel did not know.

When Nathaniel followed the edges of the cliff and around the headland down into the village he heard the familiar sounds of loose chickens squawking, and the odd shout of a villager calling for their son or daughter. Everything sounded and appeared normal to Nathaniel, and it was every Saturday at midday when many people would be preparing for the market in the village square that afternoon. In the manor house overlooking the port was the stately home of Lord Trethowan, who owned much of the land around the port. He was busy thinking, while watching the approaching ship through his telescope. It was rumored that Lord Trethowan's ancestors had been smugglers, and had made a fortune smuggling tobacco and other goods along the shores of Cornwall. Today, Lord Trethowan's family was on the right side of the law as he studiously recorded the details and the cargo of every ship that docked at the port for the Crown. He wondered where the ship had sailed from as he leaned against the lector supporting his large fatty torso. On behalf of the king it was his duty to collect any taxes due to the Crown.

Lord Trethowan peered through his telescope at the colors the ship was showing. Recognizing the ship was flying a Portuguese flag and was probably a cargo vessel, and that it posed no threat, he decided he would send his deputy Captain John Flynn to record the details of the ship.

"It's flying a Portuguese flag," Lord Trethowan said.

"Perhaps, it just wants fresh supplies," Lord Trethowan's deputy remarked.

"Maybe, all the same…go down there and record the details. I will follow you later," Lord Trethowan said.

Captain John Flynn had been Lord Trethowan's deputy since retiring from the royal navy early in his career due to ill health caused by malaria. He now managed Lord Trethowan's tin mining, farming and tax collection interests and had become an integral part of the business.

***

As Lord Trethowan's deputy and a couple of farm hands made their way down the only track from the manor house to the village they observed how quiet the day appeared. The squawking of seagulls in the distance was the only discernible sounds the three men heard as they approached the village.

"That's unusual today... its market day," one of the farmers said.

"Quiet!" the deputy demanded.

"Quick! Hide here. Did you see those men waving their cutlasses?" The cutlass was a favorite type of sword at the time used by pirates and sailors and was deadly when used correctly with its double edged cutting surface and its long thin blade able to slice through flesh with ease. From behind a small wall the three men could see men rounding up the men and women of the village like sheep being herded together into flocks.

"Who are they?"

"Pirates," the deputy replied softly, as all three men crouched behind a low wall.

From one cottage to the next the pirates spared no one as they gathered the villagers together beside the wall of the port. Some children cried for their mothers in the confusion. A look of panic and fear gripped the faces of the village folk the like he had only seen before at war, the deputy thought. He could see several bodies lying on the ground and watched as another man tried to escape, but the man escaping was immediately surrounded and killed with one thrust of a pirate's cutlass. What to do, he said to himself?"

"Who are they?" again the farm laborer quietly asked.

"Pirates," the deputy repeated.

"From where?" the farm hand asked.

All three men then felt the cold blade of iron touch their necks. "Raise your hands and get up!" the pirate demanded.

The three men turned around to see a group of pirates that had now surrounded their position. The three men saw there was no place to run to.

"Take them away and group them with the others," the pirate leader ordered. The deputy saw the fear on the faces of the village folk as he watched the commotion.

The pirate leader took a fishbone whistle from his pantaloons' pocket and began blowing it. The sound of the whistle was a signal for the pirates to get on board their vessel. Within minutes, the ship had loaded its captives and raised its anchor, and was on its way to the next port.

Below the lowest gun deck on the bottom of the ship housed like caged animals were the people captured from the village. They were caged by bamboo bars that formed a prison like cell. Nathaniel noticed, among the crowd in the cells the deputy from Lord Trethowan's office.

"What are you doing here?" Nathaniel asked in a worried tone of voice to see that Lord Trethowan's deputy among the captives.

"I got caught with two of my farm hands just outside the village," the deputy replied.

"And you?"

"I walked straight in to a melee near the Inn," Nathaniel countered.

Nathaniel explained to the deputy that he had heard shouts and screams, and then saw men with their cutlass and blunderbuss ready to use on the villagers. Nathaniel described how the pirates rounded up the villagers and had killed some that had tried to escape.

"It looks like they have everyone from the village."

"Yes, they don't want anyone to know the truth," the deputy remarked.

"Deputy, do you know where we're going?" Nathaniel asked tersely.

"No. My name is John…and you?" the deputy asked, and he had decided not to reveal his real name to the boy for now.

"My name is Nathaniel, but most call me Nat."

"They were flying the colors of the Portuguese flag," John the deputy continued, "but, I don't know where we're going."

***

Meanwhile, Lord Trethowan had decided to ride into the village accompanied by a servant on their horses. It took several minutes, before Lord Trethowan noticed how quiet the village appeared. He could see in the distance a silhouette of a ship sailing away from the port, and realized it must be the Portuguese ship from earlier. Lord Trethowan instructed his servant to dismount and start looking for his deputy.

"Start at the Inn!" Lord Trethowan shouted at the servant, with a scowl across his face as he circled astride his horse looking for life in the village.

***

"There is no one…I have found no one," the servant said grimly, and was dejected by his efforts, and was now looking up to

Lord Trethowan sat on his horse with an authority like a general commanding his forces from the saddle.

"Where is everyone?" Lord Trethowan asked out loud to himself.

Lord Trethowan at first could not contemplate the horror of what may have happened to the village folk and his deputy, who he relied on to collect taxes for the Crown and to run his farming estate and much more.

"There is no one here, sir. I have looked everywhere," the servant said abruptly.

"We must ride to the Crown office," Lord Trethowan said with urgency in his tone of voice.

As Lord Trethowan and his servant rode out of the village and on towards the Crown office they came upon the local blacksmith. He had been hiding in a field behind the blacksmith's workshop when he saw the pirates. And he was glad to see Lord Trethowan.

"Are you alright, Tom?" Lord Trethowan asked.

"Yes, I was lucky they didn't find me," Tom Smith replied.

"They were pirates," Tom Smith said with a look of horror written across his blackened face from working in the smithy that morning.

"Did you see the pirates?" Lord Trethowan asked.

"Yes, they were pirates and I saw them use the sword on a few of our folk. There were many pirates with swords and blunderbuss at the ready. Everyone was frightened, sir."

"Did you hear what language they spoke?" Lord Trethowan asked intensely.

"Some spoke a few words in English, but I think also Spanish," the blacksmith responded.

"But, you're not sure?"

"Yes, that's correct, sir."

"It was flying the colors of a Portuguese flag," Lord Trethowan said. Continuing he added, "We'll ride to the Crown office and inform them of what has happened."

***

It took several hours, before Lord Trethowan and his servant arrived at the Crown office in Truro. The news of what had happened at the village had already started to form rumors amongst the townsfolk from a travelling merchant. The merchant had witnessed from a hilltop overlooking the village the roundup of the villagers. The merchant had then made haste on his horse to Truro, the nearest Crown office.

"All the people of the village have been taken," Lord Trethowan said, at once, to the Crown official sat behind his desk overseeing the Crown's business with the authority bestowed on him by the king.

"Yes, we have heard the same. I have a rider ready to take a message to the admiralty and request help," the Crown officer said.

"The ship was flying the colors of the Portuguese flag," Lord Trethowan continued, with a worried tone of voice, "but these men were pirates. So, I'm not sure where these pirates came from. The ship looked like it was Spanish galleon."

"Do you know the name of the ship?" the Crown officer asked curtly.

"No, I didn't get a chance to get those details. I saw the ship from a distance. It looked like a Spanish galleon. They have taken everyone from the village Trethowan and also three of my men," Lord Trethowan replied abruptly.

***

It was several days, before the rider sent by the Crown office at Truro arrived with the message from Lord Trethowan at the admiralty headquarters in Portsmouth. The rider had ridden non-stop with a change of horse at several stages along the journey before reaching Portsmouth on the south coast of England.

The Lord Admiral of the navy read the message delivered by the rider and became enraged at the news. He quickly formulated a plan in his mind, and discussed its merits with his colleagues. Present in the office of the Lord Admiral was his trusted Lieutenant Gillard standing to attention awaiting orders, and two of his senior admirals, Rear Admiral Adams and Rear Admiral Chubb.

"It's happened again…a whole village has been taken off the coast of Cornwall. A village called Trethowan. Not far from Truro. This has to stop…our people are under attack," the Lord Admiral said loudly to his admirals gathered around the chart table.

The admirals studied a large map of the world and placed a small wooden model of a ship to represent the pirate ship where they assumed its present position. They also placed a small model ship on the sea chart of the world to represent the Royal Navy

Frigate HMS Antelope known to be off the coast of Gibraltar awaiting orders.

"HMS Antelope is off the coast of Gibraltar. We need to send a message to HMS Antelope," the Lord Admiral said tersely.

"Do you think your plan will work?" Rear Admiral Adams asked intently. He had doubts about the plan the Lord Admiral had previously discussed moments before.

"Yes, it all depends on what the pirates do," the Lord Admiral replied with a commanding tone of voice. "We'll know more intelligence when HMS Antelope gets to the area."

"Who is the captain of the HMS Antelope?" Rear Admiral Adams asked keenly.

"He's an excellent sailor...Captain Horner," the Lord Admiral replied.

"Good, he should find them. I know the man well," Admiral Chubb interjected.

Lord Admiral read out the message to the HMS Antelope. "Message to H.M.S Antelope: Pursue and capture pirate ship known to resemble a Spanish galleon, its name unknown, and last seen flying the Portuguese flag."

"The whole village of Trethowan, Cornwall was taken prisoner assumed for slave trade. It's important to recover as many people as possible. Return intelligence. End message."

"Lieutenant, send this message to Gibraltar," the Lord Admiral said.

At this time, the royal navy used carrier pigeons to send and receive messages as a fast means of communication for their fleet of ships. The message for HMS Antelope would arrive at Gibraltar within several days in all weathers such was the speed and determination of the pigeons used. Each ship had its own pigeon, so the pigeon knew its home as Portsmouth, and would naturally return from whence it came from. Such was the simplicity of the system any ship could easily send messages from any part of the world.

"They will receive this message, within a week," the Lord Admiral said confidently.

"Yes, we should start receiving intelligence within a couple of weeks," Rear Admiral Adams reiterated.

"If I'm right, then we should find the pirates along the Barbary Coast," the Lord Admiral said.

"That's where the pirates usually operate from. The Barbary Coast is lawless and pirates over centuries have attacked mainland Europe including England many times. It's time we put a stop to this trade and protect our coastline. Otherwise, people will be afraid to live in coastal towns and villages because we failed to catch these bastards."

At this time, the Barbary Coast was lawless because the towns between Morocco and Tripoli were ruled by self-styled independent rulers. These rulers gained their wealth from conducting raids across the Mediterranean. These pirates and individual despots were loosely controlled by the Ottoman Empire. The pirates were often encouraged to raid and attack mainland Europe because the Ottoman Empire was often at war with Christian Europe. The Mughals who ran the Ottoman Empire were not militarily strong enough to wage war against Europe, but instead encouraged the pirates to wage war on their behalf.

***

On the second day of their captivity, Nathaniel and the other captives had water and food for the first time and waited to see what would happen to them on board the pirate ship. The pirate that brought the water and food spoke no English and revealed no clues for them.

"What do you think will happen to us?" Nathaniel asked curiously.

"Call me John Flynn," the deputy said.

"Yes, sir," Nathaniel replied curtly.

As they spoke, the ship had begun to violently roll from side to side and Nathaniel and the other captives could hear the waves crashing over the ship. The storm was gaining strength minute by minute. Nathaniel wondered if the ship was crossing the Bay of Biscay where the Atlantic meets the English Channel, and an area of the sea associated with storms that he had heard about from the sailors that frequented the port of Trethowan. Nathaniel wondered if the ship was heading for Spain or Portugal. He noticed many of the captives were sick from the motion of the ship as it rocked from side to side and up and down through the peaks and troughs of the waves. Most of the captives had never been to sea before and neither had Nathaniel who also felt sick like he wanted to die. Sitting on the floor of the cell, he remembered, some of the sailors' yarns he was told at the local Inn in the village. Sea sickness they said fated everyone at some point, but eventually the body gets used to the calm or violent motion of a ship, it just depends on the person, he said to himself, with the look of death written in the color of his face. His face had turned from its normal light pinkie color to almost green with every major motion of the ship as it navigated through the storm.

Nathaniel turned again to John. "You said the ship was flying a Portuguese flag?" Nathaniel asked intently, trying to keep his mind of how he felt. At that moment, he wanted to know more from the deputy. He felt sure the deputy knew more, he said to himself.

"Yes, that is true. But, they could have come from farther afield," John Flynn replied intently.

As John Flynn held fast to the prison bamboo bars, he noticed the ship was accumulating water at a faster rate. This wasn't unusual for a ship in a storm to have to pump water from the belly of the ship, he said to himself. But, he was worried.

"Look!" John Flynn shouted with urgency in his tone of voice, as he pointed to the water pouring into the ship.

In one area of the belly of the ship a wooden plank had busted and was now allowing the Atlantic Sea to gush in. The captives screamed and shouted to be heard as the ship swayed to one side then to the other. The pirates soon heard the noise and found the leak. They were able to shore up the hole with wood planks wedged against the leak and a supporting beam, which soon pacified the captives.

"You boy," said the pirate pointing at Nathaniel.

"Come with me," the pirate said as Nathaniel was let out of the cell.

Nathaniel followed the pirate up the steps onto the lower gun gallery and then some more steps up to the upper deck and some more steps onto the ship's quarter deck. Standing ready for action was the captain of the Rag-tail. The Rag-tail was a forty-two gun Spanish built galleon ship that was recently captured by the captain during a raid down the Barbary Coast. Captain Bartolomeu Português was a Portuguese pirate and buccaneer with a gait like a wrestler. He stood taller than most men with an upright gait on the quarter deck, as the leader of an assortment of thieves and cutthroats. The width of the captain's neck was larger than most men's thighs. He had a beard and moustache to match the jet black color of his long straggly hair that straddled his shoulders. Captain Kerry as he was known to his crew and his peers always carried two pistols loaded with shot and a cutlass sword ready for action. He wore leather boots with iron studs hammered into the soles, it was said that the captain liked to hear the sound of his feet as he walked on the decks, why no one knew.

Captain Kerry was a nickname he used to confuse his enemies, especially the English, which he hated because of the recent war between England and Portugal. The scar across the captain's face from his brow to his moustache was the most prominent feature on the pirate's face apart from his deep set brown eyes that beguiled most observers.

The pirate urged the boy up the quarter deck steps and threw Nathaniel down in front of the captain.

"This boy said he could cook," the pirate said cockily.

"We need a boy for the food galley. I want you to help our cook. If you try and escape then I'll have to kill one or two of your friends from the village. Do you understand?" Captain Kerry asked.

Nathaniel nodded his head and also replied, "Yes, I understand."

"Take him down to the cook," Captain Kerry ordered.

As Nathaniel was escorted down to the food galley, he took notice of the ship and its pirates. Nathaniel had seen many ships at the docks in Trethowan, but wasn't familiar with the design of this particular ship.

"This boy is to help you cook…captain's orders," the pirate said.

The cook looked at Nathaniel and laughed. "He's only a boy and thinner than a hangman's noose," the cook said, laughing. The cook had a grin like a Cheshire cat and chuckled at his own words.

"What's your name, boy?" the cook asked abruptly

"Nathaniel Curnow, but most people call me Nat."

"Good, short and sweet…," the cook said, "I'll call you Nat and you can call me Ali."

Ali was small in stature. Nathaniel noticed the cook had dark looking features; it reminded him of some of the sailors he had seen before at the village Inn back home.

"Where are you from?" Nathaniel asked curiously.

"Too many questions, you can sleep over there. And we cook over there by the fire," Ali in broken English replied.

Nathaniel noticed the fire was built off the galley deck surrounded by bricks encased in wood to protect the fire in bad weather. The cook had a few cooking pots and one large cooking pot that probably could hold enough food to feed the crew, he thought. Nathaniel noticed the food galley was at one end of the ship between the lower gun deck and the captain's quarters under the quarter deck, which Ali had told him never to enter without permission.

"Where is the ship heading for?" Nathaniel asked sheepishly.

"Too many questions, we start cooking, now!" Ali replied briskly.

Later, the first pirates sat down to eat, and Nathaniel kept an account in his head of the number of pirates on board the ship. Nathaniel noticed that many of the pirates spoke different languages, and many of these pirates were in small groups of two to five men speaking the same language. Nathaniel was eager to get this information to John Flynn.

Nathaniel also noticed some of the pirates spoke English. He tried to speak to these English pirates for information about his fate and the lives of the village folk held captive.

"Where're we going?" Nathaniel asked intently.

"You speak out of turn," a seated pirate replied, who had two scars across his face with a bandanna around his head holding back his silver colored hair.

"Yes, you have no business asking this question?" another pirate said, who had a large gold ring hung from one ear.

A voice from the group of pirates seated around the table came out of the blue like a wind that suddenly blows from a different direction. "Your fate is tied to the captain like a ship anchored to the sea…," the pirate continued, "unless you die, your fortune is linked like the tides are linked to the moon."

"Who are you, sir?" Nathaniel asked curiously.

"I have many names, but you can call me Morgan," the pirate replied, his face and most of his body was covered with strange tattoos the like of which Nathaniel had never seen before. Nathaniel noticed his tattoos were mainly of circles and straight lines. But it was his voice that was so remarkable, similar to how Lord Trethowan spoke, Nathaniel thought.

"Where are we going?" Nathaniel asked with a curious tone of voice, and hoped the pirate was willing to talk more.

"Too many questions, you should be thankful that you are not rotting away below deck, my boy," Morgan replied scornfully.

"Why should I be thankful of being held captive on this ship?"

"Listen! You have a choice and you know which one to take. Now, fetch me some more ale," Morgan replied abruptly, and cursed the boy to watch his manners.

***

After a week had passed, the Rag-tail was close to the Gibraltar straight and had passed the English threat because of the storm. The ship continued to roll heavily to the port side then the other before the seas started to abate off the Barbary Coast. Captain Kerry gave orders for the pirate ship to fly the colors of a pirate ship with the Jolly Rodger of a skeleton head and cross bones. Near the Barbary Coast, the Rag-tail docked at the port of Rabat, Morocco and took on provisions for their next voyage.

At the port, the pirates were unloading some of their captives to be sold into slavery at the local slave market. The slave trade was well established along the North African coast to the port of Tripoli under the flag of the Ottoman Empire, which stretched from Constantinople, Turkey to the rulers along the Barbary Coast to Morocco.

"Just take the old men and women," Morgan the pirate said.

The old men and women were taken from their cell and led up to the upper deck. At first, the captives were blinded by the sunlight their eyes had not seen the sun for many days. The noise of their chains jangling as the captives were led down the plank onto the dock unnerved some of the captives.

"Where are you taking us?" one of the female captives asked, and cried for some pity.

"You ask too many questions, but don't worry you are in good hands," the pirate replied, and was laughing at the captives' dilemma.

"Take these people to the market," Captain Kerry demanded as he observed the slaves to be sold.

"Right and what about supplies, boss?" Ironman Slim asked briskly while ordering his men to hurry up.

"You'll get supplies and here's the list, and I'll wait for your return. Remember, we're in a hurry, so make haste," Captain Kerry replied.

"Will do, boss," Ironman Slim agreed.

Ironman Slim had a huge gait like a bareknuckle fighter. He got the nickname 'Ironman Slim' from his days working in an iron making works in Manchester, England. He preferred to be called 'Slim' because he was getting older and didn't have the zest for fighting as he had when people called him 'Ironman' for his fights. He was still just as tough with his crew and had to occasionally bang some heads together to keep order on the ship. But most of the time, that chore was other pirates' responsibility.

While the Rag-tail took on supplies, Captain Kerry stood on the quarter deck awaiting the return of Ironman Slim. "Did you have any problems?" Captain Kerry asked eagerly as Ironman Slim climbed over the ship's railing onto upper deck.

"No, Narin said the slaves would be sold and payment held until your next visit," Ironman Slim replied.

"Yes, that's what I'd expected," Captain Kerry said, and continuing after giving orders to set sail to his bosun. "Yes, Slim that's why we're taking the other…younger captives to Yemen. Where we can get a lot more money for the slaves we've on board."

"Sounds, good to me, boss," Ironman Slim reiterated.

"And there's the money. That bastard Narin has always tried to duct me on past slave trades. But, he has the market along the Barbary Coast. He sells his slaves mostly to the Middle Eastern clients. The Arabs like to have white Europeans as slaves. I think it's because of the Crusades when they slaughtered the Muslims. So, now, they take their revenge by encouraging pirates to make attacks to grab white slaves for their market," Captain Kerry said dismissively.

As the Rag-tail set sail, and as the days and weeks passed, the ship hugged the coastline of Africa down towards the hazardous Cape. The Cape had always been a dangerous part of the sea to navigate, because the Cape was where two oceans meet with their competing currents. Especially, in bad weather the currents could drive a ship onto the rocks around the Cape without warning. For most sailors, the fear of the Cape was legendary.

"Steer, south by southwest," Captain Kerry said to Ironman Slim.

"Steer, south by southwest," Ironman Slim said restating the order to the bosun. Morgan the bosun had also been a bareknuckle fighter in his younger days, but now controlled the pirates from day to day with only the threat of violence. Rarely did Morgan have to resort to violence to restore order on the ship.

"We'll go around the Cape, and hope we're not being followed," Captain Kerry said.

"Do you think the English will come after us?" Ironman Slim asked pensively.

"Yes, it's possibly."

"But, we have many days ahead of them," Ironman Slim stated, and then was curious to know more. "How can they catch us?"

"A bird is faster than a ship. The royal navy use pigeons to receive messages from their ships to its headquarters in Portsmouth, and they have an outpost at Gibraltar. So, perhaps, our lead is not so," Captain Kerry replied.

***

The sights and sounds of the ship were a daily reminder of Nathaniel's captivity, even though he was free to some extent to move around the ship. Life for Nathaniel had become predictable, everyday feeding the pirates and cleaning their wooden plates and spoons used to eat. The smell of gunpowder and the sweat of men sleeping in their hammocks along the gun deck often lingered for days. Occasionally, Nathaniel saw a seagull and heard the familiar sounds of their squawking as they passed near the ship, and he assumed the ship was not far from land. He had tried to get a message to the captives held below the galley, but he was always constantly watched by the pirates.

"See that bucket of fruit, Nat...takes it down to your friends below," Ali the cook said reluctantly in his broken English and with a sharp tone of voice, which showed his disgust to Nathaniel in feeding the captives with the best food he had.

"Why're they getting this fruit?" Nathaniel asked, puzzled and why his friends below were suddenly being fed with extra rations, especially fruit which was often in short supply, he said to himself.

"You ask too many questions. Just do it!"

As Nathaniel made his way down the steps in to the belly of the ship, he could smell the stench of too many people crammed together like fish caught in a net, it overwhelmed his senses. The smell of sweat and feces soon reminded Nathaniel how lucky he was not to be locked up like some sort of wild animal, he mused.

"Here's some extra fruit from the cook," Nathaniel said.

"Do you have any information?" John Flynn asked instantly. He had now assumed the leadership of the remaining captives and was impatient for news.

"Yes, I think there're forty eight pirates on board the ship. And I've heard, but not sure, that we're heading for the Cape."

"Good, the more we know the better the chance of escaping," John Flynn said.

"Listen! Find out where they keep their weapons?" Flynn asked.

"Yes, I will."

***

Nathaniel climbed the steps onto the upper deck and heard the sound of panic amongst some of the pirates. It was a cacophony of different languages all shouting to be heard at the same time. Nathaniel noticed that Captain Kerry looked worried from the scowl across his face. He looked like he had seen a ghost as he shouted out orders to his crew. Nathaniel thought, the roar of the giant man's voice echoed throughout the ship at times like the sound of church bells ringing for service.

"What's all the fuss about?" Nathaniel asked Ali.

"You ask too many questions, boy," Ali replied. His permanent wicked grin belied no immediate danger.

"Are we in danger?"

"Not in this ship," Ali replied.

"What do you mean?" Nathaniel asked.

"This ship is a Spanish galleon, which is small, light, fast and easy to steer," Ali replied confidently with a beaming smile across his face revealing his brown stained teeth, before continuing. "And the Captain is one of the best. It looks like another ship on the horizon has spooked the crew. We'll find out when the first of the crew sit down to eat. Fetch those plates!" He knew the rumors that their ship was being followed by the English navy may come to pass.

Within an hour, the noise of the crew and the captain shouting his orders had abated, and the first group of pirates had come down to the galley to eat. Nathaniel saw the pirates were laughing and smiling as they sat down to eat.

"Take this to the captain's quarters, Nat," Ali ordered.

As Nathaniel made his way to the captain's cabin with the tray of food, he wondered how long he would be a slave. The first chance he got to escape he would make a dash for freedom, he said to himself. But immediately, he thought about what the captain had said to him.

As Nathaniel entered the captain's cabin, he saw Captain Kerry and his second in command Ironman Slim in conversation stood over a map table.

"Leave the food and go," Captain Kerry stated abruptly.

Nathaniel quickly laid the food on the captain's table and made his way out of the cabin before catching a glimpse of the map the two pirates were studying without being noticed. Nathaniel wondered where the ship was going to. He knew the ship's destination was towards the Cape, but from there he had no idea where the ship was heading for.

Chapter 2

On board HMS Antelope that was just of the coast of Gibraltar, stood the captain on the quarter deck awaiting orders to proceed. The naval signals from Gibraltar were explicit to Captain George Horner. Born in Blackfriars, near London in 1615 during the reign of James VI of Scotland and as James I of England, his parents were devoted Catholics, but because of the rift between Catholics and Protestants his parents practiced their faith in secret. George's early life saw him having to secretly adhere to his parents' faith, which he showed little signs of approving. His father wanted George to follow his father's footsteps and become a lawyer, which George had other ideas. At an early age he decided to join the royal navy, which his father disapproved of after leaving university with a degree in law. At the naval academy in Portsmouth he showed great promise and was given his first commission as a Second Lieutenant upon leaving the academy. After several years at sea, he was promoted to captain and saw action in the wars between Portugal and Spain. Now, Captain Horner was overweight and rambunctious with fading grey hair, deep green eyes and had a face that some would say had a thousand wrinkles caused by too much sea and wind. He had a tendency to be boisterous and a habit of repeating words in succession.

As Captain Horner read the message from Gibraltar is grey hair curled with anger and a cold chill ran throughout his overweight body that warned him of danger. He was an experienced sailor, who had spent most of his adult life in the navy. Now middle-aged, he enjoyed his position as captain, but still had the urge for adventure.

"Lieutenant, we're to intercept and destroy a pirate ship. Believe to be called the Rag-tail, and recover the English captives held aboard the ship. These captives were taken from the village of Trethowan, Cornwall. We're to rescue as many people as we can," Captain Horner said, as he observed the rigging of the ship.

"Did you say Trethowan…Cornwall?" the lieutenant asked anxiously.

"Yes…why?"

"I've a cousin that lives there…or did," the lieutenant replied. "His name is Nathaniel Curnow."

"Well, let's hope he's alive and not been captured, and if so, we can rescue him and the other captives," Captain Horner said wistfully.

"Set a course due south."

"Yes, due south, set course south by southeast," said the lieutenant, turning to the bosun standing at the wheel house on the quarter deck.
"We shall head for the port of Rabat off the coast of Morocco. We shall aim to gain some intelligence at the port about our prey," Captain Horner said dutifully.

"Yes, captain."

***

As the days passed, HMS Antelope had all of its canvas rigged taut on the frigate, and was making steady progress towards Rabat, Morocco, when suddenly the weather conditions changed.

"Captain, the wind has turned and we're dead calm," the lieutenant said.

"Yes, we've no choice, but to wait until the wind changes," Captain Horner remarked.

In the following hours, the captain had the ship on full battle orders. The drill was to prepare the sailors for any gun battle to come. Captain Horner kept watch and timed his men each time the cannon drill was practiced.

"Ready...fire!"

"That was thirty seconds too slow. Prepare to fire again," Captain Horner ordered, as he leaned over the quarter deck railing, and shouted the order to Lieutenant Curnow on the upper deck to fire again.

"Ready...fire!"

"That's a lot better. Let's go again," the captain demanded.

"Ready...fire!"

The wind soon changed course, and the frigate was at full speed again heading towards Rabat, Morocco. Crossing the stretch between the Gibraltar sea bridge and the waters of the Mediterranean Sea and the Atlantic Sea the frigate was rocked from side to side by high winds and waves. This was always a difficult sea bridge to navigate because of the clash of different oceans. The captain was studiously studying his charts alone in his cabin as the ship rocked from side to side. He had calculated that the port of Rabat was now about a day's sailing away.

"You...sailor...fetch Lieutenant Curnow," Captain Horner demanded to the sailor standing guard outside his cabin.

Born in the village of Tintagel, Cornwall in 1637 during the reign of Charles I. Jack Curnow as young boy helped his father in their fishing business. During this time, Jack demonstrated a likeness for the sea and from an early age was eager to join the royal navy, which he did at the age of twelve becoming a midshipman after training at the Portsmouth academy. After excelling in his seafaring craft, he soon rose through the ranks becoming First Lieutenant to Captain Horner aboard the frigate HMS Antelope. His Cornish ancestry was noticeable with curly blond hair, deep blue eyes, a pinkish complexion and a thin lanky stature.

As Lieutenant Curnow entered the captain's quarters, he wondered what the captain wanted. Standing by the chart table, Captain Horner outlined what Lieutenant Curnow's mission would be once they docked in Rabat, Morocco.

"As soon as we dock at the port of Rabat, I want you to find out if that pirate ship has been seen and any other information you can glean. Is that understood?" Captain Horner asked.

"Yes, captain."

"What, what…lieutenant?" Captain Horner asked is his usual manner when he was in deep thought. Before the lieutenant could reply the captain continued pacing the cabin, while trying to understand his opponent.

"What I don't understand, lieutenant is why he takes all this risk so far and he's heading for more risk? There's to be more, a lot more," Captain Horner asked out loud, still in deep thought.

"Perhaps, this pirate is just greedy," Lieutenant Curnow suggested.

"Yes, but there's more. I can feel it in my bones like a winter wind that chills the body from head to toes," Captain Horner answered as they heard a knock at the door and a sailor entered the cabin.

"Set a course, south by southwest," the captain ordered Lieutenant Curnow, who then made his way out of the cabin and up to the quarter deck and repeated the orders to the bosun, who soon cajoled the crew into action

"Man those sails."

***

The following day, the frigate entered the port of Rabat, Morocco, and made anchor in the bay not far from the docks. Captain Horner stayed on board, while Lieutenant Curnow with four navy ratings made their way via a rowing boat to the jetty dock. Lieutenant Curnow headed straight to the local Inn, where he hoped to find the information on the pirate ship they were pursuing.

"Do you know the pirate ship Rag-tail?" Lieutenant Curnow asked the Inn owner, who was pleased with the silver coin he received for the information he was about to depart.

Sat in the corner away from the nosey clients the Inn keeper told the lieutenant what he knew about the pirate ship. "Yes, the Rag-tail docked here last week. It took on fresh supplies and unloaded some slaves," the Inn keeper said regretfully.

"How many slaves and where did they go?" Lieutenant Curnow asked.

"I'm not sure, but they were old."

"Where did they take them?"

"To the slave market in Ashkan is what I heard," the Inn keeper said.

"Where's that?" Lieutenant Curnow asked.

"Near, the port of Tunis along that coastline."

"It's many days on camels from here," the Inn keeper said.

"Do you know where the pirate ship is heading for?" Lieutenant Curnow asked.

"No, I can only guess."

"Well, guess!"

"My guess would be the slave market at Zinjibar, Yemen or Mahajanga, Madagascar. Prices are high there and worth the journey for the pirates. But, it's a high price to pay to go around the Cape," said the Inn keeper.

"Right, is there anything else you have forgotten to mention?" Lieutenant Curnow asked.

"No, only, I saw a white boy, tall and as thin as a snake," the Inn keeper said.

"Mmmm…right, I hope for your sake the information is correct," Lieutenant Curnow said before leaving the Inn.

Lieutenant Curnow and his men made the short walk to the docks. "Have you got the supplies, I requested?" Lieutenant Curnow asked one of his junior ratings guarding the rowing boat with the fresh supplies already loaded.

"Yes, sir, everything is in order," the junior rating replied.

As Lieutenant Curnow and his crew got into their small boat and rowed back to HMS Antelope, the lieutenant wondered, if the boy the Inn keeper saw was his cousin. The profile the Inn keeper had said about the boy matched Nathaniel like the colors of a country's flag. They were a match, he said to himself.

***

"What did you find out, lieutenant?" Captain Horner asked eagerly. He was quick to the point like the sharp end of a pirate's cutlass.

Lieutenant Curnow stood in the captain's cabin, and relayed all the information he had gleaned from the Inn keeper.

"This Inn keeper, can he be trusted?" Captain Horner asked skeptically.

"He knows we will be back if his information turns out to be false," Lieutenant Curnow replied.

"So, we believe the pirates are heading for Yemen or Madagascar. But first they have to get round the Cape. That may buy us some time," the captain suggested.

"What say you?" Lieutenant Curnow said.

"It takes an exceptional sailor to sail around the Cape. So, unless this pirate captain is exceptional then we have a chance to make up time. You say six days past they departed from Rabat. What more do we know about this Portuguese pirate captain," Captain Horner asked, as he poured some wine into a pewter jug. Taking a sip of wine from the jug, he continued, "What, what, lieutenant?"

"They call him Captain Kerry, but we believe he's a Portuguese pirate," Lieutenant Curnow explained, what he had been told by the Inn keeper about the fate of some of the captives, and a possible sighting of his cousin.

"What about the old men and women taken to the slave market?" Lieutenant Curnow asked keenly, and was now concerned for their wellbeing because the Inn keeper had mentioned their condition.

"For now, we chase our main order and we send a signal to help the other captives," Captain Horner replied.

"Send a signal to Gibraltar. Requesting their assistance and to intercept the slave traders," Captain Horner ordered. Later, using the pigeon they had received from Gibraltar before leaving on their mission, a message was sent by Lieutenant Curnow.

After visiting the port authority and the local Inn near the docks again. Lieutenant Curnow was satisfied he had all the information he required.

"Captain, we have a signal from Gibraltar," said Lieutenant Curnow as he made his way to the quarter deck to pass over the message to Captain Horner.

"It's from the admiralty. They stress the importance of saving the life of Captain John Flynn. They say he's important for the war effort. They must know something that we don't?" Captain Horner said as he read the message out loud. He wondered why this Captain John Flynn was so important for the war effort.

"Yes, I agree, sir," Lieutenant Curnow replied as he watched the captain pace up and down the quarter deck in deep thought. He also wondered why the life of Captain John Flynn was important for the war effort. The war with Holland seemed a long way from where they were heading, he thought.

***

After a day had passed, Lieutenant Curnow stood upright and watched as the Captain Horner paced the cabin, sometimes the captain spoke out loud trying to formulate and understand his opponent. He knew the pirate had raided the Cornish coast and was now on the run. What he didn't understand was why? Why did the pirates act this way? These were some of the questions that unsettled his mind, he said to himself, before hearing the door knock.

"We're ready to sail, sir," the sailor said.

"Set sail, south by southwest," the order came from the captain as they left the port of Rabat, Morocco.

***

HMS Antelope was now nearing the Cape after several weeks of sailing with full canvas at all times. The four-rigged frigate's speed was greatly increased by the square rigged canvas enabling it to achieve the maximum speed for the vessel with the prevailing wind. The crew managed several days' gun practice. Captain Horner's plan was to fire chain shot at the pirate ship and hope to disable their masts and rigging without sinking the ship. The pirate ship could be boarded and the captives below deck could then be saved. Captain Horner and Lieutenant Curnow knew the plan was bold and made sense, but it also depended on the fighting spirit of their men against pirates. The pirates would have nothing to lose against a hangman's noose. Most battles at sea were dictated by the number of cannon and the size of cannon ball the ship had at its disposal and its ability to maneuver. HMS Antelope had sixty-two cannon firing eleven-pound cannon balls. It had the class to out battle the pirate ship, but Captain Horner knew his Achilles' heel was the captives; otherwise, he could just blast the pirate ship until it sank. Captain Horner knew his new orders were to seek out and destroy the pirate ship and recover captives if possible, especially the life of Captain John Flynn.

"We'll aim to disable the pirate ship when we get a chance and we'll have to board it to free those captives." Captain Horner said.

"That means we've to find the pirate ship before it off loads more of its captives into slavery." Lieutenant Curnow remarked.

"Its better we find the captives on shore then we go after the pirate ship and sink it to the bottom of the sea." Captain Horner said.

"But, first, we have to stop at the first slave market at Madagascar," Lieutenant Curnow said. Continuing he added, "Otherwise, how will we know if the pirate ship is holding any captives?"

"Yes, you are correct, but either way, I would like to take the pirate captain alive and find out some more information. Like, what were his motives for raiding the English coast?" Captain Horner asked thoughtfully.

"Yes, a lot of dangers for limited reward," he continued. "It doesn't make sense, and the slave market at Mahajanga, Madagascar is another popular place for the slave trade."

"I agree," the captain agreed.

"I'm concerned about those old men and women, I wonder if they have been rescued?" Lieutenant Curnow asked sympathetically.

Captain Horner was first to notice the change of the winds as the frigate tried to clear the Cape, which could take weeks because of ocean currents and winds. The frigate began to roll into the deep swell of the waves. Lieutenant Curnow heard the cry of 'man overboard' from the deck of the ship as he stumbled to regain his balance. The ship was listing close to the sea as it tried to cross the Cape.

"Lieutenant, see to your men," Captain Horner shouted.

"Yes, captain."

"All hands," Lieutenant Curnow howled.

The crew of HMS Antelope tried several times to rescue their man overboard. But, because of the raging winds and the deep swell of the sea all attempts at rescuing their crew member failed. The following morning, the crew of HMS Antelope stood to attention, while the captain read a service from the Bible in remembrance to the man lost at sea. Captain Horner said his last word from the Bible as the crew was dismissed. He wondered how many more men he would lose on this mission. It took several more days and nights, before HMS Antelope was safely around the Cape, and heading for the island of Madagascar.

Chapter 3

In the year 1667, King Naria ruled over Siam, which had borders to the east with Laos and to the west with Burma. Siam was at war with its neighbors. Burma often made raids into Siam and enslaving anyone it came across. The slave trade was well entrenched by most countries at this time. Nations and pirates traded slaves like bushels of cotton, which was common practice amongst many countries as a means to provide free labor for any ruling despot.

Yuki a young girl living in a village far from the capital of Siam wanders down to the local river to fetch fresh water for her parents, and is captured by marauding Burmese soldiers. Her Japanese father and her Siamese mother never stopped hoping their daughter would return home one day. After several weeks and days trekking through the jungle Yuki and the other captives she was tied to found themselves at a port town in Burmese territory.

Yuki is fifteen years old and tall for her age, but still a child not yet a woman. She has dark jet black hair like the color of corking tar used to waterproof sailing vessels. She had inherited her Japanese father's characteristics around the dark brown eyes combined with her Siamese mother's rounded facial features. Yuki had a natural beauty of Japanese and Siamese features, which meant that she had a recognizable face in a crowd.

At the slave market, Yuki watched as slaves were quickly sold. Stood in the market shivering with fear waiting to be sold she could only hear the shouts of men with unfamiliar languages. Within minutes, she was sold to a Burmese pirate, and led away from the market tied by rope to a pirate, who also spoke her language she later found out.

"Take my slaves to the ship," Captain Kareem said to his second in command Purapratt.

Purapratt had been born in Bombay, India during the Portuguese rule. He had a hatred of the Portuguese from an early age. Because of how the Portuguese had badly treated the Indian population who were often enslaved to work for them under terrible working conditions. Although, not physically large, he had the courage to lead men. Small in stature with dark brown hair, brown eyes and a dark complexion he grew up learning to sail working on his father's fishing boat around the islands off the west coast of Bombay. Still only a young man, at a local Inn in Bombay, he met Captain Kareem and immediately became friends.

Eventually, Purapratt joined Captain Kareem's pirate crew with the promise of wealth and the chance to attack Portuguese ships.

Boarding the ship Yuki noticed the man who had bought her at the slave market. It was Captain Kareem who plied his trade throughout the Far East and East Africa. The man was talking with other men on the upper deck as Yuki was led aboard the ship. Yuki felt a tear roll down her face, and wondered what fate had in stall for her, and for the first time she feared for her safety amongst the men aboard the ship.

"Save those tears. Don't worry girl, you will be safe on board this ship," Purapratt said and added, "Captain Kareem has his eyes on you. He likes you."

***

Later that day, Captain Kareem with a horse and a wagon and two of his crew made their way to the local Inn house. Inside the Inn were soldiers, pirates and sailors all enjoying the local black coffee and smoking tobacco from Hookahs. Captain Kareem hoped he could purchase some bottles of alcohol, not usually found in a Buddhist country. He knew Ahmed the Inn keeper had supplies he had previously arranged to buy.

"You've the supplies I ordered?" the pirate Captain Kareem asked.

"Yes, get your men around the back of the Inn," Ahmed the Inn keeper replied.

"Take these crates away to the wagon," Captain Kareem ordered his men.

"Did you buy any slaves at the market, today?" Ahmed asked with a wicked smile that grew across his face like a slow wet trail from a snail.

"You ask too many questions, and one day it will get you into trouble," Captain Kareem replied.

Captain Kareem was no fool and was often keen to spread false information about his activities. He was a large muscular man with a bald head; a large Arabesque nose and a boisterous voice were his main features.

"A bought a few slaves to replace the men I lost recently," Captain Kareem said dismissively and added. "Do you have any news to sell?"

"I overheard two pirates talking about a pirate's treasure. They said they'd sailed on the pirate ship called the Rag-tail, which had docked here a year ago or more. The pirates said the treasure was on the island of Madagascar," Ahmed replied.

"That's a big island. Do you know where?" Captain Kareem asked pensively.

"If I did, I wouldn't be here talking to you," Ahmed replied, laughing at the silly question.

Kareem shouted, "Listen!" Before grabbing Ahmed around the throat with his two hands and persuading him to talk.

"Okay, I understand."

"Now, tell me everything you know?"

"The two pirates said the treasure lay buried somewhere near a Buddhist temple," Ahmed replied.

"How do you know it was a Buddhist temple?" Kareem asked.

"Because the pirates were drunk, and said the treasure was near a statue of a monk they called the Buddha," Ahmed replied.

"Is that all you have for me?" Kareem asked again.

"Yes."

"The information is a year or more old."

"Yes, but the treasure may still be there. So, my information is worth some silver coin," Ahmed said with a grimace across his face revealing his coffee stained teeth.

"Let's hope your neck fits the noose if you haven't told me everything," Captain Kareem said and added. "Have you told anyone else about this treasure?"

"No, just you, I swear."

Ahmed was a proverbial liar and made a habit of selling information, and at the same time embellishing the information to such an extent that he often forgot what the truth was.

As Captain Kareem and his crew rode the wagon back to the dock where his ship the Santé Maria lay docked. There his crew was awaiting his return. He wondered about what Ahmed had said. Kareem knew the Inn keeper probably sold the same information over and over again to willing ears with coin to spend. How reliable was the information, he wasn't sure. Kareem had heard about the pirate they called the Portuguese from other sailors and Inn keepers over the years. Madagascar was an island he knew only from charts and sailors' yarns, but he was determined to find out the truth for himself.

"Are we ready to sail?" Captain Kareem asked with a loud voice to his second in command as he clambered aboard his ship.

"Yes, we have stored the fresh supplies…wine and your slaves," replied the second in command Purapratt.

"Set a course, north by northwest."

As the Santé Maria a single mast sloop with one head sail in front of the mast and a main sail behind the mast made its way from the port at Burma and up the trade routes towards India the seas were rough. A late Monsoon storm had formed giant waves that crashed aboard the Santé Maria with such force that the ship would keel to one side for a few seconds before the ship righted again. The crew of the ship was busily trying to tack in the sailing canvas to avoid certain destruction. Without the canvas pulled in the ship would not avoid being sunk by crushing waves and gushing winds that could tear a man off the ship in a moment into the sea to his death.

"Close those hatches!" Captain Kareem said shouting to be heard over the noise of the storm.

"Yes, boss," Purapratt said.

"Look out!"

The captain heard the words just in time to miss colliding with part of the wooden canvas pole. The wind had ripped the wooden pole straight from its tackle aloft of the main mast of the fully rigged ship. As the captain scrambled to his feet, Purapratt was busy trying to save the ship from sinking into the ocean.

"Get that fucking tackle rigged," Captain Kareem said trying to restore some order to the chaos aboard the ship as the storm was raging around them.

Meanwhile, Yuki and the other slaves were huddled together inside the cell for comfort, but many were sick from the motions of the ship. Yuki had never seen the sea before and never experienced sea sickness.

"Go down and see if my slaves are good," Captain Kareem demanded.

Purapratt made his way down into the belly of the ship where the slaves had been housed inside a bamboo cage configured to the contours of the ship's hull. He could see and smell that many had been sick.

"Here is some water. Drink! But do it slowly, this will help you," Purapratt said.

Purapratt tied the barrel of water to the outside of the bamboo cage for the slaves to help themselves. He noticed the young slave girl lying down.

"Are you alright?" Purapratt asked.

"Yes, I am okay, just sick," Yuki replied.

"Good, because my boss must like you," Purapratt replied, smiling.

***

Over the following days, the Santé Maria made its way across the sea following the trade winds, which took the ship towards Yemen from India. Captain Kareem knew about the slave market at Yemen from other sailors, so was surprised to hear from the Inn keeper about the Portuguese pirate who plied his trade around these waters. He wondered what was so special about the slave market at Yemen. He was determined to find out, he said himself.

"This food is disgusting…throw the cook into the sea," Captain Kareem said to Purapratt.

"Yes, boss."

"And send that slave girl to the galley," Captain Kareem demanded.

Purapratt made his way below decks and opened the cage holding the slaves and retrieved Yuki to work in the galley as a cook.

"Remember, the captain had the cook thrown overboard into the sea earlier, today. So, I hope you can cook?" Purapratt insisted with a concerned tone of voice.

Yuki looked shocked at the news about the cook, but was determined to survive. She had learned from her mother how to prepare food, and was now resolute to learn fast.

"Your first task is to prepare a quick meal for the captain and feed the crew."

"How many mouths do I have to feed?"

"We have thirty six crew members and six slaves plus the captain."

"Remember, keep the captain happy and the crew…and you won't have to learn how to swim," Purapratt said with a giggle in his tone of voice.

Yuki made her way to the captain's quarters, which was guarded by one pirate with pistol and sword at the ready. As Yuki made her entrance into the captain's quarters she was fully aware of the captain's attention.

"I hope you can cook?"

"Mmmm, good taste. Now, what shall I call you?"

"My name is Yuki," Yuki replied with a sharp tone of voice.

"Good…and short."

"Now, you may go," Captain Kareem ordered.

As Yuki crossed the open deck of the ship she could hear birds squawking that she had heard at the dock in Burma. She wondered if the ship was close to land and thought about the day when she could return to her parents in Siam. Peering over the port-side of the deck she caught a glimpse of the outline of a distant land.

"What are you doing, girl?" the pirate asked.

"Just looking at…where we're going," Yuki replied. "Where're we going?" Yuki repeated.

"Ask the captain and see what he says."

"You don't know?"

"I don't need to know."

"I'm the new cook, so treat me right; otherwise, I won't feed you," Yuki said briskly. She wondered if the pirate understood her broken English, which she had learned from her father that spoke good English. Her father had learned from an English missionary that came to their village multiple times over many years.

"You'll be food for the sharks like the last one," the pirate said, chuckling as he walked away.

Later that day, Yuki spent more and more time with Captain Kareem and was beginning to like the attention from the captain. His humor beguiled Yuki and this she hadn't experienced before as a girl. She felt the urge for love as a woman taking over.

***

In comings days, Yuki spent more and more time with Captain Kareem alone in his cabin and they would talk together about their lives.

"Have you heard the story about the Dalai Lama in Tibet?" Captain Kareem asked.

"No, go on," Yuki replied hurriedly. She was anxious to hear the story.

One night, a man appeared at the gates of the Dalai Lama's palace and wanted an answer to a question that had plagued his mind like a fever.

"What was the question?"

"The pilgrim wanted to ask the Dalai Lama what was the meaning of life?" Captain Kareem replied.

"I shall go on with the story. The pilgrim appeared every year at the gates of the palace. In the end, the pilgrim waited five years before seeing the Dalai Lama."

"That's a long time to wait for an answer," Yuki said.

"Yes, it is, but sometimes that's how it is," Captain Kareem replied seriously.

"In the end, the Dalai Lama answered the pilgrim's question by asking the pilgrim why you want to know the meaning of life."

The pilgrim replied, "Because I want to know my purpose in life?"

"I guess everyone wants to know their purpose in life," Yuki said.

"Let me go on with the story," Captain Kareem said, laughing. They were becoming fond of each other's company.

"The Dalai Lama replied, "Man thinks, he is above the animal, and that he has purpose, because that is the way he is taught from birth to think, but forgets he is an animal."

"What do you think about the story?" Captain Kareem asked.

"We don't always see the answer, but it's there waiting to reveal itself," Yuki replied, smiling.

The following day, the Santé Maria docked at Zinjibar, Yemen.

Chapter 4

It had been a couple of weeks since the pirates' attack at Trethowan. As Lord Trethowan paced up and down the corridor outside the office of the Lord Admiral of the royal navy headquarters in Portsmouth, his thoughts turned to his loss of his friend and deputy Captain John Flynn. Since, the pirates' raid his ability to run his estate, which consisted of three farms, several tin mines and the local Inn had been difficult without his trusted deputy to manage his business interests. The loss of tin ore had been noticed immediately without his deputy to oversee production at the mines, which was essential for the war effort. Also, Lord Trethowan had been told that many local people were now afraid to live anywhere near the Cornish coast. People feared being attacked again by marauding pirates. He had to convince the Lord Admiral of his plan, he said to himself.

Lord Trethowan had requested an audience with the Lord Admiral hoping to secure information concerning the navy's response to the raid by the pirates. His pace had increased along the corridor as he waited to be heard by the Lord Admiral. Lord Trethowan had a plan to discuss with the Lord Admiral that he hoped would increase the chances of finding his deputy and the other captives.

"The Lord Admiral will see you, now," the Lord Admiral's captain at arms said.

"How can I help?" the Lord Admiral asked politely, as he relaxed into his chair opposite a highly polished wooden desk. Stood to one side of the Lord Admiral, the captain at arms listened intently to the conversation.

"I would like to know how the hunt for those brigands and pirates that raided my village is proceeding," Lord Trethowan asked briskly.

"Well, Lord Trethowan our business is not to give out information concerning on-going naval missions. I have sympathy and appreciate your concern, but I cannot divulge the information you may require."

"Can you at least tell me what progress you have made?" Lord Trethowan asked, struggling to hold his anger at the lack of information. His face had turned more reddish than its usual pinkish color with frustration at the lack of urgency.

"We have a ship on their tail and that is all I can safely say," the Lord Admiral said.

"I have plan, which may speed up results. I want to donate a reward for the persons who successfully brings back my deputy and the other villagers," Lord Trethowan said. He now felt he had the admiral on the hook. Money usually made people change their tune, he said to himself.

"No, no, no that is not what we can allow. You see it would be bad for moral and dangerous. You see men will change at the possibility of wealth," the Lord Admiral said.

"But, your sailors can gain wealth by taking a prize at sea," Lord Trethowan said.

"Yes, that is true and is in our rules. But, what you are suggesting would cause a rift in who gets what. You see, my man," the Lord Admiral said.

"But…"

"Stop, sir, and the answer is no reward. But, you can donate your money freely to the navy and it will be put to a good cause. When I can inform you of information I will. Please be patient. It takes time to rid this land of pirates," the Lord Admiral said.

"I know this may sound callous, but I would like to return my deputy John Flynn to my employ," Lord Trethowan said.

"You mean Captain John Flynn?"

"Yes, how did you know?"

"It's our business in the admiralty to know much business, especially former naval officers," the Lord Admiral said.

As Lord Trethowan made his way out of the admiralty office and down the steps to his waiting carriage, he could hear the sound of seagulls squawking through the morning mist that had come ashore from the bay just outside the port of Portsmouth. Climbing into his carriage he told his driver to take him to London. He had a plan and was willing to defy the admiralty and put his plan into action. He also had the information he had purchased from an insider. The admiralty insider had given Lord Trethowan the progress of HMS Antelope and its destination before the meeting with the Lord Admiral.

***

"Are we there?" Lord Trethowan asked briskly, to his carriage driver. Lord Trethowan was tired by the journey, which had taken many hours from daylight through the night to the early hours before dawn the next day.

"Yes."

As Lord Trethowan climbed out of the carriage and looked up at the sign of the Inn it said, 'The Portobello Inn' he then knew he was in the right place. The only sounds he could hear were the sound of squawking ravens that were jostling each other for position on top of the Inn's roof.

It was in the early hours of the morning and first light had not arrived, yet, the Inn was open. The Portobello Inn was infamous in some circles for always being open for business. It was said that much of any smuggling was organized from the tables and rooms of the Portobello Inn.

"Can you find me a captain willing to sail?" Lord Trethowan asked the Portobello Inn keeper.

"It may take a few days, but we will find someone," the Portobello Inn keeper replied.

"Next, I need a room and stabling for my driver and horses. Do you have both?"

"Yes."

Lord Trethowan followed the Inn keeper up several stairs to a room. The room had a view to the front of the Inn.

"Your driver, we have lodgings and stabling for the horse, which both will be taken care of."

"Good, send some wine and food, before I take my rest," Lord Trethowan said.

***

The following day, Lord Trethowan was sat at a table in the Portobello Inn, discussing his plan, with a man the Inn keeper had recommended. Beside the strange man sat a beautiful woman dressed like a pirate in pantaloons and open shirt, he thought. She wore large gold ear rings that jangled with every move and wore a perfume that captivated the onlooker like the smell of lavender flowers in a forest meadow.

"This is my woman…where I go she goes."

"My name is Maisha…I am honored to meet you, Lord Trethowan," Maisha said politely, as she held out her hand for the lord to respect her honor with a kiss.

"That's an interesting name, Maisha?" Lord Trethowan asked. He tried to understand the man and woman he was negotiating with. He knew the very mention of treasure would make some people do anything. He quietly whispered the chance of pirates' treasure without being over heard by other patrons in the Inn.

"You say...treasure?" the sailor asked quietly. He was sat at the table opposite Lord Trethowan.

Lord Trethowan knew he held all the cards. He tried to understand the sailor and his woman before he made any deal. He knew how treasure could change a person in seconds. He wanted to be sure he had the right people for the mission. Any loose talk of treasure or gold in the Inn would be like lighting a fire you could not stop. Lord Trethowan surveyed the other tables packed with patrons and sailors busily drinking themselves to oblivion, he thought. But, he had an important objective to achieve in a short time period, he said to himself.

"Yes, but more important is the rescue of the captives, especially, Captain John Flynn.

"You will pay for the ship's supplies and a reward...plus any treasure I find, we will share?" the sailor asked.

"Yes."

"How can I trust you?" the sailor asked.

"I am Lord Trethowan of Cornwall and my word is my bond," Lord Trethowan replied in a commanding tone like he was conducting his affairs during his work as a local magistrate in Truro, Cornwall. As Lord Trethowan's face turned a reddish color in anger, he then thumped the table with his clenched fist to show he didn't like being challenged, he was used to being in control, he said to himself.

"Listen! Lord Trethowan added. "I will have you hanging on the gibbet if you cross me."

The sailor looked at Lord Trethowan with the left dark brown eye, which was the only working eye he had, the right eye was covered by a black piece of leather acting as an eye patch. Most men feared Black Eye because he was a giant with a reputation that matched his image. He had a bald held with a long straggly black beard and was of African descent, he thought. The sailor sat opposite Lord Trethowan was the pirate and brigand called 'Black Eye' but only he knew his real name.

"You can captain a ship?" Lord Trethowan asked intently. "I'm curious to know your experience?"

"I was once a bosun...so I know everything there is to know about sailing the ship," Black Eye the pirate replied. "The English taught me well."

"Don't worry...my word is my bond," Black Eye said.

"When can you leave?" Lord Trethowan asked.

"As soon as…I've got fresh supplies and a crew," Black Eye replied.

"You don't have a crew?"

"Relax!"

"I have a crew, but some will naturally find other work. But most, I can find and replace those I've lost," Black Eye said.

"I have decided to come with you," Lord Trethowan said.

"Okay, just as long as you know who's in charge…and that is me," Black Eye reiterated.

"Yes, but it's my money…if I die there is no reward," Lord Trethowan replied sporting a wicked smile across his face like he held all the aces.

"Would you like some more wine?" the Inn keeper asked. He was trying at every opportunity to listen in to the conversation.

"You say this pirate ship is called the Rag-tail and is heading around the Cape towards somewhere in the Indian Ocean?" Black Eye asked. He gulped back his ale, and was already ordering another flagon of ale when gun fire suddenly erupted inside the Inn. Lord Trethowan could taste the smoke from the pistol shots as a cloud of blackish smoke enveloped the Inn.

Taking cover under the table Lord Trethowan, Black Eye and Maisha shook hands on their future relationship. Minutes later, the scene inside the Inn was back to normal with one man dead and another man claiming self-defense. Lord Trethowan noticed the crowd inside the Portobello Inn was too busy enjoying themselves to be bothered by the death of one man. It was probably a daily occurrence to witness this level of violence with this bunch of thieves and laggards, he observed. Rowdy men and women enjoying each other's company with copious amounts of mostly ale being consumed was a daily occurrence, he said to himself.

"What do you know about this pirate ship and its captain?" Black Eye asked, as he twirled and stroked his beard with one hand, while in deep thought.

After Lord Trethowan reordered some more wine from the nosey Inn keeper, he replied, "They call him Captain Kerry, but most know him as the Portuguese pirate. They are heading for Madagascar or Yemen where there are slave markets. And there is…the treasure," Lord Trethowan replied.

"Is this information, correct?"

"Yes."

"How do you know?"

"Because I paid for it," Lord Trethowan replied wistfully

"And where is the treasure?" Black Eye asked again.

"It is rumored to be vast and somewhere on the island of Madagascar."

"But, that island is vast…the treasure could be anywhere."

"That's why you have a reward for recovering Captain John Flynn and the treasure is secondary. Remember, when we find Captain Kerry and his band of pirates we can then extract the information from them. Someone will talk, they always do," Lord Trethowan said with a wicked smile that consumed his face like a man possessed with pleasure.

"Your ship…what's it called? And where is it docked?" Lord Trethowan asked.

"The ship is called the 'Portobello' and is moored on the east dock, only a short walking distance from here," Black Eye replied and continued. "I will send you a message, when we are ready to sail."

"Good, we have a deal," Lord Trethowan said as he shook hands with Black Eye and Maisha. Lord Trethowan noticed Maisha more for the first time since their brief encounter taking cover under the table from the pistol shot earlier. He had earlier noticed Maisha's youthful olive skin and dark brown eyes up close when hiding behind the table. He could see that her long black hair flowed like a river to the middle of her back and could easily beguile the observer. He could see why she went everywhere with Black Eye, he was a jealous man, and he could be unpredictable, and that was useful, he said to himself. She had hair that shimmered in the light like the flickering light of the moon upon a calm sea. She had an Arabic look from the women he had seen before on his travels in the Eastern Mediterranean during his youth, he thought.

***

The following day, Lord Trethowan and his carriage driver made their way to the east docks and boarded the Portobello. Lord Trethowan noticed the frenetic scene as some men loaded the ship with supplies and others made it ready for the voyage. The Portobello was a former Spanish galleon captured by Black Eye during the English and Spanish wars earlier that century. The Portobello had forty-two guns at its disposal that fired eleven pound cannon balls or chain shot for disabling a ship's ability to rig its sails.

"Glad you could make it," Black Eye shouted from the quarter deck to Lord Trethowan as he boarded the ship with his carriage driver.

"Your man has been given space to sleep with the rest of the crew," Black Eye shouted.

Lord Trethowan shouted back, "Good. What about my sleeping quarters?" Lord Trethowan expected to be treated differently than his carriage driver as it was his money that was paying for the voyage, and he expected to be treated like a captain.

"I've had a hammock made up near my sleeping quarters next to the galley. It's a small space, but it will do," Black Eye replied.

"Good. When do we sail?"

"Within the hour, we sail."

Lord Trethowan wondered if Black Eye would prove to be a trustworthy partner on their mission to retrieve Captain John Flynn and the other captives from his village as he got accustomed to the small cabin next to the captain's quarters. He had made sure before leaving London that he had secured the leverage over Black Eye should he require its use. As the ship Portobello made its way out of the port of London and on its journey its departure was noted by the admiralty.

"South by southeast," Black Eye shouted as the sound of squawking seagulls surrounded the ship.

"South by southeast," repeated the bosun as the wheelhouse man steered the ship towards the open waters of the Bay of Biscay that was notorious for bad weather.

As the swell of open seas began to heave the ship up and down from the raging waves Lord Trethowan felt sick and at times wished he had stayed at home in Cornwall. The nearer the Portobello got closer and closer to the Bay of Biscay the more the ship would rise in the water and then drop in the trough of the swell. The configuration of two different currents meeting in the Bay of Biscay meant that the sea was normally rough to transverse even with a skilled sailor at the helm. On the quarter deck, Black Eye stood firm to the rail and tried to bring order to the chaos.

Black Eye cried out, "Get that main sheet in."

The bosun repeated the orders to his crew as the Portobello tried to cross the Bay of Biscay "Get that fucking sheet in."

The rigging of the three mast galleon had to be exactly rigged to avoid capsizing the ship in rough weather. The galleon had a broad keel and sat high in the water, which meant that this type of vessel was prone to capsizing in stormy seas if the rigging of the sails were not suitably set. This required the experience of a captain used to handling galleon built ships. The galleon was a design of ship that was mainly built by the Spanish and resembled an upper deck with a castle tower at each end of the ship with three masts and square rigged sails. The Spanish liked the galleon design because they were agile and lightweight compared to an English frigate design at the time, which were far heavier and hence slower.

"This is Two Coin our bosun and my second in command on this ship," Black Eye said as he introduced the man who was covered with tattoos on most of his skin that was visible to Lord Trethowan. Two Coin's face and bald head were covered with tattoos as was his muscular arms that resembled that of a wrestler, Lord Trethowan thought. The two men looked each other in the eyes and courteously accepted each other.

"You look unwell, Lord Trethowan?" Two Coin asked.

"Yes, how perceptive?" Lord Trethowan remarked he couldn't help being himself when the moment presented itself. Within minutes, Lord Trethowan felt the pangs of sickness in his fat belly as he tried to steady himself against the violent motion of the ship.

"Take Lord Trethowan to my quarters and rest him up there," Black Eye said to Two Coin.

Two Coin took hold of Lord Trethowan and led him down from the quarter deck and in to the captain's quarters. Inside the cabin Two Coin sat the lord down, and began to pour some wine.

"Here, drink this."

"I don't know if I can," Lord Trethowan said, and he tried not to be sick.

"This will settle your belly, my lord."

"Wine, will that help?" Lord Trethowan asked, and then he took a sip of wine from the flagon and continued to drink the wine.

"Yes, believe me."

"How long have you known Black Eye?" Lord Trethowan asked as he started to feel like asking questions.

"Oh! You're feeling better. There's now color in your face."

Lord Trethowan felt the pangs of sickness disappear from his belly as he again asked the same question, "How long have you known Black Eye?"

"Why do you ask?"

"It's a simple question," Lord Trethowan replied, who felt Two Coin was hiding something.

"He saved my life. Let's leave it like that. I've to get back to my crew now," Two Coin said.

Chapter 5

After negotiating the Cape, the pirate ship Rag-tail passed the northern part of the island of Madagascar on its way to the slave market at Yemen. The crew and its captain were unaware that HMS Antelope was only a few days sailing behind them. Captain Kerry paced the quarter deck as the wind and rain lashed his ship. He wondered if the English were tailing him. Captain Kerry had a feeling like a chill that goes through your body that someone was tailing him. It was in his nature to be cautious, he said to himself.

"Make sure the canvas is fully taut, Slim," Captain Kerry demanded.

"Yes, boss, we are making good time," Ironman Slim his second in command replied.

"Tack those sheets, fully squared," the bosun shouted to his crew energetically, as they tried to rig the canvas against the strength of the prevailing winds.

"We will head for the slave market at Mahajanga, we should achieve a good price for each of the slaves below," Captain Kerry insisted to Ironman Slim.

"Do you still think we're being followed?" Ironman Slim asked.

"Yes, I think they're only a few days behind us if they're there. I've had a feeling we're being followed for some time," the captain replied.

"What your plan?"

"Our best plan is to sell the slaves and get out of the way of the ship following us. They probably out gun us. We have only forty-two guns available to the sixty-two guns available on an English frigate. A frigate is fully rigged squared, so she has more sail to the wind. This ship is a galleon, which we captured from the Spanish. That should tell you something." Captain Kerry replied, grinning.

"Trim those sheets," Captain Kerry shouted.

"Trim the sheets," Ironman Slim shouted out the order to his bosun.

"We want full control of this ship as we sail through this sea," Captain Kerry said.

The Rag-tail was sailing through the strait between the west coast of Madagascar and the east coast of Africa on its way to the northern port town of Mahajanga at the northwest end of the island of Madagascar.

***

When the Rag-tail entered the port of Mahajanga the seas were calm as it anchored at the docks.

"Listen!"

"I want you to inform the crew that anyone not on board this ship when we sail in the morning shall have no cut of the money from the sale of the slaves. We'll sail on time to Yemen."

"Are we going to the slave market at Zinjibar?" Ironman Slim asked.

"Yes, make sure you inform everyone to be on board by first light," Captain Kerry replied. The captain had a plan in his mind, but he didn't intend to inform his second in command. For his plan to work it had to be convincing, he said to himself.

"Get fresh supplies. I will see you in the Inn, Slim," the captain said.

After docking some of the crew loaded the Rag-tail with fresh supplies while others was busily transferring the slaves below deck to the docks ready to lead them to the slave market. Nathaniel watched from the upper deck, while the captain watched from the quarter deck as the slaves were led out in a continuous line of men and women iron chained together. There was no escape for his friends and for the first time, he felt guilty. He had the pain of guilt because he was not chained like an animal like his friends were. In his mind, he knew he had to find a way to escape.

***

That night in the local Inn by the port of Mahajanga, Captain Kerry and some of his crew sat and drank the local ale until the early hours the next day.

"Did you get a good price for the slaves?" Captain Kerry asked, as he sat and drank some ale from his flagon.

"Yes, we had a good result. All have been sold to Saria, the slave merchant, as you requested before the sale," Ironman Slim replied.

"Good," the captain added, "What about the boy, Nat?"

"He is on the ship. Ali has him under guard," Ironman Slim said and added. "He could try to escape."

"No, he's chained to the galley, I made sure he was chained just in case he tried to escape when we docked at the port," Captain Kerry said.

"Listen!" Captain Kerry said abruptly, as he leaned over the table and grabbed hold of Ironman Slim by the cuff of his shirt. "I want you to make sure the boy gets a chance tonight to escape.

Is that clear? And to make sure he overhears you talking about our plans to sail to Yemen. Those two things must happen if my plan is to succeed."

"You want to free the boy?"

"Yes, he's of no use to me, now. Just find a way for him to escape the ship, tonight. And let him hear our plans to sail to Yemen."

"You could have sold him at the slave market and be done with him."

"Yes, Slim, but for my plan to succeed. The boy is part of the gibbet, without it you cannot hang a man," the captain said.

"I don't understand?"

"You will as time passes by. Just do as I command and we'll see what happens."

Ironman Slim was puzzled by the captain's actions, but followed his orders, and later that night made sure the boy Nathaniel was unchained from the galley, and that he had overheard him give orders for the ship to be made ready to sail to Yemen the following day.

Chapter 6

The pirate guarding the gang way to the dock from the ship Rag-tail was too drunk to notice Nathaniel quietly making his escape by climbing down the forward port side rope anchoring the ship to the docks. Nathaniel soon found a way to safety. He had noticed a man with horse and cart leaving the port and wondered if he could help him.

"Can you help me?" Nathaniel asked.

"I need to find my friends. They have been taken to the slave market," Nathaniel said, as he pleaded with the man for help.

"Yes, get on!"

"I'm on my way to my home, which is several days from here. I'm a merchant."

"I need to help my friends," Nathaniel repeated briskly, as he stressed the importance of helping his friends to the man.

"I understand, but it's late, my name is Salim Nadeer. What shall I call you?" Salim Nadeer asked kindly.

"My name is Nathaniel Curnow, but just call me Nat," Nathaniel replied.

"Where have you come from?" Salim asked.

"I've escaped from the arms of pirates. The one they call Captain Kerry and his crew of brigands and thieves," Nathaniel replied.

"Where's the slave market?"

"It's to the north of the port, close by the Inn. We've already passed the market. Your friends will not be sold, until, several days have passed. They like to wash and feed the slaves after a sea journey, so that they fetch a higher price at market. Your friends are safe for now."

Nathaniel consoled himself with the news from Salim that his friends would be safe for now, until they were sold. He wondered what he could do for his friends held captive at the slave market. But, for now, he felt the pangs of his newly gained freedom throughout his body for the first time in weeks. He felt like a bird and able to fly anywhere, that sense of freedom, only gained, once you have suffered the agony of captivity like a caged animal, he said to himself.

"Where is your home?" Nathaniel asked.

"It's on the northeast side of the island. It will take several days to get there. So, tonight, we'll camp under the stars," Salim replied. Continuing, he added, "You will see a wonder, if the sky is clear."

"What do you mean?" Nathaniel asked.

Later that day, Salim and Nathaniel stopped, and made camp beside a large baobabs tree. "In Madagascar the baobabs tree is regarded by the locals here as a sign of fertility," Salim said.

"Why is that?" Nathaniel asked.

"Because the tree has a wide trunk and has the ability to live a long life." Continuing he added, "We have to make sure we unsaddle the horse from the cart for tonight."

"Why is that?"

"In case of snake attack, you cannot be too careful. There are many things that can frighten a horse. I don't want my horse to disappear with my goods, overnight. Now, do you see?"

"Yes, I understand."

"Good, let's cook and eat. And wait for the sky to clear."

"Look!"

"You can see all the stars, tonight. The sky is clear," Nathaniel said.

"Where have you come from?" Salim asked. Continuing, he added, "And put more wood on the fire. I feel the cold air, tonight."

"A village called Trethowan on the south coast of Cornwall in England."

"What happened to you?"

"I was walking into the village, when I was caught by some pirates along with most of the village folk, and then caged aboard the ship called the Rag-tail. The captain of the ship is a big burly man they call Captain Kerry. The captain made me work with the cook in the galley, but my friends were held captive in the belly of the ship," Nathaniel said sadly, as he continued to explain to Salim the plight of his friends aboard the pirate ship.

"Where is the Rag-tail going to?"

"I'm not sure, but I overheard some pirates talking about going to Yemen."

"You say, Yemen, eh?"

"Yes, that is what I heard. Some sort of cargo to pick up. That's what I heard."

"There is a slave market at the port of Zinjibar in Yemen. Perhaps, they plan to buy some more slaves," Salim queried.

"I don't know? All I know is, I have to try to save my friends from slavery."

"Of course my friend, we will see to that in the coming days. For now, do you see that star formation it forms an archer on a horse?"

"Over to your right and just above the horizon!"

"No why?"

"That's called the Sagittarius Zodiac sign."

"What's that?"

"The universe of what you see in the night sky was divided up into twelve sections and each portion given a name. Sagittarius is just one of those twelve portions."

"Who created the Zodiac and for what purpose?" Nathaniel asked.

"An ancient people called the Babylonians first created the Zodiac signs. Two thousand years before the birth of Jesus Christ."

"What was the purpose?"

"Well, that is a difficult question to answer," Salim replied.

"Why, what do you mean?"

"When we create anything it's because we need it? So, the Babylonians must have needed it, otherwise, they wouldn't have created it."

"Who and where are the Babylonians from?" Nathaniel asked

"Like I said an ancient civilization far to the east in a land between two great rivers, but I have never been there. The Babylonians no longer exist, but the Zodiac signs do," Salim replied dutifully, and tried to explain the concept of the Zodiac signs to Nathaniel.

"The Babylonians needed a way to read the night sky. To make sense of what they were seeing. In a sense, they needed a reason, why this and that happened like good and bad actions in their lives." Continuing Salim added, "It's like playing with fire you never know when you are going to get burned."

"I don't understand? What do you mean?" Nathaniel asked, as he noticed a white light streak across the sky.

"Did you see that?"

"Yes, it's called a shooting star. Some people say it is good luck to see one, although I don't believe in good or bad luck. Shall I continue?"

"Yes, I want to know all there is to know."

"My understanding is the Babylonians created the Zodiac to serve a political purpose for the mass of their population. It probably helped in giving people hope. If you haven't got the opium to quell the masses then you need another form of opium to give people hope. The people will have hope after reading part of the Zodiac that their situation may improve or about to improve."

"Give people what they want and they become pawns in the hands of giants," Nathaniel remarked, and for the first time in many weeks he had begun to relax as he gazed at the stars. He felt the pangs of guilt every time he thought about the plight of his friends, he said to himself.

"Yes, the elite of Babylonia could control and predict how people would react. So, the Zodiac signs were used for giving people hope and not much else," Salim said.

"Why are you telling me this?" Nathaniel asked. He was intrigued by what Salim had to say and was eager to learn more as he gazed at the night's sky.

"Because you have to learn that sometimes people invent things for the opposite reasons to what you probably thought," Salim added. "Do not assume anything, because we all make mistakes."

"Why are you helping me?" Nathaniel asked.

"Because I was once a slave," pausing for moment, before continuing, he added, "tomorrow, I will tell you all about it. Now, get some sleep!" Salim suggested.

The following day Salim and Nathaniel continued on their journey to Salim's home on the northeast side of the island. Salim explained to Nathaniel the days when he was a slave. He explained how he had bought his freedom from his master after many years of saving his money that he had made selling candles and food that he had made on his only day off work, which was usually a Sunday.

Chapter 7

"Make preparations to anchor," Captain Horner said.

Lieutenant Curnow gave the orders to his bosun and HMS Antelope anchored just off the docks at the port of Mahajanga on the northwest side of the island of Madagascar.

"Find out what you can about the pirate ship and get some fresh supplies," Captain Horner ordered.

Lieutenant Curnow and a crew of six sailors rowed to the docks at the port town and soon made their way to the local Portuguese's administrative office.

"Go to the warehouse and get these supplies," Lieutenant Curnow said to his bosun and gave him a list."

"Did the pirate ship called the Rag-tail dock here recently?" Lieutenant Curnow asked the man sat behind the desk in the port authority office.

"Yes, only for short time," the Portuguese official replied, who was responsible for collecting taxes from shipping that moored at its docks.

"Let me see...yes, only four days ago the ship slipped its moorings," the Portuguese official replied as he read the details from his shipping accounts.

"Do you know where the ship is heading?" Lieutenant Curnow asked.

"I understand its heading for the slave market at the port of Zinjibar in Yemen."

"Do you know what cargo it unloaded here?"

"Yes, some slaves."

"Where did the slaves go to?"

"The slaves would have been taken to the holding area close by the slave market, ready to be sold, tomorrow."

"Where are the slave market and the holding area?"

"You can't miss it. It's that large building you see at the north end of the town keeping the port to your left."

"How do you know the pirates are heading for Yemen?" Lieutenant Curnow asked.

"I understand that many of the crew from the Rag-tail was talking about the slave market at Yemen. And their captain sent a message by pigeon to Zinjibar."

"How do you know this?

"Sir, the message service is organized from this office. We often have merchants and captains sending messages via our pigeon service."

"Do you know what message the captain sent?"

"No, only that he sent a message," the Portuguese official replied.

"Is there anything else, you have forgotten to tell me?"

"Oh, yes, I understand that a boy escaped from the ship, but the boy hasn't been seen since."

"Is there any description of the boy?"

"Tall and thin as a rake, I heard one man say."

***

Later that day, Lieutenant Curnow and his men headed towards the slave market at the north end of the port town in Madagascar it was eerily quiet. They noticed a few men guarding the entrance to the camp where the captives were being held. After Lieutenant Curnow and his men fired off a few pistol shots in the air all the guards soon surrendered or ran off. The guards had no intention of risking their lives for slaves. Lieutenant Curnow's men found the captives in a pigs' stall chained together like animals ready for slaughter, the lieutenant thought. He also noticed his cousin Nathaniel was not among the captives.

"That Portuguese official was right," Lieutenant Curnow said to himself.

Lieutenant Curnow shouted, "Back to the docks."

As Lieutenant Curnow and his men with some of the freed captives made the first journey in the rowing boat back to the ship, he wondered about his cousin. His thoughts turned to what the captain would do about Nathaniel who was still missing.

"A couple more trips and we shall have all the captives freed on board, sir," Lieutenant Curnow said to the Captain Horner, who was now busy deciding his next move. Lieutenant Curnow could see the captain was contemplating something from the deep wrinkles now appearing across the captain's forehead. He wondered what the captain was thinking, he said to himself, now that he knew the plight of some of the captives.

"But, the boy Nathaniel Curnow is still missing," Lieutenant Curnow added.

"I understand your concern, but, we have a mission. That mission is to seek out the pirate ship Rag-tail and destroy it. And kill or capture any pirates we come across," Captain Horner replied.

"If your information is correct that the boy escaped, and is somewhere on the island of Madagascar, then all we can do is return here when we have finished our mission." Captain Horner added.

***

After all the freed captives were safely on board HMS Antelope, Lieutenant Curnow decided to return to see the Portuguese official. He now had orders from the captain to leave a reward for the safe return of Nathaniel Curnow.

"Will you inform the people about the reward?" Lieutenant Curnow asked as he stood waiting for a reply from the Portuguese official.

"Of course, lieutenant," the Portuguese official replied as he sat behind his desk in his office overlooking the port.

"Please inform Nathaniel Curnow that we shall return for him."

"We will look out for the boy."

As Lieutenant Curnow and his men made their way back to HMS Antelope his mind turned to the fate of his cousin Nathaniel. He wondered if Nathaniel had made his way somehow to a safe place. He knew that the island of Madagascar was under the control of the Portuguese, but this was limited, and at most the island was run by different brigands and pirates that served the interests of the Portuguese, who often turned a blind eye to the antics of the pirates. But, for now, he knew he had to put his mind back towards catching the pirates and finding out why they had attacked the English coast.

Arriving back onboard HMS Antelope, Lieutenant Curnow made his way to the quarter deck where the captain stood ready for his report.

"Captain, we are ready to sail," Lieutenant Curnow said.

"Good, steer north by northwest," Captain Horner ordered.

"Bosun set a course, north by northwest," Lieutenant Curnow repeated the order to the bosun who rang out the orders to his crew. The fully rigged ship was then set full all canvas squared for full speed.

"Have the captives given us any new information?" Captain Horner asked as he watched his crew set the rigging of the sheets.

"Second Lieutenant Shaw is conducting the process, while we wait," Lieutenant Curnow replied.

"Good. They have several days ahead of us," Captain Horner said as he paced up and down the quarter deck, occasionally, stopping, as if to say something, but then he continued in his own world just pacing up and down the quarter deck with his mind in contemplation.

The wind was strong and caught the squared rigged sheets of the ship with full force as Lieutenant Curnow looked up to see the sheets were fully taut. "We have the weather with us, sir."

"I would like to capture this pirate they call Captain Kerry, because someone sent him to our shores. They can hang him from the gibbet when we get the information we need. Do you agree, lieutenant?" Captain Horner asked.

"Yes, of course, captain," Lieutenant Curnow replied.

"I think, we will use chain shot to disable the ship and cannon if we have to."

"Yes, I agree."

"Ship on the horizon," the mid-shipman shouted from the crows' nest from the highest position on the main mast for a lookout.

Captain Horner shouted back, "Where?"

"On our port side, captain," the mid-shipman shouted back as Captain Horner took the telescope from Lieutenant Curnow who was standing against the tackle of the mast. Captain Horner noticed from the outline of the ship that it was a Spanish galleon. The three mast vessel had a distinct profile of a Spanish built galleon, which Captain Horner had had first-hand experience of during the war with Spain and the Catholic King.

"She looks like a Spanish galleon, although I can't see her colors."

"Here, see for yourself."

Looking through the telescope Lieutenant Curnow remarked, "It's Portuguese. She's flying the colors of the Portuguese flag. She could be the Rag-tail."

"If we can see them, then they can see us. Set a course for south by southwest," Captain Horner said. Continuing, he added, "And loosen the sheets; we don't want to catch up with them at this stage."

"Yes, captain, south by southwest," Lieutenant Curnow said to the bosun, who was already shouting out the orders to his crew to loosen the canvas sails.

"Let's see where there going."

"Do you agree, lieutenant?"

"Of course, captain."

"You don't sound so sure, lieutenant?"

"It's your orders, captain. It's my duty to obey your orders," Lieutenant Curnow replied.

"Look, lieutenant, I want your opinion, if you think I have missed something," the captain said in a rage because his second in command was questioning his judgement.

"We will lose time, if we chase this ship," Lieutenant Curnow replied.

"Yes, but if they are going to Yemen then we will catch up with them eventually. I say, Yemen but that information was too easily gathered. You said yourself that everyone in the town knew where the pirate ship was heading. It's too good to be true. Perhaps, the pirates wanted us to believe they were heading for Yemen." Captain Horner said.

"So, what do we do now, captain?"

"We follow them keeping a safe distance and see what they do."

"In the meantime, have those main sheets loosened again," Captain Horner said.

"Loosen the main sail," Lieutenant Curnow shouted to the bosun as the crew loosened the tackle allowing the sheets to sag and draw less wind and power.

The Rag-tail was now just a distance dot on the horizon as HMS Antelope slowly tried to maintain its distance from the possible pirate ship it was tailing. Captain Horner was now pacing the quarter deck pondering what his next move would be. He knew about the Portuguese treasure and wondered if the Rag-tail was headed there. He also knew about the rumors that told of the treasure being buried somewhere on the island of Madagascar. But, the people that told these stories knew not where. And Madagascar was a large island, the treasure could be anywhere, he said to himself.

"That ship, sir. It's heading for the coast," the midshipman shouted from the crows' nest.

"Captain, the ship we are following has turned and is heading towards the coast of Madagascar," Lieutenant Curnow said.

"Good, let's see where they go?" Captain Horner said briskly.

Chapter 8

As Nathaniel and Salim followed the coastline to Salim's home, which was on the northeast side of the island, Nathaniel had begun to know more about Salim. As each night passed, Salim would tell Nathaniel a story about his life.

"Tell me about when you were a slave?" Nathaniel asked.

"It was a long time ago, when I was a boy. My mother and father were poor and needed the money. So, they sold me into slavery when I was about twelve years old. It is a practice that is popular with poor people. I was bought by a plantation owner and made to work every day except Sunday. As the years passed I saved the money I made selling candles and food in the market on Sundays."

"What type of food did you sell?"

"I had watched my mother prepare our meals as a child. It was with only rice and corn that I made my food."

"Eventually, I had saved enough to buy my freedom. And from there I became a merchant."

"And now…you are a merchant. Is that right?" Nathaniel asked as he stoked the camp fire with more wood and waited for an answer.

***

Meanwhile, the pirate ship Rag-tail was heading to the isolated cove that led to where Captain Kerry and his crew stored their treasure. Captain Kerry stood on the quarter deck admiring the view as the Rag-tail made its way to the coast of Madagascar.

"Make sure we have no lights burning," Captain Kerry demanded.

"That ship that was behind us is still out there somewhere. With no moon they will keep away from the shoreline. If they have any sense in their heads they will avoid the shoreline, for sure?"

"Yes, boss," Ironman Slim replied.

"There it is…over there…do you see it?" Captain Kerry asked.

"Steer north by northwest."

"Slow…release the sheets."

"We don't want to bear down on those rocks," Ironman Slim said to his bosun who repeated the orders to his crew.

"Lay anchor," Captain Kerry ordered.

"Lay anchor," Ironman Slim repeated.

***

Meanwhile, as Nathaniel and Salim continued on their journey to Salim's home Nathaniel wondered if he could help his friends that were to be sold into slavery. He again felt the pangs of guilt and pondered the plight of his friends as he savored his new found freedom.

Suddenly, Salim shouted, "Look!"

"Over there, do you see, Nathaniel?"

Standing up in the horse drawn cart Salim pointed to the direction of a narrow cove along the coastline.

"Do you see that ship anchored in that cove?"

"Yes, it looks like it could be the Rag-tail," Nathaniel replied.

"It's a strange place to be anchored," Salim said.

"Yes, you're right. I need to get a closer look."

"We have to follow the track where the cliff meets the shore. We can see from there. There's an old Buddha Temple close by," Salim said.

As Nathaniel and Salim dismounted from the horse and cart and made their way through the thick jungle of lush vegetation on foot they could see the stone statue of the Buddha gradually appearing like some forgotten ancient civilization appearing for the first time in decades. Nathaniel and Salim noticed the statue was twice as tall as a man and was covered by vegetation and the roots of nearby trees. They noticed the statue had been carved from a single outcrop of rock that stood on the site.

Nathaniel had heard the cacophony of animal and bird sounds coming from the surrounding jungle and was mesmerized by its calming effect. It was totally different from the sounds he would hear in a forest back home, he said to himself.

As Nathaniel and Salim made their way down the track towards the old temple they were unaware they had been seen by one of the pirates guarding the perimeter of the temple. Why the temple was here and had been abandoned Salim didn't know, he said to Nathaniel.

"I knew the temple was here," Salim said.

"Oh!" muttered Nathaniel.

"But, I've never been here before, today."

Before Nathaniel and Salim could see the Rag-tail from the shoreline they were surrounded by pirates, they had suddenly appeared from the jungle like flies around a carcass. Nathaniel recognized several of the pirates from the Rag-tail, who were holding their cutlass and pistols at the ready.

"So, it's you, my boy!" Captain Kerry bellowed as he suddenly appeared from the jungle. When Nathaniel noticed the captain had a crooked smile on his face like a thief in the night.

Nathaniel looked at the captain with disdain and wondered what his fate would be and that of his friend Salim. With a grimace across his face he replied, "Yes."

"What do I do with you?"

"Please, do not harm my friend," pleaded Nathaniel with Captain Kerry, and he watched the pirate draw from his belt a long double edged knife.

"They call it...the cutthroat," Captain Kerry said grimly.

"No, fool, your friend is useful. But, you, I'm not sure," Captain Kerry said to the boy.

Captain Kerry shouted out his orders to his men, "You two take the boy back to the shoreline and wait there."

As Nathaniel was led away by two pirates he heard the sound of someone screaming and wondered if it was Salim. It sounded like the voice of Salim, but he couldn't be sure, he said to himself.

"Now, tell me, what you know about this location?" Captain Kerry asked. Continuing, he added, "Or the other ear comes off. Who told you about this location?"

"I know nothing, before, today," Salim replied, and tried to stop the pain from the loss of an ear by holding his hand to his head.

"I knew there was a temple and that's it."

"I don't believe you," Captain Kerry said as he flashed his cutthroat knife again in front of Salim's face. Salim felt the blood run down his face as he struggled with the two pirates holding him firm before the overbearing captain that towered over everyone like a goliath.

"Shall I start on your fingers? Tell me the truth!" Captain Kerry demanded.

"Treasure," Salim replied.

"Now, we're getting somewhere," Captain Kerry said.

"Yes, the treasure of a Spanish gold ship. Believed to be buried on this island," Salim said as he watched the faces of the pirates animate into a trance like state at the mention of gold. Salim knew the power of gold fever and intended to use it to save his life. Gold fever was like a plague, he said to himself.

"So, you know about my treasure?" Captain Kerry asked.

"There is talk of gold and treasure from many sailors with loose tongues and time to spare. Go visit the Inn near the docks," Salim replied.

"Mmmm, I guess a few would talk with ale in their bellies," Captain Kerry said. Pausing to twist the cutthroat in front of Salim's eyes, he added, "So, you know about my treasure?"

"A sailor's tale, but now I know," Salim replied, who allowed himself for the first time a minor smile to appear across his lips.

"Perhaps, I should just kill you."

"No! You need me."

"Why do I need you?" Captain Kerry asked.

"The Spanish gold," Salim replied as he again saw how the pirates reacted to the words Spanish gold. Captain Kerry had now realized Salim knew of another treasure and not his.

"Perhaps, we can make a deal. Spare my life and the life of my friend Nathaniel and I will show you where the gold is for a share of the spoils," Salim said.

"Okay, we have deal," Captain Kerry said as the thoughts of more gold filled his mind like a gusting wind in a storm. Gold fever had already consumed Captain Kerry's every thought like a plague of locusts. Such was the power of gold fever that once it caught on to you then you were forever hooked for life.

"Where is this gold?" Captain Kerry asked.

"At the southern end of the island, near a town called Tolanaro," replied Salim.

"Good, we shall head there soon, but without you" Captain Kerry said, as he cut the throat of Salim.

"We shall get back to the ship and make ready to sail as fast as possible, Slim."

"Right, boss," Ironman Slim remarked.

***

As Captain Kerry climbed aboard the Rag-tail he felt the chill of a cold wind on his face that reminded him of the danger lurking somewhere outside the secluded cove. His intuition could be right; there was a ship on his tail, he thought. The Rag-tail would make a dash for the open sea and avoid fighting a battle if it could, unless it was forced to fight, he said to himself.

Chapter 9

Meanwhile, Yuki was allowed to accompany Captain Kareem to the slave market at Zinjibar, Yemen. Yuki watched as young and old, black and white people were being sold into slavery. She felt lucky she was alive and not being bought and sold like animals at a farm market. Captain Kareem and Purapratt had Yuki tied to one of the pirates as they walked around the port of Zinjibar, which was under the control of Yemenis' pirates.

"Take two of our men and find out what you can about the Portuguese pirate," Captain Kareem said.

"Where to, boss?" Purapratt asked.

"Go around the port and the docks."

"Meet you later in the local Inn, just over there," Captain Kareem said.

As Captain Kareem with his men and Yuki entered the local Inn they ordered some drink and waited for the Inn keeper to attend to their needs. It was the custom in a Muslim country to be served. Captain Kareem knew Inn keepers were always listening to sailors' tales and could be a reliable source of information at times.

"We need information about a pirate ship called the Rag-tail," Captain Kareem said to the Inn keeper.

"Do you have coin?" the Inn keeper asked, who had a beard as long as a baby's arm that was black and grey, but mostly grey. His dark eyes lit up like a flickering candle at the thought of making money for nothing. The black bandanna he wore to hid his bald head and also hid the scars of battles he fought when he was a young lad making his way in the pirate world. Now, he was an ageing man with little to live for except adventure and coin.

"How do you know?"

"Because they sent a message via pigeon from Mahajanga, Madagascar," the Inn keeper replied.

"How did you come by this information?"

"Because my patrons who secretly drink ale have loose tongues, I hear all the news in my Inn."

"How much do you want?" Captain Kareem asked.

"Enough to retire, I'm tired of dealing with laggards and drunks," the Inn keeper replied stroking his long beard into a spiral as he spoke.

"First, tell me the news."

"The Rag-tail is due here in a few weeks. It sailed from the port of Mahajanga, Madagascar just a few days ago. With fair weather it should arrive here by the time the moon has a face."

"What else do you know?" Captain Kareem asked.

"The treasure…I know where the treasure is," the Inn keeper replied.

"Stop…say no more or I will cut you from your head to your toes and feed you to the lizards," Captain Kareem said.

***

Captain Kareem spent some time drinking with his men, before Purapratt arrived back at the Inn.

"Listen!"

"I have some news. Now, tell Purapratt what you told me earlier," Captain Kareem said to the Inn keeper.

"The treasure of the one they call the Portuguese pirate is on the island of Madagascar."

"You know this to be true?" Captain Kareem asked.

"True as the day that follows night. I was once a crew member on the Rag-tail. The treasure is near a temple, I can show you for a cut of the treasure."

"All in good time, my friend," Captain Kareem said.

"Why have you waited so long a time to get the treasure?" Purapratt asked, not willing to trust the Inn keeper.

"Because, I was waiting for a suitable partner to come to our port," the Inn keeper replied.

"You will have a share, my friend," Captain Kareem said.

Yuki could hear every word that was spoken by the Inn keeper, Captain Kareem and Purapratt, but paid no interest. She was more interested in escaping if she got the chance. She was on the other side of the world as far as she was concerned in a foreign land with little hope of escape tied to a pirate.

"We sail first light, tomorrow. We are agreed then on our terms?" Captain Kareem asked.

"Yes, we have terms," the Inn keeper replied. "And my name is Ali Ben Sur."

Ali Ben Sur was born in Palestine to Arabic parents, who had made a small fortune trading goods across the Mediterranean. His early life was spent helping his father in the import and export of goods. After his father had died, he decided as a young man to move to Zinjibar, Yemen to buy a local Inn, because of the thriving trade the port would bring, he hoped to make his fortune there. He was a small man in stature with an Arabic complexion with dark hair and brown eyes. Ali Ben Sur was also a shrewd business man, who was always willing to make a deal if he could make a profit, even if it meant breaking the rules.

As Captain Kareem and his men with Yuki boarded the Santé Maria moored at the docks the ship was a hive of activity. Yuki noticed the pirates were busy like bees around a hive loading fresh supplies of food and barrels of gun powder.

"Take Yuki to the galley and untie her and ready me some food, my girl," Captain Kareem said. He watched every move as Yuki was led down the steps from the quarter deck. And for moment, realized how much she was beginning to mean to him, he wanted her, he thought.

The last person to board the Santé Maria was Ali Ben Sur the Inn keeper. He was given a hammock close to the captain's quarters under the quarter deck. Later, Captain Kareem poured over the maps and plotted a course for the Santé Maria with Purapratt, he wondered about how trustworthy or not the Inn keeper would be. He hadn't been completely truthful with the Inn keeper, but that information was private between Purapratt and himself.

"The island of Madagascar…," Yuki heard the words.

The door opened to the captain's quarters as the pirate guarding the entrance led Yuki into the room with dishes of food. Yuki heard what the captain had said before leaving the captain's quarters. Again the captain had eyes only for Yuki.

"What do you think, Purapratt?" Captain Kareem asked.

"With the right weather, we could be there before the next full moon."

"No, I mean, what do you think about the information from the Inn keeper?" Captain Kareem asked again.

"He says, he used to sail with the Portuguese pirate they call Captain Kerry. If this is true then why did he leave?"

"Yes, there are many questions that need answers," Captain Kareem said.

"Perhaps, you should have told him what you already know."

"For now, we keep quiet. Until, we have the treasure in our hands," Captain Kareem said and adding. "Set a course south by southeast for tomorrow."

The following day, Purapratt proceeded to the quarter deck to relay the captain's orders to his bosun. The Santé Maria's pirates immediately began rigging the sheets of the sloop to catch all of the prevailing wind along the coast of east Africa.

Ali Ben Sur watched from the relative safety of the quarter deck as the crew rigged the sails taut. He wondered how trustworthy were his partners, but consoled himself that everything would work out. He had God on his side, he said to himself.

"I hope for your sake you are telling the truth," Purapratt remarked.

"You will see...when you have the treasure in your hands," Ali Ben Sur said.

"Where do you come from?" Purapratt asked as he was eager to extract more information from the Inn keeper.

"Palestine," Ali Ben Sur replied.

Chapter 10

After several weeks sailing, the Portobello galleon had made its way to the northwest coast of Africa. Lord Trethowan had given Black Eye the information he had previously bought from Lieutenant Gillard about the progress of HMS Antelope.

"The last information, I received was HMS Antelope stopped at Rabat, on the northwest coast of Africa, and then continued on towards the Cape. It's on course for Madagascar, I believe," Lord Trethowan insisted.

"This information…is it reliable?" Black Eye asked.

"Yes, it's straight from the admiralty," Lord Trethowan replied.

Lord Trethowan explained, to Black Eye and Two Coin that the royal navy had a means of communicating via the use of pigeons. This messaging service allowed the admiralty based in its headquarters in Portsmouth, England to keep track of its ships around the world. Any royal navy ship was equipped with pigeons to report their progress in any part of the world. The pigeons would naturally return to their home port at Portsmouth, England.

"I have a contact inside the admiralty that gave me the information before I left for London," Lord Trethowan said.

"The treasure was never mentioned, only the captives and where this pirate ship was possibly heading for."

"What were the orders for HMS Antelope?" Black Eye asked.

"Free the slaves and kill or capture the pirates and destroy the Rag-tail," Lord Trethowan replied.

As the three men discussed their plans inside Black Eye's quarters for the capture of the captives and the possible acquisition of the treasure the Portobello galleon had begun to list from one side then the other. Lord Trethowan stood firm holding the chart table, while Black Eye and Two Coin struggled to maintain their balance as the ship was hit with enormous waves that could be heard crashing down on the ship's upper deck like the sound of mature trees being felled in a forest. The Portobello was at the mercy of the sea as it continued to roll up and down with the motion of the waves like flotsam that had seen a thousand storms.

"Go see to your men…and make sure the rigging is set squared bow and aft," Black Eye said to Two Coin.

Grapping hold like a man possessed to the chart table, Lord Trethowan suddenly looked as pale as washed out clothing, all the color had drained from his normal pinkish complexion, which Lord Trethowan had gained from too much sun wandering about outdoors on his extensive estate of farms and mines.

"You look ill," Black Eye said.

"Yes, that's so perceptive of you," Lord Trethowan replied grimly.

"Perhaps, you should have stayed at home," Black Eye suggested.

"No, I have to keep my eyes on you," Lord Trethowan replied trying to provide a grin across his face, when all he wanted to do was crawl into a corner and curl up in agony.

"Perhaps, you should be on deck with your men," Lord Trethowan queried, with an intense look of anger across his face.

"Perhaps, we should be both on deck. You will feel better outside, Lord Trethowan," Black Eye replied stroking his long beard, while trying to maintain his balance, as the ship listed from one side to the other. They could hear the raging waves crashing onto the ship's deck above.

As Black Eye and Lord Trethowan made their way to the quarter deck they noticed Two Coin and two other pirates trying to rig the sheets on the main mast, when suddenly, they heard the sound of wood and tackle crashing to the main deck of the ship.

Black Eye shouted, "Get that fucking tackle secured."

"What happened?" Lord Trethowan asked in a panic, and watched the crew battling to control the ship in the storm.

"We have lost some of the aft rigging," Black Eye replied.

"As long as we don't sink, we'll be alright," Black Eye said with a brimming smile across his face, which were so revealing, that many of his gold teeth glistened under the fading light.

"What do I do?" Lord Trethowan asked, and held on to the quarter deck rail as the Portobello listed to one side then the other. The raging sea and winds now threatened to capsize the ship, as each moment passed.

Lord Trethowan shouted, "You don't seem to be worried, right now!"

"It's up to God or fate," Black Eye replied as he tried to steer the ship into the wind and avoid the raging waves and wind crossing each other and bringing down another rigging pole.

"I didn't think pirates thought about God or fate," Lord Trethowan said, who was thinking more about losing his life than feeling sick at this point in time. Black Eye was right, he said to himself. It was better to brave the elements on the quarter deck than feel sick below deck.

"I'm not a pirate. I'm a mercenary...a soldier for coin," Black Eye said with a wry smile on his face. Continuing he said, "What you call a profiteer, who makes their living within the law of the land. In this case, the law of our king or whoever makes the laws of the land."

"It makes no different, as long as you can be trusted. We made a bargain in England to save the captives and split the treasure if we find it," Lord Trethowan said.

"Don't worry, I will keep my side of the bargain, Lord Trethowan," Black Eye replied, and reached for a bottle of wine tucked inside his pantaloons, and then he took a giant sip to help keep the chill from his body.

"We will reach the Cape with good winds by the next full moon," Black Eye replied.

"Don't worry, we will catch them at some point," Black Eye said.

"You seem confident, you will find them?" Lord Trethowan asked, gloomily.

"When there's talk of treasure, especially gold...it doesn't take much to loosen their tongues. When people hear or see the prospect of gold their eyes light up like a flickering candle light and it's difficult to put out the candle light from that point onwards. It's like a fever that never leaves their body and mind. When they found gold deposits in Madagascar, a few years ago, the whole island became a beacon of light, which every dreamer and adventurer pursued until they became either wealthy or poor. I have seen it for myself. And paid the price," Black Eye said pointing to the patch over his right eye, while he continued to steer the ship's wheel into favorable winds and maintain his balance as the ship listed from one side to the other.

Continuing he said, "Tell a man there is gold somewhere and he his caught by the gold fever like a fish in a net, he cannot get away. People are then afraid to leave an area for fear of losing out to someone else that is... the gold fever, it never leaves some people. And mark my words our men on this boat will change overnight and become different people. Perhaps, you or maybe me, no one can be certain, how they will respond. Gold has a way of destroying people the moment they lay their eyes on it."

"You know a lot about Madagascar?" Lord Trethowan asked.

"Perhaps, it was too much."

Black Eye looked at Lord Trethowan, with a contented facial expression that expressed to Lord Trethowan that Black Eye knew a lot more about Madagascar then he previously assumed.

Black Eye shouted, "The wind is easing, secure the rigging."

***

Over the days that passed, Lord Trethowan gained more information about Black Eye's past as he shared the captain's quarters. It took much wine after sharing a meal with the mercenary before Black Eye was as lucid as water pouring down a waterfall, you could not stop him. All Lord Trethowan could do was to sit back and occasionally prompt him with another question. Black Eye explained, his days before he became an Inn keeper in London. He said most Inn keepers are known for their tales they told to their drunken clients. But Black Eye expressed his truth about his past like a pastor giving the 'last rights' to someone at death's door.

Black Eye explained that for many years gone past Madagascar was an island of pirates. The island had been claimed by the Portuguese and for many years the pirates and the Portuguese had an alliance to not essentially bother each other on or around the island. Black Eye explained that even the Portuguese at times resorted to piracy when it suited them. He explained how many Spanish ships were targeted by the Portuguese during their recent dispute over some of the islands around Sumatra.

Black Eye explained, one day when he was a crew member aboard a Portuguese ship working as a 'profiteer' they found a large amount of gold and silver. The treasure was in gold doubloons and silver ingots. The treasure was on its way to the Spanish government when our ship raided it and stole the treasure. But, before we had time to celebrate our good fortune, another ship appeared on the horizon. The ship was flying a Portuguese flag, so we relaxed, thinking we were safe.

"What happened?" Lord Trethowan asked as the Portobello started to rock again in the sea between the peaks and troughs of violent waves.

"Another time, Lord Trethowan we have business to do. We are close to the Cape and I need to see to my men," Black Eye replied as he tried to maintain his balance as the ship listed one way then another. Reaching the quarter deck he could see Two Coin organizing his crew to regain control of the Portobello. Men were on the main mast setting the rigging to catch as little of the wind as possible, without causing the main mast to fail against the stormy winds.

Black Eye shouted out loud to his men from the quarter deck, "We are at the Cape. It can be the Devil's daughter you have to caress."

Black Eye knew from experience, that whichever way you were going around the Cape that made no difference. The skills of a sailor that could traverse the colliding currents were your only savior. The Cape collided with two seas that meet for the first time and even in calm waters the two different currents are always going to be treacherous to cross. The proof of this was the number of ship wrecks Black Eye could see along the Cape coastline. In calm or stormy waters it was a difficult crossing for any skilled captain.

It took many more hours of treacherous seas before the Portobello had safely sailed around the Cape. The ship had been lucky the crossing had been favorable with the masts and the rigging. The Portobello managed only to lose one aft pole and some minor rigging, which was later soon replaced. Black Eye then made his way to his quarters where Lord Trethowan had already made hast as soon as he saw the ship had been brought under control by the crew.

When Black Eye had settled down in his chair, Lord Trethowan was ready with questions about what happened next to the gold.

"It was like I said. At first, we thought we were safe, as the ship was flying the flag of Portugal. The captain of our ship allowed the other ship to pull alongside ours. That was when, everything went bad. They fired cannon shot at us, all their guns and ripped us apart. Most of the crew lay dying or were already dead. I managed to escape, the force of a cannon shot sent me flying into the sea. It was all I could do to hang on to some floating timber, and eventually, I made it to the shore."

"So, you abandoned your mates?" Lord Trethowan asked with a cruel grin across his face.

"No, once in the water, there was nothing I could do. And besides, I was a mercenary employed by the government. What would you have done in the same circumstances?" Black Eye countered with a determined tone of voice.

"Do you want to hear the rest or are you going to rake my balls?"

"No, go on."

"When I made it to the shore of the island I followed the progress of the ship as it sailed around the coast of Madagascar. It wasn't easy, because some of the jungle extends to the very edge of the cliffs."

"What made you think the ship would sail around the island?"

"It was just a good guess. I assumed that the pirates would store the treasure close by. Somewhere, and perhaps where they had been before. It was just a hunch."

"What happened next?" Lord Trethowan asked, who was now showing signs of gold fever, Black Eye thought.

Black Eye explained to Lord Trethowan that after several days following the coastline through the thick jungle, he caught sight of the ship at anchor in a small cove. It was several hours before; I could see the pirates on the beach making their way into the jungle carrying caskets. Before, I could get any closer, I saw several pirates roaming the jungle and I took cover."

"What happened next?" Lord Trethowan asked who was now like a man possessed with fever.

"It was now late and the moon gave some light. I saw in the distance the light of fire and assumed they had made camp. I fell asleep and awoke to see the pirates rowing back to their ship. I then waited as the pirate ship way anchor and sailed away. After several hours through the jungle, I saw a giant statue of the Buddha and made my way around the temple. I saw where they had made camp, but I could not find any tracks leading to the treasure. I looked for days, but found nothing for my troubles. But, it must be there somewhere, I thought. So, I decided to wait for another ship to pass by that I could signal for help and that's what I did."

"This pirate ship that attacked you...was it the same pirates that attacked my village?" Lord Trethowan asked.

"Yes, I believe...the one they call Captain Kerry," Black Eye replied.

"We're at least two weeks behind their ship. But, when we get to Madagascar we can find out from the locals where they may be heading."

"There're always a few loose tongues willing to talk for some coin," Black Eye said, grinning.

"First, tell me about your experience as a sailor."

"I believe I was born on the island of Madagascar. As you can see I'm as black as the ace of spades," Black Eye said with a wry smile that had crept along his face like a passing storm. Lord Trethowan and Maisha looked on with agreement shrugging their shoulders and waited for Black Eye to continue.

"My parents were free people and so was I. When I was old enough to work I started working on a tobacco plantation under contract, then the English came one night to our village and press ganged every fit man into the navy they could find. At that time, the island was under the control of the English Crown."

"So, you have an axe to grind against the English. Is that not true?" Lord Trethowan asked wondering where his partner's allegiance lay.

"No…listen to the end," Black Eye replied, who could see the impatience of his ally as Lord Trethowan's face had begun to start to get redder as time went by.

Black Eye continued to explain his experience to Lord Trethowan and Maisha only stopping to take a gulp of wine before continuing his story. The gentle movement of the ship as it sailed towards their destination was like the rhythm of a pendulum it was a constant reminder to Maisha and Lord Trethowan of where they were.

"After several months and years I worked my way up the ladder and became a bosun on an English frigate. By that time, I knew everything there was to know about sailing, well at least that's what, I thought. I have learned since that the sea can always surprise you, when least expected. But, that's another story for another day. I couldn't become an officer in the English navy because of my color."

"Their loss your gain," Maisha shouted, as the minor parrot perched on her shoulder repeated the words several times, "Their loss your gain, their loss your gain."

"Shoooosh…damn bird has a mind of its own," Maisha said. Then Lord Trethowan poured himself some wine into a pewter jug and with a large gulp, acknowledged the status quo with a shrug of his shoulders and the words, "Their loss your gain."

"Like I said, it's their loss my gain. I believe I've helped many an English captain with my skills as a sailor. And we will need those skills as a sailor if we're to capture our pirate, and to live to tell the tale," Black Eye said, and then pausing to collect his thoughts, before continuing. He noticed that Lord Trethowan from his body posture and facial expressions was a man of little patience and that Maisha looked enthralled on his every word. He had not previously discussed much of his past life with Maisha because he felt it wasn't that important, he said to himself. He could see the difference between the two they were like chalk and cheese, Lord Trethowan the chalk and Maisha the cheese.

"So eventually, after I served out my time in the English navy I became a soldier of fortune. What I mean is... willing to buccaneer within the law of the English Crown. I captured this ship we sail in...from the Spanish and I renamed her Portobello. Most of the time, I sail between ports transporting a range of goods, these crossings which are plagued by pirates incur higher costs for the merchants, and so I make my money this way."

"An interesting story, please go on."

"As a buccaneer many Spanish ships were attacked."

"Tell me more about the gold ship?"

"Like I said, we were attacked by the pirate known as Captain Kerry. I followed the ship, until the next morning, only to see the ship leave the cove. I saw where they had camped in the jungle near a large statue of the Buddha the height of two men combined, but found no tracks leading to any treasure or gold. But, I know where the cove is and can lead you there. Perhaps, you can find the treasure." Black Eye replied.

"First, we have to get to the island. And find out some more information on our prey. Some coin spread in the right places should help our cause," Lord Trethowan said, who could already see the treasure waiting for him in his mind.

"You could be right." Maisha said, at about the same time her parrot perched on her shoulder started repeating her words.

"You could be right...you could be right...you could be right," squawked Spotty the parrot.

***

When the Portobello docked at Mahajanga the crew was busy loading the ship with fresh supplies, while Black Eye, Maisha and Two Coin joined Lord Trethowan on a mission, to find out information on the pirate ship they were hunting. As they walked to the local Inn the port was a hive of activity. Black Eye noticed some seagulls fighting and the squawking was like the rattle of pots and pans as the birds fought over the spoils from the fisherman docked at the port. He saw the guts of fish spread all over parts of the docks as the seagulls fought over the spoils the fisherman threw away.

"Let me do the talking," Black Eye said to his three companions, who were sat around the table at the local Inn, near the port.

"You're the Inn keeper?"

"Yes, why do you ask?"

"We would like information on the pirate ship called the Rag-tail," Black Eye replied.

"There are many ships that dock at this port. There is a slave market just at the edge of town. It's a busy port for trade in slaves and goods. Do you have coin?" the Inn keeper asked.

"Yes, for the right information," Black Eye replied in a commanding tone of voice.

"Yes, the Rag-tail was here and off loaded some slaves. I understand that a young boy escaped."

"When did the ship set sail?"

"Aye, no more than a few days," the Inn keeper replied, as he took a long sup of ale from a flagon.

"Do you know where the ship was heading for?"

"The ship sent a message forward to Zinjibar, Yemen. There is a slave market in this place, too."

"You say…they sent a message?"

"Yes, using the pigeon service operated by the Portuguese authority. You will find they have an office opposite the docks. You will see the Portuguese flag outside the building. You can make enquiries there."

"What can you tell me about the captain of the Rag-tail?" Black Eye asked, as Maisha, Two Coin and Lord Trethowan listened carefully to every word of the conversation.

"They call him the Portuguese pirate and also known as Captain Kerry. What his real name is, no one knows? It is said that he is Irish, but no one really knows. He works for the Portuguese government as a profiteer, but like I said, none of us really knows."

"And, there is talk of treasure."

"What treasure?"

"The treasure that came from a Spanish galleon hauling gold and silver," the Inn keeper replied.

"Do you know where?"

"If I did I wouldn't be sitting here…," the Inn keeper replied with a wide grin across his face.

"Yes, but you would have heard stories," Black Eye said. He was keen to know as much as possible from the Inn keeper.

"Somewhere, on Madagascar that is what I've heard, but where I don't know."

"Here is some coin for your troubles."

"Oh, by the way, you are not the first in recent days to ask about the Rag-tail. There was an English lieutenant asking much the same questions."

"You, say English navy?"

"Yes, it's on the Rag-tail's trail like a dog on heat," the Inn keeper replied, and then took another long sup of ale, before belching so loud, that the Inn fell silent for a moment, while the Inn keeper gently stroked his barrel shaped belly in joy.

"Thank you, for the extra information."

"Let's head back and make a visit at the port office," Black Eye suggested.

***

"We understand that the ship Rag-tail sent a message from here some days ago. Can we see the message information," Black Eye asked, as Maisha, Lord Trethowan and Two Coin watched their leader negotiate with the Portuguese's port authority official.

"That information is private," the Portuguese official replied.

"Here is some coin to sweeten the taste," Black Eye said, smiling.

"Or…perhaps the tip of my sword," Maisha said, as she withdrew her cutlass from her side, and pointed the sword at the throat of the port official, who was sat behind his desk frozen like a statue.

"Now, tell me what I need to know?" Black Eye asked.

"Let me see…here it is. The message says: Rag-tail heading for Zinjibar," the Port Authority Official replied eagerly.

"It's just a short message."

"So, the Rag-tail is heading for Yemen, eh," Black Eye said out loud.

***

Before Lord Trethowan, Maisha, Two Coin and Black Eye boarded the Portobello, Black Eye was curious to know, if any of the crew had found out any information about the pirate ship.

"Ask the crew if they found any information on the pirate ship."

"While fetching supplies, our bosun found this man," Two Coin said, and held the man by the arm and stood before the captain on the docks. The man explained, he was a former African slave, who had been given his freedom by his previous master.

"What is your name?" Black Eye asked.

"My name is Okaye Obi Tan…most people call me Tan," Okaye Obi Tan replied.

"What can you tell me?" Black Eye asked.

"On my way here to visit the market…on the track that leads around the north end of the island, I saw a ship at anchor and men rowing to the shore in a cove several days' ride from here."

"I didn't wait to see what they were doing, because I wanted to make the weekly market."

"Is that your ride…that mule?" Black Eye asked.

"Yes, she's a good animal, but a bit slow," Tan replied.

"Is there anything else you can tell me?"

"Yes, there is a large statue of a monk near the cove, but I have never seen it. I have been told the statue exists. But, there are many statues and temples all over the island. Many have been forgotten and the jungle has taken over."

Black Eye gave the black man some coin and sent him on his way, before boarding the ship, which was now ready to sail. Standing on the quarter deck, he shouted, out his orders and the Portobello set sail from the port of Mahajanga.

"Set a course north by northeast and hug the coastline," Black Eye said to Two Coin, who immediately repeated the instructions to his bosun.

"It looks like a ruse. Everyone and I mean everyone knows too much about the comings and goings of the Rag-tail. What do you think, Two Coin?" Black Eye asked, and waited for an answer. He wanted an answer to the question, which had been bothering him, since leaving the port of Mahajanga. A pirate on the run tells everyone his plans, is too much like a ruse, he could smell its stink, he said to himself.

Lord Trethowan interrupting said, "Yes, I've had the same feeling. Everyone knows too much like the Inn keeper."

Two Coin looked at Lord Trethowan with a scowl across his face like a man, who had little time for pleasantries of the landed gentry. "You could be right, Black Eye. It could all be a ruse. What will we do?"

"If I'm right, then we're only a few weeks at most behind the Rag-tail. We shall find the cove and hopefully find the treasure. If that was the Rag-tail in the cove then they must be hiding or retrieving their spoils.

"Don't forget...the captives, especially my right hand man, Captain John Flynn," said Lord Trethowan.

"Oh, yes...I haven't forgotten," Black Eye said with a commanding tone of voice.

"We have a contract between us," Lord Trethowan said.

"Yes, yes...I know we have," Black Eye said firmly.

"How do you propose we free the captives and Captain John Flynn?" Two Coin asked thoughtfully.

"We will have to board the Rag-tail and fight for their freedom," Black Eye replied dismissively.

Chapter 11

"Yes, Palestine," Ali Ben Sur repeated.

"How did you end up in Yemen?" Purapratt asked.

"It's a long story, and one I will tell you another time," Ali Ben Sur replied.

***

After several weeks the Santé Maria entered the seas off the north coast of Madagascar, the weather had turned almost overnight, from calm blue seas to a mix of dark green and white, the colors of a raging sea. The storm had lasted for several days before Captain Kareem could continue his hunt for the treasure of the Portuguese pirate.

"Bring me some food," Captain Kareem ordered Yuki, as she stood inside the captain's quarters, listening, to every word spoken by the captain and his second in command, Purapratt. By now, Yuki had gained the captain's trust and was treated as one of the pirates. She had been taught how to use a pistol and a cutlass by Captain Kareem, on the many days when the weather permitted. Yuki had also trained with the crew during their trial firing of their guns from the upper deck.

As Yuki entered the Captain's quarters with a tray of food she could hear the commotion above from the crew. Captain Kareem could also hear his men as one man shouted, "Ahoy...there on the starboard bow."

"Captain, a ship has been sighted off our bow," the pirate said as he rushed into the Captain Kareem's quarters to relay the news from his bosun.

As Captain Kareem, looked up from the charts he was studying of the island of Madagascar, he wondered, if the ship sighted was friend or foe.

"We better take a look, Purapratt."

On the quarter deck the captain could now see the ship was flying an English flag and from its outline could make out the familiar design of a naval frigate ship. The ship was a typical fully rigged square sail vessel used by the English navy.

"Here...take a look!"

Through the telescope, Purapratt could see the gun port holes of the ship and recognized that the ship had many more guns at its disposal. It outgunned the Santé Maria and they were probably better trained then his ensemble of pirates, he said to himself. He felt a cold chill creep up his spine like a slithering snake. The English ship was getting closer by the minute.

Yuki also noticed, the English ship was getting closer, as she stood by Captain Kareem on the quarter deck. Yuki also felt her heart beating louder, as she watched the crew, rushing to make the ship ready for any action. Up until now, it had been an adventure; she had consoled herself with, and one that was thrust upon her when she was taken for a slave. Her memories were fading, as the days passed, of her time before her capture. She was now, accepted as part of the crew. And Captain Kareem had become her lover in many ways.

"It's the English navy...a war ship. What are they doing here?" Purapratt asked anxiously.

"Perhaps, their looking for treasure as well," Captain Kareem replied in a curt and sarcastic manner. His thoughts turned to what action if anything he could do.

"It looks like war."

"Man the guns. And get that main sail taut." Captain Kareem shouted out to his crew.

"The ship is turning," Purapratt shouted.

"Good!"

"Stand the men down," Captain Kareem shouted, as he watched the English naval ship turn around and sail into the opposite direction to the sail of the Santé Maria.

"Get Ali Ben Sur up here," Captain Kareem stated to Purapratt. As Purapratt went below deck to fetch the Inn keeper from his sleeping quarters, which was next to the captain's cabin, he wondered, how reliable the Inn keeper's information would be. Purapratt had a distrust of Arabs because of his early experience as young man watching Arabs buying and selling slaves, and their tendency to lie about everything given the chance. Arabs could not be trusted, he said to himself.

"The captain wants you on the quarter deck, now!" Purapratt said to Ali Ben Sur.

"What's the hurry?" Ali Ben Sur asked briskly.

"Just get your fat ass off that hammock and follow me. We are off the coast of Madagascar. I hope your information is good, otherwise, you could end up as fish bait for the sharks," Purapratt replied in a commanding tone of voice, and with a wry smile across his face.

"You will see for sure the treasure," Ali Ben Sur said to Purapratt as they passed the galley where Yuki was busy preparing food over the fire. She had heard, what the Arab had said, to Purapratt, before they climbed the stairs to the quarter deck. If the pirates were distracted by the search for treasure, then, it could be her chance to escape, she said to herself.

"Here take the telescope and take a look, we are off the north coast of Madagascar," Captain Kareem said to Ali Ben Sur.

"Do you see the cove?"

"Yes, it's just beyond those high cliffs," Ali Ben Sur said.

"Where is it?" Captain Kareem asked.

"The cove is next to those high cliffs on the right," Ali Ben Sur replied curtly. And he continued, "From the cove you will see the temple."

As the Santé Maria drew closer to the cove entrance a shout rang out from the mast tower. "Ahoy, a ship sails."

Captain Kareem, Purapratt, Yuki and Ali Ben Sur all watched, from the quarter deck, as the ship sighted was heading towards their ship at great speed. Looking through his telescope at the approaching ship, Captain Kareem had no time to react before he heard the sound of cannon fire.

"The English ship is firing on the ship coming our way," Captain Kareem said.

"Is that the Rag-tail?" Purapratt asked in disbelief.

"I don't know?" Ali Ben Sur replied.

"We better get out of the way, before we end as chop sticks floating in the sea," Captain Kareem remarked.

"Turn north by northeast," Captain Kareem shouted at his bosun, who was at the wheel house trying to steer the ship.

"Get those fucking sheets rigged now," Captain Kareem demanded to his crew, as they tried to steer the Santé Maria away from the course of the approaching ship, which appeared to be heading their way. Before Captain Kareem could say another word to his crew, cannon fire hit the water around the Santé Maria, and then the sound of cannon shot splintering across the masts and the sheets of the ship.

Captain Kareem shouted, "Man the cannon."

"Captain, we are out gunned by the English ship. We need to out run the English, it's our only hope," Purapratt stressed, who was desperate to change his captain's orders.

As the Santé Maria turned broadside to HMS Antelope the order to fire was given by Captain Kareem, "Fire!"

A blast of cannon fire hit HMS Antelope as the Santé Maria maneuvered to steer clear from returning cannon fire. The quarter deck of the Santé Maria was hit by cannon fire as the ship tried to escape the terror of the English navy.

"Captain, are you alright?" Purapratt asked. He had escaped without any severe injuries.

"Yes, check Yuki."

"She's alright, wounded, but alive. The cannon had a direct hit. The bosun is gone and so is the wheel house. We are dead in the water. We can sail, but not steer. What are we going to do?" Purapratt asked in desperation.

"But up the white flag. And cease firing," Captain Kareem shouted, and then Purapratt helped the captain to his feet.

Purapratt shouted out the orders to his crew, "Cease firing and put up the white flag, now!"

***

At the same time, the pirate ship Rag-tail, with more cannon than the Santé Maria, and more to lose, continued to out maneuver HMS Antelope.

"Fire at will," Captain Kerry shouted, as his crew continued to maneuver the Rag-tail with her square sheet rigging, which enabled the ship to avoid much of the return cannon from HMS Antelope.

"Steer south by southeast!" Captain Kerry shouted as the Rag-tail headed towards the mist that could be seen from the quarter deck in the south.

"Get the ship ready to disappear in that mist," Captain Kerry said to Ironman Slim.

"Did you see the damage of that other ship?" Ironman Slim asked. He continued to view through his telescope the damage to the other ship, which was now attempting at fleeing from the English frigate.

"Yes, I don't want to end like they did. Our plans are to make our way to Yemen as originally planned," Captain Kerry replied.

"What about our treasure? Is it safe?" Ironman Slim asked, franticly.

"You know it is. The only people that know are us," Captain Kerry replied, dismissively. "Fetch, Nat to my cabin."

As Captain Kerry and Slim made their way from the quarter deck down the stairs to the captain's quarters, to discuss their plans, the ship was being made ready to disappear into the mist. This meant all candle light would be extinguished by the crew on the Rag-tail, to evade the trailing HMS Antelope.

Nathaniel was brought by a pirate from the galley, where he had been busy preparing food for the captain and Slim.

"So, your friends…the English are on our tail," Captain Kerry said to Nathaniel.

In the early evening light of the moon Nathaniel could make out the outline of the captain and Slim in the shadows of the captain's quarters. "What do you want me to say?" Nathaniel replied.

"Always, the truth…my boy," Captain Kerry replied as drew his cutthroat knife from his belt and laid it on the table in front of Nat.

"Yes, they want all the captives and that includes me back and they may know about the treasure," Nathaniel replied as he still shook from fear after the ship's encounter with the English ship.

"You are shaking?" Captain Kerry asked as he noticed Nathaniel visually shaking as he stood before him.

"Yes, from the battle. Cannon shot hit near the galley and killed several men," Nathaniel replied.

"It's like that in battle…you never know who gets killed. Now, what to do about you? You escaped and then we caught you near the temple," Captain Kerry said.

"Perhaps, we should just throw him overboard and let the sharks have a taste," Ironman Slim said with a grin so wide, that Nathaniel could now see more of his gold teeth appear, like flickering candles of light in the darkness, he thought.

"What do you know about the treasure?" Captain Kerry asked impatiently.

"To know that there is a treasure," Nathaniel replied, who was now beginning to calm down from the after effects of battle.

"You will continue to help the cook in the galley, as before. Until I decide otherwise," Captain Kerry said.

"Take Nat back to the galley," Captain Kerry stated to the pirate, as Nathaniel was escorted back to the galley to work.

"The boy knows too much," Ironman Slim said the moment the boy had been led out of the captain's quarters.

"Perhaps, but I doubt where the treasure is buried," Captain Kerry replied. Continuing he added, "We will find out soon enough."

***

The next day, Nathaniel was summoned by Captain Kerry to his quarters. Captain Kerry had discussed with Ironman Slim the previous night what to do with Nathaniel. Captain Kerry's employer had not said anything about what they should do with the captives, only, the time, location and why the attack on the village of Trethowan was worth the bounty. The race was now on to get to Yemen and make the rendezvous previously agreed. Captain Kerry had wondered why the village of Trethowan had been chosen by his employer to attack and not another village along the English coast. His employer, the mysterious sheik had the answers, he said to himself.

Ironman Slim said, "You sent for the boy?"

Nathaniel placed a tray of food on the captain's table and waited to hear his fate. Nathaniel had feared the worst, but knew the captain to be a man you could make a deal with, and he had knowledge he could bargain with, he said to himself.

Captain Kerry shook his head in agreement and said, "Nat, I have decided not to throw you overboard," with a smile across the captain's face, like that of cat that wants something he continued. "Tell me, what you know about the treasure?"

Nathaniel's thoughts for a moment were of what to say, he had considered his options, if he told the truth the pirates may just kill him after they had the information they wanted to hear.

"I know there is a treasure," Nathaniel replied, and continued, "because you told me there was treasure, you said treasure, not me."

Captain Kerry realized the boy was brave, but would soon talk under torture, he said to himself.

"Eh, why then is the English navy…urgent in their ways?" Captain Kerry asked, with a scowl across his face. And he had an intuition that the boy knew more. It was like a scratch you had to itch, he said to himself.

Over the weeks since the attack, he had wondered, why the English navy had been close to his tail. His intuition had been proved right. But, he was startled when the English fired without warning. He was now puzzled, why the English navy were so keen to capture the Rag-tail, rather than sink the ship. The Rag-tail was hit by cannon shot, and not by cannon ball, their aim was to disable the ship, by means of cutting the rigging with the cannon shot and not to sink the ship, he said to himself.

"I don't know," Nathaniel replied, and he found it hard to lie.

"But, you do…I can see it," Captain Kerry said.

"Perhaps, your friends down below know," Captain Kerry queried. "Who do we have below?"

"Only a few slaves most were sold when we docked in Rabat and Mahajanga," Ironman Slim replied.

Captain Kerry looked straight at Nathaniel, while he took a sip of wine and said, "No...you know...I wager a barrel of the finest rum...that you are lying."

"Take one of his fingers off!" the captain ordered Ironman Slim, who had already pulled his butchers' knife out, when Nathaniel acquiesced. So, you do know something...is that right?" Captain Kerry asked, as he stood over Nathaniel, wanting answers.

"Yes, it may be John Flynn they want," Nathaniel replied, who had resisted as far as he was prepared to do. He had already witnessed the screams of the possible murder of his friend Salim Nadeer, the merchant who had tried to help him, he said to himself.

"Have the slave John Flynn brought here," Captain Kerry shouted.

"Eh, take Nat down to the cage and point him out."

Ironman Slim repeated the orders to two pirates who escorted Nathaniel to the cage in the belly of the ship. Nathaniel hadn't been down to the cage for several days to see his friends because his movement aboard the Rag-tail had been restricted since his recent capture. Nathaniel noticed all the captives were sat down inside the cage.

"John Flynn stands up...or your friend will lose a finger," the pirate shouted through the cage.

Nathaniel looked straight at John Flynn who was already prepared to reveal himself without Nat pointing him out.

"I'm John Flynn," Captain John Flynn said as he struggled to stand up from the lack of food.

"Good, the captain wants to see you," the pirate said as he opened the cage door and then he helped Captain Flynn through the belly of the ship, and up the steps to Captain Kerry's quarters.

For a few minutes, Captain Flynn was temporarily blinded by the extra light in Captain Kerry's quarters. He had not seen the pirate since his capture. Once his vision returned, he could see the captain and his second in command sat at the table enjoying their food and wine.

"I am Captain Kerry and this is Ironman Slim my second in command. Now, who are you?" Captain Kerry asked abruptly.

"My name is John Flynn."

"Why is the English navy right behind us?" Captain Kerry asked, who had a hunch the man stood before him knew more than he was saying.

"Perhaps, you will talk freely when more is at stake," Captain Kerry proposed.

"Bring the boy Nat in here," stated Captain Kerry to one of the pirates standing guard at the door.

***

Nathaniel was busy helping the cook in the galley when a pirate stormed in to the galley and took hold of him and then escorted him to the captain's quarters.

"Now, I will only ask once…before the boy will lose a finger."

"Now, why did the English not sink us the other day?" Captain Kerry asked. He was gradually losing his patience with the man who was stood before him.

"Because they want to save as many of the captives as possible, I believe," Flynn replied.

"Is that all you have to say?"

"Yes…unless they know about the treasure."

"No, you are not telling the truth. Hold the boy's hand to the table," Captain Kerry shouted to Ironman Slim, as Nathaniel tried to struggle free, as Slim with his butchers' knife and another pirate held the boy's right hand to the table and sliced his right little finger off. The echo of Nathaniel's scream could be heard throughout the ship.

"Stop…stop, you bastards!" Flynn shouted.

"Now, tell me the truth. Why are the English here?" Captain Kerry asked.

"Because of me, my full name is Captain John Flynn, formerly of the English royal navy. I now work for Lord Trethowan on his estate. I manage all his farms and mines."

"As a former captain in the royal navy they would rather capture this ship than sink her, because of me."

"Go on…explain what you mean?"

"It's a well-established unwritten rule that the navy will seek to help any English naval officer above the rank of lieutenant currently serving or an officer now retired," Captain Flynn replied.

"No…there must be more," Captain Kerry suggested as he took a long gulp of wine straight from the bottle. Continuing he said, "Perhaps, more fingers."

"Let's take a toe," Ironman Slim said cheekily, as he struggled with another pirate to hold Nathaniel's foot to the cabin floor.

Captain Flynn shouted, "No...there is more." Continuing he said, "Plus the English must know a lot about your movements since your attack on the village. And if I know Lord Trethowan, he would have made waves with the English admiralty to get us back. He is a man of means...is Lord Trethowan."

"Tell me about Lord Trethowan?" Captain Kerry asked. He was intrigued to know about the man with the same name as the village he had been told to attack. That had been the specific instructions given by the sheik, he said to himself, as he tried to size up the man stood before him and Slim.

"What do you want to know?" Captain Flynn asked.

"Why is this lord so important?" Captain Kerry asked. He was now losing patience with Captain Flynn.

"Because, of his tin mining interests in Cornwall, England."

"I said...there was more," Captain Kerry bellowed with a broad grin that beguiled the observer, into thinking, he was a contented man. But, he had no qualms about torturing or killing anyone that got in his way.

"Go on."

"It's the only available location in the whole of Europe where tin is found. Tin is used to combine with other ores to make many different irons. You could say tin is more precious than gold in many ways. It's an essential part of the war effort," Captain Flynn replied.

"What war?" Captain Kerry asked, who was now intrigued to know how this was related to his orders to attack the village port of Trethowan in Cornwall.

"The war with the Dutch," Captain Flynn replied.

"It seems England is always at war. And, we are now at war with the Dutch. Those tin mines are very important to the war effort, so any attempt at disrupting their operation, would be considered as sabotage." Continuing he said, "I manage all of the tin mines for Lord Trethowan. Without me, he is a man lost. As a previous captain in the royal navy, I'm used to handling many men and operations, so the lord employs me to handle everything concerning his farms and mines. He's fond of the title, but he lacks the ability to handle men."

"You have to remember the English navy has a means of message between ships." Captain Flynn explained how the English Admiralty could communicate between ships and countries throughout the world. They did this by means of pigeons, a message would be attached to the bird's leg and the pigeon would fly to its destination. The English navy had a well-developed message service for its time, such that a message would sometimes only take a few days to arrive at the admiralty in Portsmouth.

"I was right about the boy…I said, he would be useful," Captain Kerry said as he paused, and took another long sup of wine. And continuing his orders, "Now take Nat to the cook, he will fix his wound."

***

Meanwhile, HMS Antelope had stopped its pursuit of the pirate ship Rag-tail and was ready to board the Santé Maria, which had been crippled in the battle and unable to steer. Lieutenant Curnow and Captain Horner watched from their quarter deck as their armed sailors rounded up the pirates from the Santé Maria, and began to transfer the pirates to HMS Antelope across a plank tied between the two ships.

"Yuki, make sure you tell the English you're not a pirate and that I bought you as a slave. I will try to rescue you later," Captain Kareem said anxiously.

"We found this young girl," the sailor said to Lieutenant Curnow as he surveyed the girl. Yuki looked on with fear as she saw Captain Kareem and the other pirates led away down into the belly of the ship.

"She doesn't look like a pirate," Lieutenant Curnow said.

"We have their captain and lieutenant," the sailor said.

"Bring the captain and the lieutenant with the girl to Captain Horner's quarters," Lieutenant Curnow demanded. Continuing, he added, "bosun, get that pirate ship ready to sail."

"Yes, sir."

***

"What about the Rag-tail?" Lieutenant Curnow asked Captain Horner, as they sat around a chart table in the captain's quarters discussing their course.

"We know their heading for the port of Zinjibar in Yemen," Captain Horner replied, before pausing to take a sip of wine from his pewter goblet. And continuing he said, "What, what…we will catch them there or somewhere else."

Yuki was still shaking, when the sailors brought her to the captain's quarters. She was first to see the captain and the lieutenant sat at the table discussing their plans. She had heard the port of Zinjibar was their destination.

"So, you're a pirate or a slave, which is it girl?" Captain Horner asked.

"First, I can speak your language. My name is Yuki. I was captured and sold as a slave," Yuki replied, who knew the fate of pirates that were caught would end up on the gibbet. Her only chance for survival, she had told herself, was to convince the captain that she wasn't a pirate.

"So, you're not a pirate? Then, what did you do on that pirate ship?" Lieutenant Curnow asked. He was beginning to believe the girl.

"I cooked for the crew and the captain," Yuki replied.

"Okay, then…you shall cook and we shall see…what, what" Captain Horner said.

"Take the girl to the galley. You can cook for your supper," Captain Horner said. And continuing he said, "You shall work with our cook. Take her away."

As Yuki was led away from the captain's quarters to the galley, she caught sight of Captain Kareem and Purapratt and briefly smiled. They were barely standing as they waited to hear their fate. She still had feelings for the pirate, but she knew it couldn't last, she said to herself, and then she felt a tear run down her face.

The two pirates then stood before Captain Horner and Lieutenant Curnow with their hands chained together like men awaiting their prison sentence. Both men looked like broken men who now had resigned themselves to their fate on the gibbet.

"Which one of you…is the captain?"

"It's me…I'm Captain Kareem and this is my second in command Purapratt," Captain Kareem replied.

"We decided to save your ship for the prize money," Captain Horner said, who knew the ship they had captured would fetch a fair sum. He had already begun to count, in his mind, the amount a captain's share would amount to.

"You and your men will hang. As soon as you and your men have a fair trial the better…what, what," Captain Horner said.

"Perhaps, we can make a deal."

"What deal?" Captain Horner asked.

"The treasure of the Rag-tail," Captain Kareem said.

Captain Horner and Lieutenant Curnow were intrigued to hear what the pirate had to say.

"Go on!"

"Do we have a deal?" Captain Kareem asked.

"What are you offering?" Captain Horner asked.

"For a share in a pirate's treasure of gold…a Spanish gold ship, this was attacked by the pirate Captain Kerry. The Spanish gold ship was carrying thousands of gold coins and other gold relics taken from their conquest of parts of Africa and transported to the coast."

The moment he heard the talk of gold, Captain Horner was hooked like a fish to a hook and line.

"Why should we make a deal with you? We could just torture you."

"Because without me you will never find the gold," Captain Kareem replied.

"Okay, you have a deal," Captain Horner said.

"But…on what terms? We have not discussed terms?" Captain Kareem asked.

"On these terms, we let your lieutenant and you live…with a captain's share and that is all."

"But what about my men," Captain Kareem asked as he looked at Purapratt with disbelief, but his men knew their fate the moment they sailed as pirates. Any pirates caught would normally hang on the gibbet.

"Your men will have a fair trial. Someone has to hang…what, what." Captain Horner replied, before he took a sip of wine from his goblet.

"Deal…my God, be with you." Captain Kareem replied as he bowed before the captain and the lieutenant, who now were the masters of his and Purapratt's fate, he said to himself.

"Take these two to the cells," Captain Horner said to the three marines guarding the pirates.

"What about our orders?" Lieutenant Curnow asked.

"My orders haven't changed, but you have." Captain Horner replied briskly, who was shocked to be questioned by a lower rank. Captain Horner then continued, "We seek out and destroy the Rag-tail after we have freed the captives."

"Sorry, sir."

"Look lieutenant, don't question my orders again," Captain Horner said harshly.

Lieutenant Curnow had listened to the negotiations between the captain and the pirate and had played no part in them, as this was the protocol to follow during naval training, that a senior officer will always lead negotiations whomever that may be with, until, that senior officer asks for a lower rank's advice shall they speak, he said to himself.

"What are your orders, captain?" Lieutenant Curnow asked.

"We will sail within hours. The gold can wait," Captain Horner replied.

***

Meanwhile, Ali Ben Sur watched as Captain Kareem and Purapratt were pushed into the cell, which had iron bars fixed from the floor to the ceiling of the cell. There was no escape.

"What comes of us?" Ali Ben Sur asked, as he could feel the ship starting to list from side to side.

"We need to know where the treasure is buried." Captain Kareem asked.

"We have made a deal with the captain," Purapratt said, He knew the truth was different and continued, "our lives depend on it. No gold then we hang on the gibbet for sure."

"Take me to the temple in that cove where the Rag-tail sailed from. And I will find the treasure," Ali Ben Sur replied.

"If I die then the secret goes with me," Ali Ben Sur said, and he now realized from their first meeting that Captain Kareem and Purapratt had gold fever.

"We could kill you with our bare hands," Captain Kareem said.

"Yes, but if I die…then you will never find the treasure."

"Okay, you win."

"Do you know our destination?" Ali Ben Sur asked. He was now eager to make a deal with captain and get him and his comrades' better sleeping arrangements.

Ali Ben Sur shouted out, "I need to speak with the captain. It concerns gold." Ali Ben Sur wanted everyone to hear, soon gold fever would strike the crew and its captain, and that's when he would have the advantage, he said to himself.

***

It was the following day, when Ali Ben Sur stood before Captain Horner and Lieutenant Curnow, who were eager to hear what the man had to say.

"You wanted to see me?" Captain Horner asked.

"My name is Ali Ben Sur. I am an Inn keeper from the port of Zinjibar, Yemen. I'm not a pirate. You must believe me. I had a deal with Captain Kareem for half share in the treasure of the Rag-tail. It's the Portuguese pirate's treasure on the island of Madagascar. I know where the treasure is hidden," Ali Ben Sur said.

Captain Horner looked at Ali Ben Sur and wondered if the man was telling the truth or not. "How do I know you're telling the truth or not?" Captain Horner asked.

"My life is in your hands. The gold is from a Spanish gold ship attacked by Captain Kerry the pirate. The gold is on the island of Madagascar. I know where," Ali Ben Sur replied, as he felt sweat drip down the side of his face. He could feel his face swelling as he bargained for his life and the others.

Captain Horner chuckled at what he had heard. He now had another man claiming to know where treasure was hidden. "So, Captain Kareem needs you and you need me, what, what?"

"Yes, for a half share, I will show you where it is hidden," Ali Ben Sur replied.

"But, first release me from the cell. I'm not a pirate," Ali Ben Sur said passionately.

"Okay, I will release you…you can sleep with the crew for now."

"You may go," Captain Horner stated.

"Do you believe him?" Lieutenant Curnow asked.

"We shall soon see, but first we have to complete our mission. Do you agree, lieutenant?" Captain Horner asked.

"Yes, captain."

***

"We are ready to sail," the bosun stated to Lieutenant Curnow as he stood with the Captain on the quarter deck viewing the crew making preparations for the ship to sail.

"We are ready to sail," Lieutenant Curnow said to Captain Horner as he viewed through his telescope the Santé Marie being sailed away now by his men back to Gibraltar, where the prize money for the vessel would be settled by the admiralty for him and his crew.

"Set a course for Zinjibar, Yemen," Captain Horner stated.

"North by northwest," Lieutenant Curnow stated to the bosun.

"When we reach Zinjibar, we will find out where our pirate is heading. In the meantime, we will prepare our crew," Captain Horner said.

"We shall practice our cannon fire."

"We will need to board the Rag-tail, so our men need to be ready for a battle, what, what?"

"Yes, sir," Lieutenant Curnow replied, who knew the captain was serious about boarding the Rag-tail, rather than blasting the ship with cannon fire, and sinking the ship to the bottom of the sea.

***

The voyage to the port of Zinjibar, Yemen for HMS Antelope and its crew had been mostly favorable with only a few days when the sea was in a rage.

Lieutenant Curnow was first to notice the wind change from a mild breeze to a gusting wind. The only light was the full moon, as he stood on the quarter deck as he tried to gauge the approaching storm, which could hit the ship within hours, he said to himself. His first thoughts were to get the rigging changed to suit the changing weather conditions.

"Loosen those sheets," Lieutenant Curnow shouted to the bosun.

"Aye, aye, sir," the bosun replied, as he shouted to his crew to loosen the sailing sheets and set the rigging of the sails.

In what seemed only moments, the ship started to heave up and down and from side to side as each raging wave hit the vessel. The wind was now gusting, and forcing HMS Antelope to list, as the force of the wind and the sea crashed down on its upper deck, and with such a force that men were throne about the deck as if like toys.

"Lieutenant, fix those aft sails down," Captain Horner stated, as he tried to maintain his hold of the quarter deck railing.

"Yes, sir," Lieutenant Curnow replied, who hadn't noticed the aft sail rigging hadn't been loosened, yet.

"We've lost a man overboard," the bosun shouted.

"Bosun, get that aft sail down," Lieutenant Curnow shouted at the bosun, and he now knew a man had been lost overboard.

"Good, the ship does not list now, what, what?" Captain Horner asked, and continuing, "I will retire to my cabin."

"Yes, captain."

As the sound of the gusting wind roared, like the sound of converging yells of men fighting in battle. Lieutenant Curnow began to feel the change of the gusting winds on his body. The rain had ceased to pepper his face like confetti, and he now noticed the black and grey clouds had started to disperse as HMS Antelope returned to its normal rhythm of a ship in pursuit of the pirate ship. As Lieutenant Curnow made his way from the quarter deck to the captain's quarters he saw Yuki entering the cabin with a tray of food. On entering the captain's quarters Lieutenant Curnow noticed the captain eagerly tasting the dishes Yuki had prepared with the help of the ship's cook.

"Ah, Lieutenant Curnow, join me in some food will you?" Captain Horner asked, as Yuki stood waiting for the captain's approval of the food.

"Yes, it's different," Lieutenant Curnow said as he sampled some of the food Yuki had prepared for the captain.

"This is delicious! You are indeed a cook, my girl," Captain Horner remarked.

"Now, we have to decide on your fate. What say you, lieutenant?" Captain Horner asked, although, the captain had already decided the fate of Yuki.

"It's not my decision, sir. But, she is only a young girl. Sold as a slave and bought by the pirate we have locked away below," Lieutenant Curnow replied.

"Yes…it is my decision as captain of this ship," Captain Horner said.

"May, I ask what is your decision?" Lieutenant Curnow asked.

"The girl is free from slavery. And when a suitable opportunity arises we will endeavor to return her to her homeland. In the meantime, she will pay for her keep by working with the cook in the galley."

"Yes, captain."

"Thank you, captain," Yuki said, who had stood and listened to the exchange between the captain and the lieutenant and had understood most of what was said.

"Now, return to the galley," Captain Horner stated, before he took a large gulp of wine from his pewter jug, and ushered the girl to leave with a wave of the other hand, which flapped like the wings of a bird.

"What have you to report?" Captain Horner asked.

"We lost two men in the storm. And sustained minor damage to the starboard side rigging, which is currently being repaired," Lieutenant Curnow replied.

"You said…two men lost?"

"Yes, captain."

"A pity...those men have families," Captain Horner said grimly. And continuing he added, "Record the details and the navy will compensate those concerned." Its standard practice for sailors that sign on, Lieutenant Curnow thought, as he wondered, about the fate of Nathaniel.

"Yes, captain."

"Are you thinking about your cousin?" Captain Horner asked. He knew his lieutenant, at times, showed signs of being in another world. This had worried the captain, as soon as he knew his lieutenant had a personal connection to the outcome of their mission.

"No, sir," Lieutenant Curnow replied quickly, who wasn't about to reveal his deepest emotions or the truth of what he was thinking to the captain. At times, he had worried about the sanity of the captain, especially when there was talk of treasure. He felt sure the captain had gold fever like much of the crew.

"Do you think Ali Ben Sur is telling the truth?" Lieutenant Curnow asked.

"Between the three of them, we will soon find out. Our main mission is to pursue the Rag-tail, until we can board the ship and rescue the remaining captives. I've done much thinking on the matter. We need to catch the pirates like we hook a fish on a line," Captain Horner replied, grinning.

"How do we do that, sir?" Lieutenant Curnow asked. He was now intrigued by the captain's idea.

"What, what…it's simple? A hook of course," Captain Horner replied boasting with a wide grin across his face.

"What do you mean?"

"A hook that will force the pirates our way will be irresistible."

"What's that, sir?" Lieutenant Curnow asked.

"The treasure…eh, what, what," Captain Horner suggested and added. "We have all the aces. They don't know we have all the aces."

"But, we haven't found the treasure, yet." Lieutenant Curnow stated.

"They don't know that…besides we have three men who say they know where the treasure is buried. They are our three aces and the other will be the pirate Captain Kerry himself. Before he swings on the gibbet, we will help him reveal his secret."

"But, surely the pirate deserves a fair trial?" Lieutenant Curnow asked, who was now shocked at what the captain had proposed to do with the pirate if captured and not killed.

"Don't have mercy for this scum," the captain remarked. Pausing and then added, "Remember your cousin."

"Yes, I know…but…," Lieutenant Curnow said before the captain had interrupted his reply.

"There is no mercy from me. We have lost several men already and likely more before this mission is successful. We're duty bound to retrieve this treasure for the Crown, and a share divided amongst the men. Are you with me, Lieutenant Curnow?" Captain Horner asked.

"Yes, but our mission is to rescue the captives on the Rag-tail," Lieutenant Curnow said.

"I haven't changed the mission…we'll act as I command. Do you understand?" Captain Horner asked angrily. He was now outraged again by the lieutenant for challenging his orders. His face had turned red within seconds, and a rage of anger consumed his body like a cold chill that spreads throughout the body of the person on a wintery night.

"Yes sir."

Lieutenant Curnow stood to attention as Captain Horner studied the sea charts. "What are your thoughts about our arrival in Zinjibar?" Captain Horner asked.

"We have made good time. I believe, with favorable weather, we should arrive by the next full moon."

"I agree I've worked out the same."

"Oh, send for the girl and bring some wine," Captain Horner demanded.

Lieutenant Curnow repeated the order to the sailor standing outside the captain's cabin.

As Yuki entered the captain's quarters with more wine she noticed the sea charts on the table, and recognized the outline of India. She had previously been taught by Captain Kareem the main countries of the world, and wondered, if India was their next destination.

Chapter 12

Meanwhile, the Rag-tail had entered the port of Zinjibar, Yemen after several weeks of sailing through good and bad weather. As Nathaniel watched from the upper deck he noticed, how busy the port was as the ship laid anchor some distance from the docks. He wondered why the ship had not docked at the docks, and now, could only be reached by rowing in a small craft to the jetty. On the quarter deck watching proceedings stood Captain Kerry and Ironman Slim.

"Make ready the rowing boat," Captain Kerry ordered Ironman Slim to lower the rowing boat into the sea. "I mean to go ashore, and bring the boy and three men."

"Aye, aye, captain."

As the six of them climbed down into the rowing boat and set off towards the port docks, Captain Kerry and Ironman Slim watched from the stern of the rowing boat as Nathaniel and the three pirates rowed towards the docks.

"Where is our rendezvous with the sheik?" Ironman Slim asked.

"In the local Inn near the docks," Captain Kerry replied, continuing he added, "the message I sent by pigeon from Mahajanga should have been received."

"I thought Arabs don't drink ale or wine?" Ironman Slim asked.

"Some lie. Before we sit down at the table...tie that boy to one of your men," Captain Kerry demanded.

They all sat down at a table in the Inn, and Nathaniel watched, as two men at another table were fighting each other. The brawl continued, until another large heavy set man began to throw both men out of the Inn. Within moments, a man was serving Captain Kerry with his order.

It was almost an hour before the sheik arrived at the Inn and sat down between Captain Kerry and Ironman Slim at one end of the table far enough away from his men and Nathaniel so they could not hear what was being said.

The sheik was dressed in a white robe with a cutlass and pistol fastened around his waist. He had typical Arabic features of a large nose, dark eyes, dark skin and black hair.

"We have been waiting a long time," Captain Kerry said.

"Yes, so have I," Sheik Abu Ben Ali said with a smile that crept along his face like a dark crack in a wall. Continuing he added, "Did you accomplish your mission?"

"We did everything you asked," Captain Kerry replied.

"Where is my proof?"

"We have your proof, locked away aboard our ship. We also have Captain John Flynn who works for Lord Trethowan. We attacked the village like you wanted. We have sold some slaves. But, you can have the boy…see at the end of the table. His name is Nathaniel. We now, want our money," Captain Kerry said briskly.

"You shall have your money, when I have seen the proof," Sheik Abu Ben Ali replied. Pausing before adding, "Is that why you did not dock at the port and instead chose to lay anchor out in the bay?"

"Yes, that's right, I don't trust you," Captain Kerry said sharply.

As Captain Kerry, Ironman Slim, Sheik Abu Ben Ali, Nathaniel and the three other pirates made their way back to the Rag-tail via their rowing boat a sudden flux of sea gulls could be seen circling and squawking the Rag-tail. Nathaniel was first to spot the cook throwing waste food from the upper deck into the sea.

"I hope you haven't spoiled the broth," Captain Kerry said to the cook, as he climbed up and over the rope ladder onto the upper deck. "Bring some food and wine for our guest."

***

As Captain Kerry, Ironman Slim and Sheik Abu Ben Ali sat around the table in the captain's quarters waiting for their food and wine to be brought in by the cook and Nathaniel, they could hear the squawking sea gulls outside fighting over their food floating in the sea.

"You have the proof?" Sheik Abu Ben Ali asked. He was now eager to see what he had been waiting months for.

"Yes…it means so much to you," Captain Kerry said.

"Go fetch Captain John Flynn," Captain Kerry stated to one of the pirates stood guarding the door to the captain's quarters. Continuing, he added, "Why did you want this man so much?"

As Nathaniel prepared food and wine for the captain's table, he noticed, his friend Captain John Flynn in chains being led by pirates to the captain's quarters.

Nathaniel shouted out to Flynn, "We are in Zinjibar, Yemen."

"Good to know. Don't worry…we'll overcome this," Captain John Flynn answered abruptly, as he struggled to walk with the chains around his hands and feet to the pirate's quarters.

"Here's the man you wanted."

"Hold the man up," Captain Kerry said to the two pirates on either side of the weakened Captain John Flynn.

"So, you are the famous Captain John Flynn?" Sheik Abu Ben Ali asked with glee in his tone of voice.

"You know me?" Captain John Flynn asked.

"I know of you. You work for Lord Trethowan...managing his business interests."

"Yes."

"Why is Lord Trethowan mining business so important?" the sheik asked. He wanted to know the truth from the captain.

"Cornwall in England is the only available source of tin ore in the western world, apart from finding a different substance most of the mines in Cornwall are owed by Lord Trethowan."

"You said...a different substance. What did you mean?" Sheik Abu Ben Ali asked.

"Talk!"

As Nathaniel entered the captain's quarters, he saw his friend, Captain John Flynn stood before the pirates and the sheik.

"Give this man some food and drink." Sheik Abu Ben Ali said, as he pointed, to the bulk of the captain stood before him like a towering tree that overshadows everything in its vicinity.

"What about our money?" Captain Kerry asked. He now had listened long enough to the sheik interrogate the captain.

"You will get your money."

"You said a different substance. What did you mean?" Sheik Abu Ben Ali asked again.

"You need tin to mix with other irons to harden them. The English navy uses the tin to make cannon balls. Without tin you can't make cannon balls." Pausing to eat Captain Flynn added, "We're at war with Holland. The tin mines are a major asset for the war."

"Take the captain away."

"Where is our money?" Captain Kerry asked as he watched Captain Flynn struggle to walk as he was led away by two pirates.

"Yes, you have done well. Your money, I have waiting. I will signal my coach driver to deliver your money on the docks."

"Yes...do this, but you stay here, until we have our money," Captain Kerry said bitterly.

With a small piece of glass the sheik signaled his driver on the docks. Captain Kerry and Ironman Slim watched, from the quarter deck as the sheik with a small piece of glass signaled his driver on the docks to transfer the money to the pirates. As the pirates loaded the rowing boat with the wooden casket they all wondered what it contained as they made their way back to the Rag-tail. Captain Kerry, Ironman Slim and the sheik made their way to the captain's quarters with two pirates carrying the wooden casket. Captain Kerry was first to open the casket and reveal its contents.

"It's all here…yes?" Captain Kerry asked, as he smiled like a child with a new toy, as he observed the gold and silver coins. With his cutlass drawn the captain rammed the blade inside the casket from side to side, until, he was satisfied the casket was full.

"Wait, Slim…let's tip the casket."

"We have many mouths to feed," Ironman Slim said cheekily, as he tipped the casket over on the table to reveal its contents.

"I do not cheat," the sheik said. As the sheik turned to exit the cabin he added, "We are done."

"Wait!"

"Why did you want the village attacked?" Captain Kerry asked intently.

"Like the captain said…tin is very important," the Sheik Abu Ben Ali replied wistfully, who knew the truth. His employers were the Dutch, who were eager to disrupt the English war machine as much as possible.

As Sheik Abu Ben Ali was taken back to the docks, he wondered how long Captain Kerry had before the English navy caught up with him and either killed or captured the pirate.

"What do you think?" Ironman Slim asked as he watched from the quarter deck with Captain Kerry as Sheik Abu Ben Ali was rowed back to the docks.

"What do you mean?" Captain Kerry asked, as his thoughts, turned to what the sheik had said about the importance of his captive Captain John Flynn.

"What the sheik had to say," Ironman Slim replied as he passed the telescope to Captain Kerry who saw the sheik returning to his awaiting carriage.

"Yes, it seems we have been but minor pawns in a game of chess. The English navy wants what we have. We now have an edge. The captain below will be our bargaining purchase. In the meantime, we need to set sail for Madagascar," Captain Kerry replied.

"What about our captives for sale?" Ironman Slim asked who knew the slaves would fetch a good price at the slave market in Zinjibar.

"Yes, send all the captives to the slave market except Captain John Flynn and the boy Nathaniel when the men get back with the boat. Sell the captives to the slave market without waiting for the next sale. When our men are back set sail for the island. I expect the Rag-tail to way anchor as soon as possible," Captain Kerry replied.

As Captain Kerry retired to his cabin, he wondered why the English frigate had not pursued the Rag-tail when they had the upper hand. His only ace was Captain John Flynn and he would need to produce his ace at the appropriate time, he said to himself, as he mulled over the coming confrontation with the English navy with a bottle of wine. Standing in front of him was Nathaniel, who had been spared the slave market for reasons only he knew.

"Tell me about, Captain John Flynn?" Captain Kerry asked, as he paused, and took a long sup of wine from his pewter jug.

"But, you know everything...I told you everything," Nathaniel replied.

"Yes, but there is always more. You are from the same village. Come...tell me more."

"He works for Lord Trethowan as his deputy. I know of him, but have no call to see him," Nathaniel replied, who was getting nervous and fearing the worse, he didn't want to be tortured again. His voice was starting to tremble like he had a winter chill.

"What do you know about Lord Trethowan?"

"Not much, he owns several farms near our farm," Nathaniel replied.

"What about his tin mines?"

"I don't know about that," Nathaniel replied.

"Okay, fetch me a bottle of wine," Captain Kerry demanded, as he waved away Nathaniel, and awaited the return of Slim. He was eager to get underway and hopefully avoid the English navy if he could, he said to himself.

Chapter 13

As Ironman Slim and his men climbed on board the Rag-tail they immediately started to winch the rowing boat on board the ship. Ironman Slim gave orders to way anchor and release the sails and set the rigging. As he entered the captain's quarters he saw Captain Kerry actively studying his sea charts as the Rag-tail started to list from one side to the other side as the ship crossed from the relative calm of the port bay area into the choppy waters of the Indian Ocean.

"We're on our way, captain," Ironman Slim said as he poured himself a jug of wine.

"Set a course for Bombay."

"Not Madagascar?" Ironman Slim queried.

"We're making a detour," Captain Kerry replied with a wry smile as he took a sip of wine from his jug.

"Tell the bosun to set a course north by northeast," Ironman Slim ordered the pirate guarding the cabin door.

"What's the plan, boss?" Ironman Slim asked, and then he sat down to enjoy his wine.

"I let some sailors know that we're heading for Madagascar before we departed the port. If I'm right, then the English navy will dock at Zinjibar and find out the false information. Hopefully, we can avoid the English and eventually sail to Madagascar. In the meantime, we head for Bombay and drop off our gold and silver from the sheik. It's the only option. I don't trust storing any more treasure at Madagascar, too many people now know too much," Captain Kerry said.

"What do you think of the sheik?"

"The sheik hasn't been fully truthful with us. It seems we were part of a Dutch plot to disrupt the English war effort. Now, we have the English navy on our tail, and out to kill or capture us and they won't let go until they find us. The English frigate out guns us, but we have Captain Flynn and the boy, so they will want to disable us with chain shot and not sink us. I also think they have gold fever and will want to capture us for the treasure." Pausing to drink some more wine the captain added, "Slim, what say you?"

"We'll drop off the chest of gold and silver at Bombay and then sail for Madagascar and retrieve our treasure before someone finds it," Ironman Slim replied.

"Yes, we must do this, Slim, otherwise, our secret will be known."

"What will we do if the English navy catches us?" Ironman Slim asked.

"Negotiate; negotiate...until we have them hooked on gold like a plague of fever."

"Yes, boss."

"Give the order...no lantern light, tonight; we need to avoid the English like the plague. And tell the bosun to make haste to Bombay."

As Ironman Slim made his way to the quarter deck he saw the bosun at the wheel house talking to the cook.

"The captain wants no lanterns, tonight. Make haste to Bombay," Ironman Slim said.

"Yes," the bosun said.

Shouting at the crew, Ironman Slim said, "Get those sheets taut and fix the rigging."

"Get those fucking lights out...now!" the bosun stated.

"If you need me...I'll be in the captain's quarters."

"Okay, Slim."

When the Rag-tail began to list to one side, Slim held onto to the lower part of the aft mast in the captain's quarters as he tried to maintain his balance against the motion of the ship. He noticed the captain asleep hunched over the table like a baby without a care in the world.

"Everything, okay?"

"I thought you were asleep, boss."

"I was for a while until you spoilt my dreams."

"Yes, everything is okay."

"The cook tells me that some of the crew is asking for their share of the gold and silver. Some want to leave us at Bombay. They are worried about the English navy. They don't want to end up dead or on the gibbet," Ironman Slim said regretfully.

"Oh! You tell the men they'll get their share when we get back from Madagascar and not until then. Anyone that wants to leave at Bombay leaves without a share. Is that understood?" Captain Kerry said.

"Yes, boss."

"In the meantime, bring Captain Flynn here. And get the cook to bring some food and more wine. I fancy the captain has more to say," Captain Kerry said gleefully.

As Ironman Slim made his way to the galley he saw Nathaniel and the cook preparing food for some of the crew. He wondered how long it would be before some of the crew would mutiny.

"Have Nat bring some food and more wine for the captain's table," Ironman Slim stated to the cook, before he returned to the captain's quarters.

As Nathaniel entered the captain's quarters with food and wine, he saw his friend Captain Flynn sat talking with Captain Kerry and Slim, and wondered what they were discussing.

"Enjoy some food and wine, Captain Flynn," Captain Kerry said as he waved with a hand for Nathaniel to leave.

***

Several weeks had passed, before the Rag-tail had reached India and began to follow the coast south towards Bombay. On reaching Bombay, Captain Kerry gave orders for the ship to lay anchor in the bay rather than dock at the port jetty. He was worried about being attacked by the locals if they found out his ship was carrying treasure. After rowing to the jetty, Captain Kerry, Slim, Ali and six of his crew secured a horse and cart for the journey into the jungle. They had provisions and were armed with cutlasses and pistols for a journey they had made many times over the years.

Captain Kerry and his men made their way along an old track on the outskirts of Bombay far from any nearby village to avoid being seen. Along the route they cut into the dense jungle with machetes using the nearby mountain as a guide to their destination, and making sure they were not being followed as the jungle soon provided cover as they disappeared into the dense green camouflage. It wasn't long before Captain Kerry had found the elephant track that he had used before that led to the mountain. The track was just wide enough to plough through without needing much work with machetes.

"We should be there before dark and make camp for the night," Captain Kerry said to Ironman Slim.

"Yes, boss."

Early, the following morning, Captain Kerry had the casket of gold and silver safely stored away without disturbing the vegetation that hide the opening. Later the following night, Captain Kerry and his men were on the Rag-tail and sailing out of Bombay towards Madagascar.

***

Meanwhile, HMS Antelope had reached the port of Zinjibar, Yemen and made anchor at the docks. Lieutenant

Curnow watched, from the quarter deck, as the crew tied the ship to the docks, while he waited for orders. He noticed there were several ships at anchor in the bay and some ships tied up at the docks, but none as big as HMS Antelope. The English frigate out gunned most ships at sea, and would soon find the Rag-tail, and make amends, he said to himself.

"Go ashore…and find out what you can about the pirate ship. And see if any captives have been taken to the slave market," Captain Horner said to Lieutenant Curnow.

Lieutenant Curnow soon returned to the ship with more information about the whereabouts of the Rag-tail.

"What's your report, lieutenant?" Captain Horner asked briskly.

"It seems the Rag-tail docked here five days past, and there's a rumor that it's heading for Madagascar. And it seems that four captives were sold at the slave market and their whereabouts unknown."

"Again probably false information about their destination wouldn't you agree, lieutenant?"

"Yes, captain."

***

Meanwhile, as the Portobello sailed into the cove at the northern tip of Madagascar, Black Eye remembered, the day he was blown into the sea by cannon fire, and that he was lucky to escape the clutches of the pirate Captain Kerry and his men.

"Sail around the point and lay anchor. We will be hidden from prying eyes here. Also get the boat ready to row," Black Eye ordered Two Coin as he stood with Maisha and Lord Trethowan on the quarter deck of the Portobello. Peering through his telescope Black Eye could see the statue of the Buddha, which he had seen all those years before. He noticed some seagulls, which were already circling the ship and were squawking for food. Also, he could hear the sound of a raven squawking in the distance, which was an ominous sound, he said to himself.

"Here take a look!" Black Eye said to Maisha as he passed the telescope to her.

"Straight ahead…the statue of the Buddha…do you see it?" Black Eye asked.

"Yes…I see it," Maisha replied, as she passed the telescope to Lord Trethowan, who had patiently waited his turn to use the telescope. And he was not pleased at being third in line, when he was used to being number one. Lord Trethowan's face had a scowl that clearly showed his distaste at being last inline.

"There straight ahead...not far from the shore...just below those cliffs to the right," Maisha said as she pointed with her out stretched arm the direction of the statue to Lord Trethowan.

"Yes, I can see it. The statue is huge. The jungle has consumed most of it," Lord Trethowan said.

"I still think we should've gone straight for Yemen."

"Never mind, Lord Trethowan...he stills thinks...he's the boss," Maisha said.

***

Later that day, as Black Eye and his men cut their way through the jungle to the giant statue of the Buddha, he wondered if the pirate's treasure was still in the same area. It had been many years since the day he watched the pirates leave the cove. He had spent many days then looking for the treasure and never found any clues to where it may be buried. Perhaps, his luck had changed, he said to himself.

In a clearing, where previous camps had been made they stopped to make camp before nightfall. Black Eye watched from the top of a temple wall the outline of the Portobello recede into darkness as the steep cliffs around it cast a black shadow over the ship.

"What are you thinking?" Maisha asked intently, as she stood beside Black Eye watching the Portobello.

"I have ordered a crew change every day to make sure we keep the men ready for action. Otherwise, we risk mutiny. We can't have that," Black Eye said to Maisha.

"Do you think your men will mutiny?" Maisha asked.

"It's better to take no chances."

"What happens if we don't find the treasure?" Maisha asked briskly.

"We find Captain Kerry and his men and make them talk. Someone always talks...when they have the point of a sword at their throat."

Lord Trethowan thought it was a welcome sound the chorus of the jungle rather than the sounds of a ship at sea. The monotony of listening to creaking wood, as the ship rode the waves, was completely different to the cacophony of sounds emanating from the jungle. The sounds of monkeys, birds and insects all competing, in a chorus of the jungle story, was enough to send you to sleep, he said to himself.

***

The following morning, Black Eye and his men started searching for the treasure. "What do you think, Two Coin?" Black Eye asked as he stood in the center of the abandoned temple wondering where the treasure could be hidden.

"I say, we group three men together and let them search. You say, you looked for days and never found anything. So, it must be well hidden to be used today as a place to bury treasure. You found no trace of the treasure here in the temple. But, what if the treasure is buried close by and the statue of the Buddha is only a marker for the place where the treasure is buried. We need to search in the jungle far from the Buddha statue and look for any signs of recent disturbance," Two Coin said.

"I agree, with you," Black Eye agreed.

"I'll lead one group," Two Coin said.

"And I'll lead the other."

"Lord Trethowan can go with you, Two Coin."

"Okay, boss."

"Maisha and I will take the right side and you start your search from the left of the statue," Black Eye said.

As Black Eye led Maisha and his men through the jungle they stumbled upon two human skeletons that bore the signs of pistol holes to their clothing that still hung from their bones. It was a sign that they may be on the right track, Black Eye said to himself.

"Those skeletons were most likely pirates," Maisha said.

"You could be right," Black Eye agreed.

"Should we signal to alert the other group?" Maisha asked.

"Not right now…let's continue."

As they continued, to cut their way through the jungle, Black Eye wondered how Lord Trethowan's patience was holding up. Especially, now he had to take orders from Two Coin in the other group.

***

"Fire a pistol shot." Two Coin said as he stood over the remnants of human skeletons.

"It looks like at least three people have died here. One or two from pistol shot from the holes in their clothing," Lord Trethowan said.

For a moment, after the noise of the pistol shot there was an echo of silence before the sounds of the jungle roared into its frenetic action again.

"They have found something." Black Eye said as he quickly ordered one of his men to take a message to the other group.

"Did you hear that pistol shot?"

"It was unmistakable," Maisha replied precocious as ever.

"I wonder what they have found."

"Hopefully, more than we have," Maisha remarked.

***

Later that day, Black Eye received the message from the other group. And he later decided to return to their camp at the temple as it was getting dark.

"They have found another three human skeletons with pistol holes to their clothing. What do you think, Maisha?" Black Eye asked as he sat round the camp fire waiting for Two Coin and the other group to return.

"Someone didn't want anyone to know the whereabouts of the treasure. Is that too much of a stretch?" Maisha replied.

"Yes, you could be right. At first, I had one idea then another. And now, well it's the only real answer. The pirate Captain Kerry has kept this place his secret for a long time. Now, we are closer, but we still haven't found anything."

"Two Coin and his men are late getting back. Let's hope they don't get lost," Maisha said sullenly, before she supped more wine from her pewter flagon.

"That jungle during the day is hard enough to get through and misplace your bearings. At night, the jungle is when most of the predators emerge to feast," Black Eye said.

"My men seem happy. What say you?" Black Eye asked.

"I'm well, thanks for asking," Maisha replied in her precocious manner.

"No…the men…what do you think?"

"Yes, I know…I was just being myself. Yes, the men are in good spirits for now," Maisha replied.

"They're getting payed."

"Yes, but they have gold fever and I think you have. Is that true? Tell me the truth. Do you have gold fever?" Maisha asked intently.

As Black Eye listened to the sounds of the jungle, he heard the familiar sounds of seagulls squawking in the distance.

Taking a sup of wine from his flagon, he considered his reply to Maisha's question.

"Yes, I think I have gold fever. It's hard not to have gold fever. But, hopefully, I can control it," Black Eye replied.

"Listen!"

"Did you hear that?"

"What…I don't hear anything?"

"So, what did you find?" Black Eye asked out loud, as he saw Two Coin and his men emerging from the surrounding jungle.

"Did you not get the message I sent back?" Two Coin asked, as he sat down around the camp fire and tried to get warm.

"Yes, I received your message. What was your delay in getting back here?" Black Eye asked as he watched the stars in all its majesty in the sky.

"We got lost because in the jungle it's hard to know where you are," Two Coin replied.

"We found three human skeletons that showed they were killed by pistol shot, from the clothing still clinging to the bones. These people looked like they were once pirates."

"What makes you make that observation?" Black Eye asked.

"Most people die from at home and not from pistol shot. And we know the pirate Captain Kerry hid his treasure somewhere out here."

"I guess you're right."

"What do we do from here?" Maisha asked.

"Tomorrow, we continue our search. I feel, we are close to finding the treasure," Black Eye said.

"Are you sure…you're not thinking straight? Gold fever…it never fails," Maisha said.

"I think, we have spent enough time looking for treasure. When we should be looking for Captain Kerry and his crew," Lord Trethowan suggested.

"Well, it's lucky I'm in charge," Black Eye said.

"Yes, but it's my money paying your wages," Lord Trethowan remarked.

"What happens if the pirate decides to come back while we're here?" Maisha asked.

"Let's hope we can over power them. If Captain Kerry's ship has sailed to Yemen it could be weeks before he's back here," Black Eye said wistfully.

***

The following morning, Black Eye woke to the sound of pistol shot coming from his ship anchored in the cove. Black Eye viewed from the top of the temple wall the outline of a ship approaching the entrance to the cove through his telescope. He noticed the ship was flying the colors of the Portuguese flag, the same colors the pirate ship Rag-tail sailed under, and it was heading straight for the cove, it was the pirate ship, he said to himself. He had only a few minutes to react. His orders could mean the death of him and his crew.

"Let's get back aboard our ship, now!"

***

"When we get aboard...get her ready to sail and fire." Black Eye said to Two Coin as his men franticly rowed their boat to the Portobello.

"Set those fucking sails, now!" Black Eye shouted as he climbed aboard the Portobello and tried to ready the ship to sail.

"Cut the fucking anchor!" Black Eye shouted.

"We need as much time as possible to catch the wind, Two Coin."

"We need to make open sea."

As the Portobello headed towards open sea the ship was hit by cannon chain shot, which cut across much of its sail and rigging. The Portobello had lost much of its movability before it had a chance to return fire.

"Open fire!" Black Eye shouted.

"Move hard to port," Black Eye shouted to Two Coin, who repeated the order to the bosun at the wheel.

"We need to catch that sail," Black Eye said.

"We'll end up ramming them broadside," Two Coin said, who was at that moment puzzled by the order.

"That's right, right into their middle, where they cannot fire on us. Just get us ramming their ship and quick before we lose the advantage. And get three of your best men with muskets up in the crows' nest ready to fire down on the other ship when we collide." Black Eye stated to Two Coin, before he made his way to the lower deck to pick his men.

"Maisha, I want you to take cover in my quarters," Black Eye said to Maisha, who had other ideas.

"No, where you go I go," Maisha replied.

"What?"

"Besides, I'm a better shot than you," Maisha replied precocious as ever.

As Black Eye viewed the pirate ship through his telescope he could see the frantic scene aboard the Rag-tail as its crew tried to maneuver their ship out of the way. Black Eye's unexpected maneuver had gained the upper hand, and now his ship was about to hit the Rag-tail straight in the middle on their broadside, which would either severely disable the pirate ship or sink her. Either scenario was desirable under the circumstances, where his ship had fewer cannon and more likely less men to fight a hand to hand battle, he said to himself.

"We were lucky the sea waves made it difficult for their cannon fire to hit their target. Most of their cannon shot failed to hit us because of how much the roll of the sea played its part.," Black Eye said to Maisha.

"Hold on to something, we're about to hit."

The Portobello crashed into the Rag-tail like a hot knife into butter. The bow crushed the Rag-tail's lower and upper decks into thousands of splinters of wood. The Rag-tail now had a huge cavernous gap the width of several men just above sea level.

"Bang, bang…bang," the sound of pistol shot.

"Fire!" Black Eye shouted.

The noise of muskets shot, littered the air, like squawking birds, as Black Eye's men up the crows' nest with their muskets fired relentlessly down onto the pirates on the Rag-tail's upper decks. The pirates were sitting ducks as they had no cover from the musket fire. Within minutes, Black Eye gave the order to board the pirate ship when he considered the odds were in his favor.

"Two Coin, take control of the Portobello, I mean to board the Rag-tail."

***

As Captain Kerry rallied his crew to fire upon the ship that came from the cove, his own ship was struck broadside by the bow of the other ship. Captain Kerry felt the Rag-tail shudder and heard the noise of wood cracking and splintering from the direct blow to the broadside. Above the noise of musket fire, Captain Kerry shouted out orders to his men as he took cover from the musket fire.

"Damage report?" Captain Kerry asked.

"We have a large gap just above sea level," Ironman Slim replied.

"Get some men down on the lower deck to make urgent repairs, before we sink."

"But, we are about to be boarded," Ironman Slim said.

"Yes, I know. If we don't fix the gap we won't have a ship to sail," Captain Kerry replied.

"We need to steer into the wind. So, we can fire our cannons straight into their broadside," Captain Kerry said.

"Look!"

"There's another ship on the horizon coming our way," Ironman Slim said as he passed the telescope to Captain Kerry, who was trying to avoid the musket fire from the other ship's crows' nest.

"It's an English frigate, fucking hell!!"

Just as the Rag-tail turned into the wind, Captain Kerry shouted out to his men to take cover, as the first of several cannon shots hit the Rag-tail's sails and rigging.

"We're being cut to ribbons," Ironman Slim said franticly, who was now worried about the odds of defeating two ships. "You're injured, boss."

"Yes, it's only my arm," Captain Kerry said, as his left arm hung like a bone needle on cotton thread, it was lifeless.

***

"Fire!" Captain Horner shouted as HMS Antelope opened fire with all available cannon shot at the pirate ship's sails and masts.

"We could hit the other ship," Lieutenant Curnow said.

"Yes, I know, but it's the chance we have to take," Captain Horner replied.

"But, it's flying the colors of an English ship," Lieutenant Curnow said.

"Yes, I know. We have to take a chance," Captain Horner repeated.

"It's our chance to capture the pirates. It's what we have been ordered to do, what, what. Keep firing, until the pirate ship can't sail," Captain Horner shouted out.

"Yes, captain."

"Bring her into the wind. Now, get your men ready to board the pirate ship, lieutenant," Captain Horner said briskly.

Lieutenant Curnow felt the blast of cannon fire hit the quarter deck as he was blasted off his feet. Lieutenant Curnow saw the captain struggling to stand on his feet when other cannon shot hit the quarter deck sending shards of wood splinters in all directions.

"The captain has been hit. Get the captain to the doctor." Lieutenant Curnow shouted frantically.

"Bring her broadside, bosun."

"Yes, sir."

"Fix anchors and board, now!" Lieutenant Curnow shouted as his men started to climb aboard the pirate ship as musket and pistol fire peppered the scene amongst the sounds of swords and cutlasses clashing and the cries of dying men.

"We have the captain," a marine shouted.

"We have rescued the captives!" Black Eye shouted out to Lord Trethowan, who had stayed aboard the Portobello watching the battle from the safety of the quarter deck.

"I'm Lieutenant Curnow, my captain is injured. So, I'm in command for now," Lieutenant Curnow said.

"My name is Black Eye and I'm the captain of my ship the Portobello. I'm in the employ of Lord Trethowan," Black Eye said firmly. Continuing he added, "It looks like we will have to share the prize."

"Yes, that seems fair," Lieutenant Curnow agreed for now.

"More than fair," Maisha said.

"Oh…this is my woman, Maisha."

"This is not a place for a lady," Lieutenant Curnow remarked.

"What makes you think I'm a lady," Maisha said flippantly.

"We have a young girl aboard our ship… a former slave called Yuki. The captain wants to return the girl to her country if we get the chance," Lieutenant Curnow remarked.

As Nathaniel waited below deck for the noise of the battle to cease, he heard the familiar sound of a voice he recognized, it was the voice of his cousin Jack Curnow above deck shouting out his orders, he thought.

When Lieutenant Curnow viewed the scene of the battle from the quarter deck of the Rag-tail, he caught sight of his cousin Nathaniel, on the upper deck, who was about to be rounded up by his marines with the pirates that had survived the battle.

Lieutenant Curnow shouting, "Wait, release that boy!"

"Nathaniel, so glad you survived."

"Jack, it's me! Yes, I'm alive and well," Nathaniel shouted back.

"You know this boy then?" Black Eye asked.

"Yes, he's my cousin and was captured with the other captives from England by the pirates," Lieutenant Curnow replied.

"He's lucky he was not sold into slavery," Black Eye said.

"Yes, very lucky indeed," Maisha reiterated.

"Well, what have you to say, Nathaniel?" Lieutenant Curnow asked.

"Luck had nothing to do with it," Nathaniel replied, who now had a smile across his face, which matched his pleasure of being rescued and of seeing his cousin for the first time in many years.

"See to that hole in our ship," Lieutenant Curnow said to the ship's carpenter. "Make good any damage before we try to sail our ship back to port."

"Aye, aye, sir," the ship's carpenter said.

"You plan to sail your ship back to port?" Black Eye asked. He was curious to know the lieutenant's plans, now, that the lieutenant was in command.

"We have all the pirates secure below deck," the marine said.

"We lost six sailors and two marines in the battle, sir," Lieutenant Hawkes said.

"Yes, well get those men ready for burial and clear the decks of the dead pirates. We'll sail our ship back to Mahajanga when it's ready and finalize repairs there. From there you will send a signal to the admiralty of our success in capturing the pirate ship the Rag-tail and releasing the captives. Notify the admiralty that we have saved the lives of Captain John Flynn and some of the captives. Is that understood?" Lieutenant Curnow asked.

"Yes, sir," Lieutenant Jones replied.

"I leave you in charge," Lieutenant Curnow said.

"Ready the rowing boat."

"Would you care to join me aboard HMS Antelope we have much to talk about?" Lieutenant Curnow asked. He was now in total control now that Captain Horner was incapacitated and in the care of the ship's doctor.

"Yes, but what about Lord Trethowan on the Portobello?" Black Eye asked.

"Leave the bastard there," Maisha said, who was keen to have her say.

"Who is this lord?" Lieutenant Curnow asked.

"He is Lord Trethowan and our employer. He hired us and our ship to rescue Captain John Flynn," Black Eye replied.

"Of course, Trethowan the village where the pirates raided and where my cousin lives," Lieutenant Curnow said.

"Two Coin get the Portobello ready to sail, and have the rowing boat ready to bring Lord Trethowan to HMS Antelope," Black Eye shouted across to Two Coin on the Portobello.

"There is no haste," Maisha said, smiling at Black Eye. Her distrust of the lord was born from her ability to size up a person, like a soothsayer who would make predictions with a crystal ball.

As Black Eye, Maisha, Nathaniel, Captain John Flynn and Lieutenant Curnow made their way back to HMS Antelope via the rowing boat they were quickly reminded of the battle by the damage the ship had suffered. Large cannon holes could be seen along most of the port side. And as they climbed aboard the ship they could see the damage to the wheel house, which was now being repaired by the ship's carpenter.

"Escort Captain John Flynn and Nathaniel to the ship's doctor and have them checked out." Lieutenant Curnow stated to the mid shipman that was standing to attention as the lieutenant made his way to the captain's quarters followed by Black Eye and Maisha.

"Take a seat, we have much to discuss," Lieutenant Curnow stated to Black Eye and Maisha.

"Yes, we've no time to waste," Black Eye said, who was eager as ever to start the search for the pirates' treasure.

"So, you're in command," Maisha said as precocious as ever, who didn't trust anyone, especially the English navy. She was eager to flee the scene because she feared how people react when they have gold fever. She had watched at an early age when her father had uprooted the family to prospect for gold in the 'Becker Valley' only for it to end in tears and poverty. She saw at first-hand how her father could not let go of his dream of finding gold and becoming rich. Her father had had gold fever and feared that if he packed up then someone else would find his gold, and this he could not allow even to the point of going broke.

"You must forgive my woman, she sometimes speaks without warrant," Black Eye said looking at the lieutenant with a wry smile that meant he didn't disapprove of what Maisha had said.

"I understand, we all have our axes to grind," Lieutenant Curnow said, who knew that his captain had had the same motives, until his injury during the battle, and this now meant he was no longer in command.

"Are we together on finding the pirates' treasure?" Black Eye asked, who was now, wondering, what the lieutenant had in mind now that he was in command.

"We've Captain Kerry and his second in command below deck on the Rag-tail. We can transfer them to the HMS Antelope and see what they have to say. Most men talk when they have a choice. What say you?" Lieutenant Curnow asked.

"We could cut off their balls," Maisha said.

"They will talk, we just need to show them what to expect if they don't," Black Eye said.

"But first, we need to agree between ourselves how to split what we find. Don't forget the Crown will want its share and the men on your ship and mine," Lieutenant Curnow said.

"Don't forget Lord Trethowan, he'll want his share of the booty," Black Eye said.

"Leave the bastard to stew, he then may boil over and die," Maisha said.

"No, no. Mid-shipman, arrange a boat to fetch Lord Trethowan and the pirates Captain Kerry and his second in command to our ship. Make sure the pirates are suitably shackled, we don't want to lose the pirates at this late stage of operations," Lieutenant Curnow ordered.

"Yes, sir," the mid-shipman replied, before he exited the captain's quarters.

***

Before the door to the captain's quarters opened all present in the cabin could hear the sound of what sounded like distant thunder, which had a rhythm. It was like someone clapping their hands only the beat was stretched with one clap then another, it was Captain Kerry's boots as he walked along the wooden decks. The iron studs on the pirate's soles of his boots announced his presence long before he and Ironman Slim entered the cabin along with Lord Trethowan leading the way.

"I am Lord Trethowan," Lord Trethowan said in a commanding tone of voice.

"Greetings Lord Trethowan," Lieutenant Curnow said as the lord was led into the captain's quarters by a mid-shipman and two marines guarding the two pirates who had their hands clasped in iron chains.

"Please, take a seat Lord Trethowan, we are about to interrogate these pirates," Lieutenant Curnow said.

"First, I would like to see Captain John Flynn. I understand he's well considering his ordeal," Lord Trethowan said, who was eager to see the man he had spent a small fortune and considerable risk to his own life to rescue.

"He's fine and in good health and at present with the ship's doctor having a check over. If you wish you can go below and check for yourself. But, I thought you would be interested in what these pirates have to say," Lieutenant Curnow said.

"Could you send a message to Captain Flynn to join us as soon as possible?" Lord Trethowan asked. He was also eager to hear what the pirates had to say.

"Yes, of course."

"Mid-shipman, go below and ask Captain Flynn and my cousin the boy Nathaniel to join us as soon as possible. Oh, also ask the cook to bring us some food and wine for six of us." Lieutenant Curnow ordered as he tried to size up the pirates standing in front of him across the captain's table.

"Yes, sir," the mid-shipman replied as he tried to regain his balance as the ship begin to list from one side to the other.

"Oh, find out how progress is going with repairs?" Lieutenant Curnow asked as the ship started to list more frequently.

"It looks like a storm is approaching and we are still dead in the water until the wheel house is repaired," Lieutenant Curnow said as the mid-shipman exited the captain's quarters.

"Perhaps, we should start our integration before the ship sinks," Maisha said in a rhetorical manner.

"This is a frigate and well used to this kind of weather," Lieutenant Curnow said.

"I hope so," Maisha said snappily.

As HMS Antelope rose and sank in the swell of the sea, the crew was busy frantically trying to make urgent repairs, as giant waves crashed over the upper decks, making it difficult for the crew to maintain their balance and avoid being washed overboard.

"Sit the pirates down and stand guard at the door." Lieutenant Curnow ordered the two marines guarding them.

"I'm Lieutenant Curnow and in command of this ship. We want to know where you have the treasure buried."

"I'm Captain Kerry and this is my second in command, Ironman Slim," the pirate replied.

"Yes, yes, we know that. Are you prepared to cooperate?" Lieutenant Curnow asked. He knew his mission was nearly over and wanted to avoid unnecessary bloodshed if he could.

"Why should we?"

"Well, you have two choices. Either, you tell us what we want to know and lead us to your treasure or risk the end of the gibbet and hang until you die. It's your choice," Lieutenant Curnow stated.

"There's another choice, we could torture you until you squeal like a pig," Black Eye interjected, who was already tired at the sight of the pirates and hadn't forgotten his previous miss-fortune with the pirate all the years before.

"Let's start cutting some flesh," Maisha said.

"You see, my friends have a different method to make you talk," Lieutenant Curnow said, who was eager to take back control of the interrogation and avoid bloodshed if he could, but he knew his friends had other ideas that didn't fit with his code of honor.

"They have cost me a small fortune and considerable risk and I want my share," Lord Trethowan demanded, before he slammed the table with his fist in anger.

"If I tell you where the treasure is hidden what guarantee do I have from you?" Captain Kerry asked as he coughed up some blood, and then as he gazed at the lieutenant he began to spit it out on the floor of the cabin.

"My orders were to kill or capture you and sink your ship, which I cannot change. But, I could offer you a chance to live and not hang on the gibbet, which you deserve," Lieutenant Curnow said as he tried to reason with the pirate.

"Eh, it's Nathaniel my cousin and Captain John Flynn," Lieutenant Curnow said as he stood up to greet the boy with a brief hug, and he then noticed the boy was missing his right little finger.

"How did you lose your finger?" Lieutenant Curnow asked with concern noticeable in his tone of voice.

Nathaniel then pointed to the pirates and said, "It was them, they tortured me to speak about Captain Flynn. At first, I didn't say a word, until one of his men sliced off my finger.

"I see, so these men are responsible," Lieutenant Curnow said, who was now in an angry mood and not willing to waste any more time.

"We should pay the favor back," Maisha said.

"With interest," Lord Trethowan interjected.

"Let me do the honors," Black Eye said as he pulled a long curved knife from his belt buckle and plucked his finger across the blade, which immediately drew blood.

"Okay, Captain Kerry last chances before you suffer the same as Nathaniel. What is it to be?" Black Eye asked as he stood beside the pirate captain sat at the table with his hands cuffed in iron chains. Black Eye was just waiting for the nod from the lieutenant to exact revenge.

"What is it to be, Captain Kerry?" Lieutenant Curnow asked as he looked straight into the captain's dark brown eyes that showed no sign of emotion and nor did his facial expression amongst his over grown beard.

"Okay, I will help you, but what about my side of the bargain? There has to be something in it for us. For me and Slim, otherwise, if you kill us you will never find the treasure.

"Yes, we saw how you dealt with your own crew on the island," Maisha said.

"Yes, we saw several skeletons near the statue of the Buddha with pistol holes in their clothing," Black Eye added.

"We have no intention of killing you and Slim, but we could just torture you and Slim until one of you begins to loosen their tongues," Lieutenant Curnow said.

"Let us go with your word of integrity and we will show you where the treasure is on the island," Captain Kerry said as he spat out some more blood from the injury he suffered during the battle.

"But, someone has to hang on the gibbet; otherwise, the admiralty will have my head in a stock," Lieutenant Curnow said, who knew the admiralty had given Captain Horner specific instructions on what to do with the pirates, especially what they wanted done to Captain Kerry and his pirate ship the Rag-tail. Kill or capture the pirates and sink the pirate ship Rag-tail were their specific instructions from the admiralty. Sinking the Rag-tail when his men had risked their lives without the chance of claiming the ship as a prize, didn't make sense to him and nor would it be to his men.

"Okay, you have my word of honor. But, unfortunately we cannot claim the Rag-tail as a prize for my men. I have orders from the admiralty to sink your ship, which will be done as soon as we have transferred the prisoners and any useful goods to HMS Antelope.

"Lieutenant Hawkes, see to it the prisoners and any useful goods are transferred to our ship and prepare the Rag-tail to be scuttled." Lieutenant Curnow ordered.

"Wait! We were part of capturing the Rag-tail, we should have a say," Black Eye interjected.

"Yes, what gives you the right to scuttle the ship?" Maisha asked angrily.

"Because, I have orders and orders are orders. The admiralty wanted it done; otherwise, we will have to account for our actions. It's the only action we can perform that will please the admiralty and it must be done," Lieutenant Curnow replied.

"It doesn't make sense to me," Lord Trethowan said.

"What doesn't make sense?" Black Eye asked as he stared into Lord Trethowan's eyes with such an evil look that for a moment Lord Trethowan was truly frightened by the African giant for the first time. Even Captain Kerry and Ironman Slim felt the fear of the black man.

"Sinking the ship when it would have made a handsome prize for the crew," Lord Trethowan said, who knew it would make a handsome prize even though the ship needed major repairs.

"Forget about it. Now, tell me Captain Kerry why you attacked the village of Trethowan?" Lieutenant Curnow asked.

"Come now, talk you have my word no harm will befall you. Remember, we have a deal," Lieutenant Curnow said, who was eager to find out as much information as he could before they set foot on Madagascar.

"We were paid by an Arab to attack and raid the village," Captain Kerry replied coughing up blood as he spoke.

"Why attack the village of Trethowan?"

"Our main aim was to capture Captain John Flynn if we could and make it seem that it was just a raid on the village," Captain Kerry replied.

"This Arab, what was his name?"

"Sheik Abu Ben Ali."

"Do you know why the sheik wanted Captain John Flynn?" Lieutenant Curnow asked.

"No," Captain Kerry replied, who had decided not to reveal the truth, at that moment, figuring it may prove useful later to bargain with.

"Take Captain Kerry to the doctor and Ironman to the cells," Lieutenant Curnow ordered the two marines standing guard over the pirates.

"And return Captain Kerry to the cells after he's finished with the doctor."

"Aye, aye, sir," said the marines.

"Oh, make sure the pirates are watered and feed."

"Aye, aye, sir."

"What happens now?" Maisha asked. She was eager to know the lieutenant's plans now that Captain Kerry had agreed to lead them to the treasure. She was sure the lieutenant and most likely the crew were already in the throes of gold fever. Just as she was ready to ask another question, the door to the cabin opened, and in walked Yuki and the cook with trays of food and bottles of wine.

"Great! What a sweet smell," Black Eye said, who recognized the smell of spices he had experienced when growing up in Africa where the use of spices were routinely used on game caught in the jungle that needed added spices to make most meat palatable.

"Yes, I can taste the presence of turmeric, which is often used in the Middle East and Asia," Maisha said.

"Yes, we picked up those spices on the west coast of Africa, when we docked for supplies and information," Lieutenant Curnow said.

At the first sight of the girl with the cook, Nathaniel was mesmerized by her beauty. All thoughts of his recent miss adventure escaped his body like steam rising from a cooking pot. His eyes watched every motion of the young girl as she arranged the trays of food on the table in front of the lieutenant. Her long dark hair that reached halfway down her back gently caressed her body like the touch of silk upon the body, he thought.

"This is the girl I spoke about before, her name is Yuki and Captain Horner would like the girl returned to her own country. She told us she was captured by Burmese solders and sold into slavery. She was eventually bought by a pirate called Captain Kareem, which we have in our cells below deck," Lieutenant Curnow said.

"It sounds like she has been through the wars," Maisha said, who understood the plight the girl had been through, and immediately had sympathy with her experience and took a liking for the girl.

"She has indeed," Black Eye said who also took a liking for the girl because she reminded him of the plight he had suffered as a former slave.

"Yuki is such a good cook, I think the captain will be sad to see her go…and me," Lieutenant Curnow said as he took a sip of wine from his pewter flagon.

As Yuki struggled to hear and understand what was being said by those present, she caught sight of Nathaniel sat at the end of the table. She immediately identified with the young boy and shyly smiled at him for a brief moment without being noticed by the men and the strangely dressed woman present sat around the table. She was relieved to see another female aboard the ship, not that she felt threatened since Captain Horner had given explicit instructions to the ship's crew that any man or men trying to interfere with her would be severely disciplined.

Maisha smiled, as she noticed Yuki's brief smile at the boy, and recognized the first throes of a possible friendship between the two. It rekindled the first meeting she had had with Black Eye, when she knew she had met her soulmate.

As HMS Antelope began to sway more and more as the waves bounded the ship from side to side, Lieutenant Curnow considered his options.

"Fetch more wine," Lieutenant Curnow said to the cook and Yuki as they exited the cabin for the galley.

"It looks like we are in for a storm," Lord Trethowan said, when everyone gathered around the table were thinking the same.

"What are your plans, lieutenant?" Lord Trethowan asked. He was eager to find the treasure and get back to England, as soon as possible.

"Sir, we've had to abandon the Rag-tail to the storm," Lieutenant Hawkes said as he rushed into the cabin with the news.

"Have you transferred all the prisoners to the cells below?" Lieutenant Curnow asked in a sharp tone of voice, who was concerned the pirates would cheat the hangman's noose upon the gibbet.

"Yes, lieutenant, we have all the prisoners aboard our ship in the cells and most of the supplies from the Rag-tail. The waves are too big now to handle in the rowing boat," Lieutenant Hawkes replied as he steadied himself against the wooden mast that ran down through the captain's cabin to the belly of the ship.

"Good, there is no time to waste. Have your men blast the Rag-tail with fire and let her sink and burn. Have the bosun set sail for that cove on our port side as soon as the Rag-tail sinks," Lieutenant Curnow ordered.

"We should return to our ship," Black Eye said.

"There's no time for that," Lieutenant Curnow said instantly and added, "and send a signal to your ship to follow ours into that cove. We will need the cover of the cove against this storm that is approaching."

**

"Follow me, Maisha," Black Eye stated as they made their way onto the quarter deck. Using a special mirror to catch the sunlight between the clouds, Black Eye sent a message to Two Coin to follow HMS Antelope into the protected cove.

"Do you trust the lieutenant?" Maisha asked as she watched the Rag-tail gradually burn and sink into the sea.

"We have no other choice," Black Eye replied.

"Remember, the English cannot always be trusted," Maisha said, who recalled her previous experience dealing with the English navy and wanted Black Eye to be careful.

"It's okay, Maisha, I have already thought about that and have an ace in my hand," Black Eye said with a wry smile, that crept across his face, as he stroked his long black beard and, at the same time, curling his beard into a point like the shape of a funnel.

"What's that?" Maisha asked. She thought she knew all what Black Eye had in store.

"I will tell you later. In the meantime, don't worry about Lieutenant Curnow or Lord Trethowan; they are like jelly in my hands. If I decide to use the ace they will not see it coming," Black Eye replied, and then started laughing at his own remarks.

"Okay, I won't, but be careful that's all I ask, you know I don't trust the English," Maisha said reinforcing her opinion again.

"Let's get inside...the cold wind is biting at my person like the smell of death that lingers in the air," Black Eye said to Maisha as they made their way from the quarter deck to the captain's quarters.

**

"Eh, you're back," Lieutenant Curnow said still sat at the table with Lord Trethowan, Captain Flynn and Nathaniel eating and drinking as Black Eye and Maisha entered the captain's quarters.

"Yes, lieutenant, my ship will follow yours into the cove," Black Eye said.

"Good."

"Have you any food for us," Maisha said in a rhetorical manner.

"Yes, of course, help yourself."

"How is Captain Horner?" Black Eye asked curiously to know if the captain would be fit to retake command of the ship, any time soon.

"The latest report is he's conscious, but unfit to command, at the moment, due to the injuries he suffered during the battle. The doctor says he should be fit within a few days once he has regained his strength. He lost a lot of blood with two direct hits to his person," Lieutenant Curnow replied.

"Will he have a different view towards the pirates when he's fit to command?" Black Eye asked.

"I don't think so. I've carried out the admiralty's orders, so far as it relates to the pirates. The treasure will be shared and the Crown will get its share in due course," Lieutenant Curnow replied harshly, as he didn't like his command challenged, but wasn't about to let anyone know how he felt.

As HMS Antelope and the Portobello sailed into the deserted cove and lay anchor before the day's light had faded, they were now protected from the worst of the approaching storm. The heavy rain and gusting winds straddled the ships, but the cove acted like a protected port, allowing the sailors of both ships to relax and enjoy the evening without fear of being caught by the storm that raged without mercy out at sea. They could hear men laughing and enjoying themselves as the crew talked about the coming day and the thought of treasure, and what they would do with their share had spread like a plague amongst the sailors.

"Tomorrow, first light we will go ashore and see what Captain Kerry has tried to protect all these years," Lieutenant Curnow said triumphantly.

"I can hear your men and our men enjoying the prospect of gold. They already have gold fever, especially on our ship," Maisha said.

"Our men are more restrained," Lieutenant Curnow said, who immediately rebuked what Maisha had said.

"Are they…are you sure? What about below deck? Don't forget most of your crew is press ganged into service with your navy," Maisha said. The English navy was always short of men to crew the frigates and other ships because of the harsh conditions and poor pay they received. Because of this lack of men to serve the English navy they were rounded up by force using gangs of serving sailors or marines to force or press men into service.

"Don't worry, Maisha," Black Eye said as he tried to reassure her that everything was going to be alright, even though he also had miss-giving's about the pirates and the lieutenant. He had little trust in the English, and there was something bugging him, like an itch you had to keep scratching, but now was not the time or place to reveal to Maisha how he felt. Later, when he and Maisha were safely aboard the Portobello he would discuss the problem with Two Coin.

"At first light, tomorrow, we will head for the shore make camp and see if the pirates are telling the truth or not," Lieutenant Curnow said.

"Good, the quicker we get the treasure and share our spoils the quicker I can get back to England," Lord Trethowan said.

"You miss England then?" Lieutenant Curnow asked, before he drank some more wine from his flagon.

"The only reason I came all this way was to rescue my friend Captain John Flynn who runs my business like a clock," Lord Trethowan replied.

"I guess I can tell you, why the pirates attacked your village. Now, that we have finished our mission," Lieutenant Curnow said.

"Isn't early to be counting your chickens," Maisha said, as precocious as ever.

"Go on, never mind my woman," Black Eye said, who was eager to know as much information as possible from the lieutenant.

"They attacked your village, Lord Trethowan to strike fear into the local men and women that live near the coast and work in the tin mines, which are worked mainly along the Cornish coast. Tin is used as an additive with iron ore to strengthen the casting of cannon balls. They found that by using the tin ore with iron ore the cannon ball will not fall apart as it is fired by the cannon. And as we're at war with Holland it was their plan to disrupt production of tin ore, and Cornwall is the only place in Europe where tin ore is found. Since, the attack at Trethowan, production of tin ore has considerably been reduced. People were afraid and moved away from the coast, so their raid worked," Lieutenant Curnow said.

"What about Captain John Flynn?" Lord Trethowan asked. He already really knew the answer, but was eager to know what the English navy knew.

"I think you already know, Lord Trethowan. The capture of Captain Flynn was part of their plan to disrupt the operation and production of tin ore at your mines. And they succeeded because your mining business is local to Cornwall. The only other tin mining operation is in Turkey, which is currently controlled by an Arab business man," Lieutenant Curnow replied.

"How do you know all this?" Lord Trethowan asked as he gorged on the food on the table and made a noisy belch before taking a large gulp of wine from his flagon.

"From our naval intelligence," Lieutenant Curnow replied as he watched the overweight lord eat as though he hadn't had food and drink for a while.

"I don't think…we should take the rowing boat back to the Portobello tonight," Black Eye said as he watched the plates of food slide across the table before stopping at the raised edges of the table.

"You can stay aboard here. Maisha can have the captain's bed and Black Eye can sling a hammock over there between the mast pole and the wall. Lord Trethowan can also sling a hammock over there between that cannon and the wall," Lieutenant Curnow said.

"Hopefully, it will hold your weight, Lord Trethowan" Maisha said as everyone present laughed except Lord Trethowan who just turned redder in complexion.

"After sleeping in the jungle and fighting off insects and mosquitoes the hammock will feel like heaven," Lord Trethowan said as he gave out another loud belch and felt he was getting drunk on the wine.

***

The next morning, as two rowing boats headed toward the shore of the secluded cove fully ladened with people and provisions they all caught sight of the giant statue of the Buddha in the distance. As they all scampered above the shore line and into the jungle, which was thick with trees and vegetation Lieutenant Curnow wondered what awaited them. The excitement of finding treasure had already swept through the crew of HMS Antelope, and so fast it was like a plague had struck all on board. He had wondered about his cousin Nathaniel, who had decided to stay on board the ship with Yuki and most of the crew that had been ordered to stay and keep a watch for other ships.

If there had been a path to the treasure the jungle had now grown over that and the use of men with machetes were needed to cut a way through the dense vegetation as Captain Kerry and Ironman Slim guided the treasure seekers to their goal. As the party got closer and closer the figure of the giant statue got bigger and bigger, Lieutenant Curnow thought.

"Is it much farther?" Lieutenant Curnow shouted to Captain Kerry and Ironman Slim, who were at the head of the party.

"Not much more," Captain Kerry shouted back, as he entered the ruins of the temple, which covered the jungle with the remains of the temple as far as the eye could see. A scattering of the remnants of cut and worked stone was now mostly covered by trees roots and vegetation, where once stood a Temple to the Buddha. Upturned and broken large pieces of stone lay where they had fallen and now the jungle was gradually consuming them like the sea does when a ship sinks.

As Lieutenant Curnow passed in front of the statue of the Buddha, he could see the remnants of burnt wood where Black Eye said they had previously make camp looking for the treasure.

"We better make camp here as you did," he said to Black Eye and then ordered several of his men to stay behind and keep watch.

As the party continued on through the jungle, for several more hours, when Captain Kerry, who had led the group just stopped and pointed with his arm to an opening next to a large outcrop of rock.

"There…over there by that large outcrop of rock…there is an opening covered by the jungle," Captain Kerry said as he pointed with his bandaged right arm to the spot and smiled like a Cheshire cat.

"But, that's no bigger than the size of infant," Black Eye said as he cautiously inspected the opening fearing there was an animal waiting to emerge from the hole.

"Is this your idea of a joke?" Lieutenant Curnow asked as the smile on Captain Kerry's face had not diminished nor was the smile across the face of Ironman Slim.

"You made a deal, you laggards," Lord Trethowan said, who was busy trying to rid himself of the mosquitoes that seemed to be attracted to him like flies upon carrion.

"I have kept my side of the deal. You just need a man or boy small enough to get inside the hole," Captain Kerry said.

"Perhaps, we should just kill them here and now," Maisha said.

As Lieutenant Curnow quickly scanned his men and Black Eye did the same their eyes turned to Maisha. She was the only member of the group who would possibly be able to fit inside the hole.

"Don't look at me!" Maisha said, continuing, "I have a fear of such a place."

"But, the treasure is there," Black Eye said, who hoped he could persuade his woman.

"How far into the hole is the treasure?" Lieutenant Curnow asked. He was showing visible signs of his anger as his face had turned redder every moment he looked at the two pirates.

"It's about as far as I can throw you, not far, then you will see a pile of fallen rocks. It's under that pile of rocks," Captain Kerry replied, who still had a merry complexion as did Ironman Slim.

"The cave becomes larger after several feet, large enough for a man to move around, but the entrance will only suit someone who is small in stature," Ironman Slim said, who was willing to bear the wrath of Lieutenant Curnow, he continued, "We always brought our cook along, but he died in the battle from cannon fire."

"We could make the entrance wider with gun powder," Lord Trethowan said.

"It's no good, we would risk collapsing the cave," Lieutenant Curnow said, who was still angry, which showed on the Cornish man's face as it became redder by the moment.

"Maisha, you will have to go into the cave and retrieve the treasure," Black Eye said demonstrably, trying to convince his woman there was no other option.

"No way am I going into that cave, you know how I feel about that. I've told you what happens to me in the past. Treasure or no treasure, I'm not going in and you can't make me. You will have to figure out something else," Maisha replied, who was willing to die at the point of a cutlass or pistol and stand her ground, because she knew what would happen if she was confined in a small space. She would freeze up like ice and they would have to pull her out without the treasure.

"What about the girl Yuki?" Lord Trethowan suggested.

"Yes, she's small enough to get in there," Lieutenant Curnow said, who was feverishly figuring out what to do in his mind.

"Yes, she could do it," Black Eye said, who was eager to confirm Lord Trethowan's suggestion would work, which was something he hadn't imagined agreeing with since knowing the lord.

"Okay, we will make camp here and I will send Slim with three of my men back to our ship and fetch Yuki," Lieutenant Curnow said, who wasn't willing to let Captain Kerry out of his sight until he had the treasure in his grasp.

"Mid-shipman Jones, take two marines and guard Ironman Slim and make your way to the temple and tell the marines at the temple to accompany you to our ship and fetch the girl Yuki back here. You have enough daylight to retrieve the girl and make it back to the temple and camp there for the night. At first light, tomorrow, make your way back here as soon as possible, is that understood?" Lieutenant Curnow asked. He had every confidence in his junior officer to carry out his orders.

"Just remember Ironman Slim our deal with your captain and you. If you try anything, we will execute him on the spot, is that understood?" Lieutenant Curnow asked gazing straight into the eyes of Ironman Slim and waiting for an affirmative answer from the pirate.

"Tell him, Captain Kerry that his life depends on him making it back here with Yuki and Lieutenant Curnow's men all alive," Black Eye said who was also keen to stress the point.

"He knows my life depends on him, he will do as instructed," Captain Kerry said, and then nodded with confirmation his second in command would do as instructed.

Precocious as ever, Maisha interrupting said, "Yes, I'm just itching to cut off his balls and feed them to my pet for supper."

"You may get the chance if Ironman Slim doesn't return," Lieutenant Curnow said, smiling.

***

As mid-shipman Jones and his men climbed aboard HMS Antelope with Ironman Slim they were met by the familiar face of the boy Nathaniel, who was waiting to hear news of the treasure.

"What news of the treasure?" Nathaniel asked. He was eager as any on board the ship to hear about the treasure.

"Where is the girl Yuki?" mid-shipman Jones asked. He was eager to get back into the rowing boat with the girl and make it to the temple and make camp before nightfall.

"She's down in the galley preparing food for the crew," Nathaniel replied, who was curious to know why the mid-shipman wanted to know Yuki's whereabouts.

"Why do you want to know?" Nathaniel asked without getting a reply as the mid-shipman quickly made hast below deck with his men only Ironman Slim stayed behind guarded by two marines.

"The girl is to be taken to the island to help retrieve the treasure from a cave that is too small for a man to crawl into," Ironman Slim said just as Captain Horner walked onto the deck, and up to the quarter deck, to survey the state of the ship.

"I say you pirate, what goes?" Captain Horner asked as he braced the railing around the quarter deck like a man ready to give orders.

"Lieutenant Curnow needs the help of the girl because she's the only one small enough to climb into the cave opening and retrieve the treasure. I'm here to make sure I lead your men back to the cave." Ironman Slim said looking up to the captain on the quarter deck from the upper deck.

"Argh, there's Jones," Captain Horner stated as mid-shipman Jones emerged with Yuki who was protesting at her removal from her duties in the galley.

"Captain, we are here to take the girl to the cave and retrieve the treasure. Those are my orders from Lieutenant Curnow," mid-shipman Jones said as his men wrestled with the girl who was trying to escape.

"I will miss your cooking, but Lieutenant Curnow needs your help and you will concede," Captain Horner said, who was eager to sail as soon as Lieutenant Curnow and his men returned with the treasure.

"Captain, can I go with Yuki?" Nathaniel asked.

"What, what?"

"They may need my help as well," Nathaniel added.

"You may go, but make hast," the captain said.

"Thank you."

"Mid-shipman Jones tell Lieutenant Curnow to make hast," Captain Horner stated as he watched mid-shipman Jones and his men with Yuki and Nathaniel climb down into the rowing boat. He wondered how long it would take before he could sail away from the cove, because he feared being discovered by unfriendly forces like the Dutch. Through his telescope he watched the rowing boat make the shore, and he hoped for a quick turnaround.

As mid-shipman Jones accompanied by his men with Ironman Slim, Nathaniel and Yuki leading the group into the jungle they all soon became aware that the daylight was fading. The chorus of diverse sounds from a range of animals could be heard competing for attention as the group hurried to get to the temple and make camp for the night.

"It's not far, now," Ironman Slim said.

"Where're we going to?" Yuki asked.

"We're heading towards the Temple of the Buddha. We're planning to camp there for the night. Tomorrow, we will head deeper into the jungle to the cave where the treasure is hidden," Ironman Slim replied.

"Don't worry, I will look after you," Nathaniel said as he smiled at Yuki.

"What's that sound?" mid-shipman Jones asked.

"It sounds like a lemur they live high up in the trees like monkeys," Ironman Slim replied.

"Is it dangerous?"

"No. The locals refer to them as the 'hairy men' of the jungle," Ironman Slim said.

"Watch out for snakes," Nathaniel said. He had been told about dangerous snakes by his friend Salim Nadeer, the man who had helped him escape from the clutches of the pirates when they docked at Mahajanga.

"How long before we get to the temple?" mid-shipman Jones asked. He was eager to rest after dealing with the heat of the jungle.

"I can see the statue of the Buddha in the distance, we are nearly there," Ironman Slim replied.

The sky had turned black and the only light was the full moon when the group reached the center of the abandoned temple complex. It wasn't long before a fire was made and the group settled down to eat and sleep. It was during the night when they heard the loudest scream.

"What was that scream?" mid-shipman Jones asked out loud to the group gathered around the camp fire.

"It's one of your men, he's been bitten by a snake. It's a rattle snake," Ironman Slim said.

"Did you see it slither away...there it goes. Catch it and kill it!" Nathaniel said.

"Here take this sword and kill it before it comes back," mid-shipman Jones implored.

"Your man has been bitten on his leg. Quick, tie this rope around his leg above the bite...as hard and tight as you can. We have to stop his blood," Ironman Slim said to the marine.

"It's too late. He's dead. We need to bury him before the smell of carrion attracts other animals," mid-shipman Jones said.

***

The following morning, the group, once more headed out deeper into the jungle. As the group followed Ironman for several hours, before they reached the other group camped outside the treasure cave.

"Did you have any trouble getting here?" Lieutenant Curnow asked.

"We lost one marine to a rattle snake last night," mid-shipman Jones replied.

"I tried to save him, but it was no use," Ironman Slim sighed.

"I see my cousin Nathaniel came along," Lieutenant Curnow said.

"We could not separate the pair," mid-shipman Jones said as they both watched Yuki and Nathaniel talking together like a couple in love. They could see the couple was inseparable like peas in a pod.

"Well there's no time to waste let's get Yuki over here and start exploring the cave," Lieutenant Curnow said. Continuing, he added, "Yuki, we want you to crawl into the cave and there you'll see a pile of rocks according to Captain Kerry, where the treasure is buried. As soon as you have discovered the treasure give a shout out to us. Is that understood?"

"Be careful, Yuki," Nathaniel said to Yuki as she crawled through the narrow entrance to the cave and disappeared from view with only a small oil lamp to light the way.

As Yuki followed the entrance into the cave the cave soon opened up large enough for a man to stand up in. There to the left of her in a corner of the cave, she glimpsed the pile of rocks that Lieutenant Curnow had spoken about. She made a call to the group waiting outside that she had found the pile of rocks. As she moved the rocks out of the way she could see the wooden chest, which was locked shut.

"There's a wooden chest, which is locked shut and I can't open it," Yuki shouted to the men outside the cave. She continued, "And the chest is too heavy for me to carry."

"Can you push it out?" Lieutenant Curnow asked. He was at fever pitch at the anticipation of treasure only a short distance away.

"No, I can't the chest is too heavy for me," Yuki replied.

"Captain Kerry, do you have the key to unlock the chest?" Lieutenant Curnow asked.

"I did, but it was on the Rag-tail and its now at the bottom of the sea," Captain Kerry replied.

"Search him for the key," Black Eye said, who didn't believe what the pirate had said.

"Make a search of both of the pirates," Lieutenant Curnow ordered. He was inclined not to believe the pirates.

"Sir, we have searched both men and found no key," the marine said.

"Okay, Yuki come out, we have to think of something else to do," Lieutenant Curnow said.

As Yuki crawled through the narrow entrance and saw the men waiting patiently for the treasure, she wondered, what they would do to retrieve the treasure. She first saw Nathaniel waiting to pull her out of the cave with relief on his face that she was safe.

"We need some rope and pull the chest out," Black Eye said, who was as eager as the other men to see the treasure.

"We don't have any rope, not here, but on the ship," Lieutenant Curnow said, who was now frustrated at the situation.

"Why don't we make some rope from the vegetation that's all around us," Maisha said.

"That's a good idea," Lord Trethowan said.

"Okay, let's get started," Lieutenant Curnow said as he ordered his men to gather the twine.

"I will show you how to make rope," Yuki said. She knew how to make rope from plants since a child.

As Lieutenant Curnow's men gathered the vegetation, that Yuki had showed them what to collect; they started to twist the vines into a rope that could be strong enough to pull the heavy chest through the cave and into the hands of the group. After several hours, the rope was ready to use, and again Yuki crawled through the narrow entrance into the cave with the rope.

"Have you tied the rope around the chest?" Lieutenant Curnow asked.

"Yes."

"As we pull, can you push the chest towards the entrance?" Lieutenant Curnow asked.

"Yes, I can," Yuki responded.

"Is there anything else buried?" Lieutenant Curnow asked.

"No, there's no more."

"Captain Kerry, is there anything else buried in the cave?" Lieutenant Curnow asked again.

"No, that's it, just the chest," Captain Kerry replied.

"Okay, we have your word?" Lieutenant Curnow asked. Perhaps, the pirates were telling the truth, and had previously moved most of the treasure to another location, he pondered.

As Lieutenant Curnow's men pulled the rope, the chest moved slowly as Yuki guided the chest towards the opening, and within minutes, the treasure chest was out of the cave. Yuki emerged from the cave with a loud cheer from the group, with Nathaniel amongst the loudest.

"We now need to open the chest to see what we have," Lieutenant Curnow said.

"Yes, yes," Lord Trethowan said. He was eager as ever to get off the island, and return home with Captain Flynn and continue with his life running his business interests.

"Get that rock and knock that lock off," Black Eye said urgently. He couldn't wait to see what was inside the chest.

"It's open," the marine said as he managed to dislodge the lock open with the end of a sword.

The group of men gathered around the chest as the lid was opened to reveal a chest full of gold Spanish doubloons, which glowed as the daylight was fading. The group of men had never seen so much gold and many had already started dreaming again of what they would do with their share.

"It's too late to start back, we will camp here, tonight," Lieutenant Curnow said.

"How will we share this treasure?" Black Eye asked briskly.

"Not here, but when we get back to the ship," Lieutenant Curnow replied, who had already ordered his men, to tie the chest shut with some of the rope they had used to pull the chest from the cave.

"I hope you guard it well," Maisha said. She could see how some of the men had gold fever, and knew how gold fever could change what a man was prepared to do to acquire it.

"Don't worry, Maisha. I'll have three men guarding the chest all night," Lieutenant Curnow said forcibly.

"That may not be enough," Maisha said, who was as precocious as ever. She smiled at Black Eye with the look that she knew he had gold fever, and may be prepared to do anything to get his hands on the gold.

"I don't trust anyone," Lord Trethowan said.

"Does that include you?" Maisha asked as Lieutenant Curnow looked on and felt the same about the lord, but could not countenance challenging the lord in the same manner.

"Don't worry, Maisha we all have our weaknesses," Lord Trethowan said. He had got used to the articulate woman challenging him. She was like a fly that keeps on buzzing around you, until you snap and have to kill it, he thought.

"Mind your manners," Black Eye said to Maisha, who respected the woman he loved, even though she could sometimes get out of hand with her witty remarks.

"Is there more treasure to be had, Captain Kerry?" Black Eye asked. He didn't trust the pirate, as far, as he could spit, he said to himself.

Captain Kerry shook his head and said, "Not now. We traded most of our treasure over the years for supplies. How would we survive without provisions for many men without trading our treasure?"

Black Eye had a gut feeling the pirate knew more, it was like the sense you get when someone is standing behind you even though you cannot see them. He trusted his gut feelings more than he trusted the pirates were telling the truth. He would have to have a word with the lieutenant about how he felt and what they could do to extract the information they required.

When the men sat around the camp fire the only words you could here were about how they would spend their share of the treasure. Maisha could see how the sight of gold had stirred the men to think about the gold and she could see the fever had its grip like the claws of a vice.

During the night, one of the marines had tried to persuade the men guarding the chest to let him untie the chest and steal some doubloons, which he said would not be missed as the gold doubloons had not been tallied yet. Gold fever had taken over and all sensible reason had been forsaken by this marine. The episode was reported to Lieutenant Curnow in the morning and the marine was put on watch until punishment could be ministered on the ship later.

"I understand there was an attempt to steal some gold last night, is that true?" Black Eye asked as he tried to get an answer from Lieutenant Curnow.

"Yes, there was, but nothing was stolen and I have dealt with the matter for now until we get back aboard HMS Antelope," Lieutenant Curnow replied.

"Never mind about that, get ready to move out," Lord Trethowan said.

"I'm just curious about what happened, that's all," Black Eye said.

"We need to make haste to our ship," Lieutenant Curnow said snappily.

Chapter 14

It was hotter than usual, that morning, as the group made their way into the jungle back to the shore. The mosquitoes were a constant discomfort, especially for Lord Trethowan, who could be heard chattering to himself and cursing the jungle, which Maisha and many of the marines and sailors found amusing. Lieutenant Curnow wondered if the pirates had been truthful about the treasure, but he had no time to waste on the matter and consoled himself with what Captain Horner would do. Black Eye also had doubts about the pirates and surmised with a gut feeling there was more treasure to be had.

After several hours, trekking through the jungle, a pistol shot was heard by the group, which meant that something was amiss aboard HMS Antelope. Lieutenant Curnow ordered his men to make haste through the jungle and told the pirates not to dally or a cutlass would be at their backs.

"How far is it now?" Lieutenant Curnow asked as he shouted out towards the pirates leading the group through the jungle?

"Captain Kerry turned around and shouted back, "We are nearly at the temple, after that not long."

***

As the group passed the temple they knew they were not far from the shore. Lieutenant Curnow constantly encouraged his men and pirates to make haste out of the jungle; he knew Captain Horner would not have sent a signal by firing a pistol without good reason. He could only speculate what the urgency may be, perhaps another ship had been sighted, and he mused. After a while, he heard the shout from the pirates leading the group that the sea could be seen.

***

Within minutes, the group was climbing aboard HMS Antelope to a cheer from the crew as the news that treasure had been found.

"Lieutenant Curnow, we have a problem," Captain Horner said as he stood on the quarter deck to greet the return of his men and the treasure.

"Sir, what's the problem?" Lieutenant Curnow asked as he watched the treasure chest being taken to the captain's quarters.

"Captain Black Eye you should return to your ship, we are about to leave this cove," Captain Horner said.

"Not until, we have our share of the treasure," Black Eye shouted as he too watched as the treasure was taken to the captain's quarters.

"No time for that just now," Captain Horner said.

"Then, I stay onboard your ship until my share is sorted," Black Eye replied. He wasn't about to let the treasure out of his sight without securing his share.

"Captain Horner, I feel the same," Lord Trethowan said, who had invested time and money in the adventure and felt the same as Black Eye.

"Okay, you may stay as well," Captain Horner said calmly.

"Steer this ship out of the cove and set a course north by northwest," Captain Horner ordered the bosun at the wheel house.

"Captain Black Eye, tell your crew on the Portobello to follow. There's no time to waste," Captain Horner said hurriedly.

Black Eye soon shouted out the orders to Two Coin across the decks to the Portobello, which had been anchored close by HMS Antelope. Within minutes, the two ships were heading out towards open seas away from the cove that had concealed the two ships from any enemy eyes.

"We have to lose that Dutch ship, which has been scouring the coast for us for several days," Captain Horner said to Lieutenant Curnow as they stood on the quarter deck overseeing their escape from the Dutch war ship.

"This Dutch ship is after us, then," Lieutenant Curnow said as he tried to see through his telescope if the Dutch ship was near and added, "We need to make haste."

"The ship is out there somewhere and looking for us. They probably had intelligence from the port of Mahajanga. Most likely the Portuguese gave them the information that we were around. There out to sink us," Captain Horner said.

"Captain, why don't we stay and fight?" Lieutenant Curnow asked. He was in no mood to run like a frightened chicken, he thought.

"Lieutenant Curnow, we have barely completed our repairs. The ship's crew are in no state to go to battle. While you were on the island many men went down with a mystery sickness and are not fully fit. So, now do you understand my reasoning?" Captain Horner replied. He was angry with the lieutenant for challenging his authority. He respected the lieutenant for his bravery, but nonetheless, he was in no mood for a discussion on his actions.

When the two ships crossed into open waters there was a mist over the sea, which was now ideal to escape the eyes of the Dutch war ship. Captain Horner had a set a course to the port of Zinjibar, Yemen to rescue the last remaining captives, which Captain Kerry and his pirates had sold into slavery. Captain Horner hoped there was still time enough to rescue the captives and fulfil his orders as instructed by the admiralty. The intelligence he had gathered from the pirates locked away below deck while Lieutenant Curnow was on the island gave him confidence the captives would still be in one place and not scattered to far flung locations. He also had promised to return Yuki to her home country if possible or find someone who could do so. He also had another problem, too many mouths to feed and a mystery sickness that plagued his ship. He had his suspicions, where the sickness had come from and was contemplating his next move.

"Lieutenant, make sure we sail without any lights. Captain Black Eye, signal to your ship to do the same. And then join me in my quarters," Captain Horner stated before he made his way to his quarters.

"Yes, captain."

"Bosun, total blackout no lights."

"Aye, aye, sir."

"It's a risk in this mist. What about the Portobello, sir?" Lieutenant Hawkes asked.

"You heard the captain," Lieutenant Curnow replied angrily, continuing, he added, "Lieutenant Hawkes, take over," before he made his way below deck with Black Eye, Lord Trethowan and Maisha following him.

When the two ships headed farther out to sea the waves began to get higher and the swell deeper in every trough of the ocean waves. It began increasingly difficult for the Portobello to follow HMS Antelope without lights in the heavy mist that hung above the water like a wet blanket in a storm. Lord Trethowan was glad to be aboard the ship and out of the jungle and the unforgiving relentless attacks by mosquitoes.

"I didn't request your presence, Lord Trethowan or indeed your presence Maisha," Captain Horner said as he sat at the table and tried to stop his flagon of wine sliding across the table.

"I go where my man goes," Maisha said. Continuing, she added, "As I said before."

"Captain, we need to discuss the sharing of the treasure so I can return home with Captain Black Eye and Captain Flynn," Lord Trethowan urged.

"I have more pressing issues to deal with at this moment," Captain Horner insisted.

"Yes, captain but we want our share," Black Eye demanded. He was getting tired of the adventure and the excuses.

"That's right my man wants his share, so we can get the hell out of here," Maisha said intently, who was eager to get back on board the Portobello and sail for home.

"Listen, we have a sickness on board this ship that we have to deal with before we have to fight another battle with the Dutch. We will be out gunned, because half my crew are either in the sickbay or recovering from the sickness. Up to now, no one has died but that could soon change. And we have too many mouths on board to feed. I propose that we drop off all the pirates at the first port. Those cells below are not fit to cater for the number of men we have locked up. And we cannot adequately feed them, what, what," Captain Horner suggested.

"You want to let them go," Lieutenant Curnow said resentfully. He was furious with the captain's suggestion, which went against admiralty orders.

"Listen, if we don't let them off this ship, we risk the whole ship's crew getting this sickness and potentially losing the ship in battle," Captain Horner said.

"I agree we could all get this sickness. The conditions in those cells are likely breeding the sickness," Black Eye said. He could see the reasons the captain wanted to off load the pirates as soon as possible.

"Yes, I agree too. You have completed your mission and sunk the pirate ship and saved most of the captives," Lord Trethowan said.

"Well that's what we are going to do. I have plotted a course to the port of Zanzibar, where we will off load the pirates. Is that understood, lieutenant?" Captain Horner asked.

"Yes, captain I will change the course," Lieutenant Curnow said before heading outside for the quarter deck to tell Lieutenant Hawkes and the bosun the new course.

"Can we now share out the treasure, captain?" Black Eye asked.

"Yes, now," Lord Trethowan agreed.

"It's about time!" Maisha said precocious as ever.

"Yes, but you know half will have to go to the Crown," Captain Horner said.

"That's a lot!" Maisha said.

"We have no choice."

"Captain Black Eye, tell the marine on guard outside the cabin to fetch scales and weights from the galley," Captain Horner said as he poured some more wine into his flagon.

As the gold doubloons were carefully weighed a reckoning was noted by the captain and half of the treasure was placed back into the wooden chest for the Crown and securely tied shut with hemp rope and marked with red wax to prevent anyone trying to steal some of the chest's contents. After dividing the remaining gold, between Captain Horner, Captain Black Eye, Lord Trethowan and the crews of HMS Antelope and the Portobello,z the men were now rich enough to buy a cottage and more. Even the lowest rank crew member had enough to retire and live a comfortable life on their share of the treasure.

"Listen, are you now satisfied Lord Trethowan, and you Black Eye?" Captain Horner asked. He was eager to rid his ship of unwanted guests, and make plans to defend the ship against a possible attack from the Dutch who were still searching for them.

"Yes, indeed, captain," Lord Trethowan replied, whose share would cover the cost of the adventure many times over. His complexion had turned a bright red at the anticipation of what he may spend his share of the treasure.

"I'm well pleased," Black Eye replied. He already had plans in his mind what to do with his share of the treasure. He always wanted a small farm where he could meek out a comfortable living with Maisha and retire from sea adventures for good.

"Come on Captain Black Eye, you need to signal the Portobello to send a rowing boat before another storm derails our departure," Lord Trethowan insisted. He was now more than ever eager to return to the Portobello and return home with his business partner.

"That's right!" Maisha said. She couldn't wait to return home and away from men who had gold fever in their blood. She didn't think she would be agreeing with Lord Trethowan, but he was right, she said to herself.

As Black Eye and Maisha exited the cabin for the quarter deck to signal the Portobello, a shout could be heard from high up in the crows' nest. But, it wasn't the Portobello, which was nearly parallel to HMS Antelope.

"Ship ahoy, on the portside," said the sailor in the crows' nest.

"What flag is she flying?" Lieutenant Curnow asked. He quickly saw the danger before anyone else, but it wasn't quick enough as cannon fire and shot hit HMS Antelope like a strong wind hits a canvas sail.

"Get down and take cover!" Lieutenant Curnow shouted to the crew above deck as another barrage of cannon shot ripped through the canvas sails like an ill wind on a cold night.

"Get the captain, now!" Lieutenant Curnow shouted to Lieutenant Hawkes as he scrambled to the deck below to get to the captain's quarters.

"It's a Dutch war ship," Lieutenant Curnow said hurriedly to Captain Horner as he climbed the steps to the quarter deck.

"Turn the ship into the wind, now!" Captain Horner ordered Lieutenant Curnow as he bellowed out the orders to the crew and the bosun.

"She'll have to follow, allowing us to avoid her cannon," Captain Horner said.

"The Portobello is firing at the Dutch," Lieutenant Curnow said briskly.

"Good, it will give us time to get ready. Get the gun crew ready to fire when we turn out of the wind and onto to her broadside. We will fire everything we have at them with cannon ball and chain shot at her sails," Captain Horner said.

"Get ready to fire men with cannon and chain shot," Captain Horner shouted preparing the men for battle.

"She's turning into the wind, sir," Lieutenant Curnow said.

Get ready. Fire, now!"

"Get ready to fire again at will, now!"

She's trying to avoid our cannon by turning again, captain."

"Good, she's losing sail, captain," Lieutenant Curnow said as he viewed the carnage aboard the Dutch ship with his telescope.

"Turn to port and get ready to fire again," Captain Horner stated.

"Turn to port," Lieutenant Curnow said to the bosun.

"Get ready to fire and blow this ship to pieces," Lieutenant Curnow shouted to his gun crew as the orders were relayed by a series of junior ratings below deck.

As HMS Antelope turned to port, Nathaniel and Yuki were in the belly of the ship, huddled together, away from any enemy cannon fire.

"We're safe here, Yuki," Nathaniel said.

"How do you know that?" Yuki asked as she looked into Nathaniel eyes to see if was telling the truth or not.

"The cannon on the enemy ship is usually pointing above the water line, unless they have positioned the cannon to fire below the water line to sink the ship, which never usually happens because they like to take the ship as a prize," Nathaniel said.

"I hope you're right."

"Don't worry Yuki, I will look after you."

They both felt the shudder of the ship as returning cannon fire rang out one blast after another. Nathaniel held Yuki close to him as the battle raged above them.

"It sounds like our ship is winning," Nathaniel said.

"How can you tell?"

"We haven't heard or felt a blast of cannon fire from the other ship."

"Do you hear those men are cheering," Yuki said, who now had a smile on her face.

"Yes, it's our men."

"Shall we go up?" Yuki asked.

"No, we wait until we hear from our men," Nathaniel replied.

***

"Tell the gun crews to sink that ship," Captain Horner ordered.

"What, sir?" Lieutenant Curnow asked.

"You heard…sink that ship, now!" Captain Horner demanded. He was angry at his orders being challenged by Lieutenant Curnow.

"Sink that ship," Lieutenant Curnow shouted at the gun crew.

The gun crew raised and tilted the cannons so that they would fire at the ship below the water line and sink the ship. The crew were not happy at passing up the opportunity of the prize, and reluctantly obeyed the orders, as the cannons blasted the Dutch ship with fire, which sunk the Dutch ship within minutes.

"What about any survivors, captain?" Lieutenant Curnow asked.

"Send out the rowing boats for survivors," Captain Horner stated.

Two rowing boats were sent out to search for survivors, which the captain hoped he could gain valuable intelligence from survivors about the Dutch's presence in the region. He knew he had insufficient food to feed any survivors, but felt it was his duty as a sailor to respect the code of war.

"Why did you order the sinking of the Dutch ship?" Lieutenant Curnow asked. He was puzzled by the order, which went against normal practice of taking an opposing ship as a prize.

"We don't have the men to take the ship and sail her to a friendly port. Out here we're on our own," Captain Horner replied.

"Lieutenant Curnow, you have consistently questioned some of my orders. I appreciate your concern, but to question a senior officer is almost an act of mutiny. Luckily for you, I have an understanding nature, and you are a young man still learning the skills you need to be in total command, so I will take your impertinence as a youthful characteristic, which I will not report," Captain Horner said.

"Now, follow me to my quarters, we have some business to discuss," Captain Horner stated. He then led the lieutenant to his quarters.

"Lieutenant Hawkes, take over," Lieutenant Curnow said before he made his way down to the captain's quarters wondering what business the captain had in mind.

As Lieutenant Curnow entered the captain's quarters they both sat down at the table where a large amount of gold doubloons had already been divided into shares for the senior officers and the crew, which lay on the table.

"This is your share and this is to be divided equally among the crew," Captain Horner said as he pointed to the potatoes' sack full of gold doubloons.

"We all have enough to retire from the navy and live a comfortable life. Now, do you see why I didn't want to risk any of my crew securing the Dutch ship, because we don't have the men to sail the Dutch ship to a friendly port," Captain Horner said with a smile of recognition that the young lieutenant would one day learn how to command in difficult times.

"Sir, I never doubted your command, but sometimes my eagerness to learn overtakes my actions," Lieutenant Curnow said. He knew the captain was right in his assessment of his qualities.

"Let's have a drink together to celebrate our victory, and our new fortune," Captain Horner said as he poured some wine into his flagon and the lieutenant's flagon as the ship started to list from side to side as an approaching storm was on its way.

"The rowing boats should be back soon with survivors, and we can then get on our way to Zanzibar," Lieutenant Curnow said as he took another gulp of wine from his flagon.

"I understand your cousin, Nathaniel wants to stay aboard?" Captain Horner asked. He had already spoken with Nathaniel on the matter and knew why the boy wanted to stay.

"You know more than me. I haven't spoken to him since we got back from the jungle," Lieutenant Curnow replied.

"I think, lieutenant you need to seek out your cousin and understand his reasons," Captain Horner said as he nodded his head in agreement with his advice to the lieutenant.

"Yes, captain I will."

"Now, I want you to interrogate the Dutch survivors as soon as they are brought aboard. Remember, we have a mystery sickness aboard the ship and it would be prudent not to mix the survivors with the pirates in the cells," Captain Horner said as a knock on the cabin door was heard.

"Enter!"

"Yes, what is it?"

"Lord Trethowan, Captain Flynn, Captain Black Eye and the woman have taken to their rowing boat," the marine said.

"Okay, let's have some food, lieutenant," Captain Horner said. He was glad they had finally gone from his ship. Two burly marines stood guard outside of the captain's cabin as Lieutenant Curnow and Captain Horner sat down to eat.

"Did they have their share of the treasure?" Lieutenant Curnow asked. He had noticed the wooden chest now tied with hemp rope and sealed with wax placed on the floor in the corner of the cabin.

"Yes, of course. The chest you are looking at contains the gold for the Crown," Captain Horner replied.

Chapter 15

"There is something you should be aware of, captain. I think there is more treasure, but it's not on the island," Lieutenant Curnow remarked.

"What makes you think that?"

"Well, you can't trust the pirates to be telling the truth."

"Are you suggesting we need to get the truth from the pirates, lieutenant?"

"Yes."

"Well, get Captain Kerry and Ironman Slim from the cells," Captain Horner said to Lieutenant Curnow.

"Fetch Captain Kerry and Ironman Slim from the cells and bring then here," Lieutenant Curnow said to the two marines guarding the cabin.

"Are you sure their hiding more treasure?"

"Yes, you can't trust these laggards."

"I prefer to get the lot off this ship as soon as possible, before the whole ship's crew come down with this mystery sickness," Captain Horner said anxiously.

"What does the doctor say?" Lieutenant Curnow asked.

"He doesn't know what the sickness could be," Captain Horner replied.

"So, we're in the dark as to what the sickness is?" Lieutenant Curnow asked. He was also worried about the welfare of the crew and officers on the ship. Continuing, he added, "We're about three days with fair winds away from Zanzibar. It looks like we're in for a storm."

"Lieutenant, you're right on the peg. At least we're ready, but we have to fix the sail sheets most have been holed and some of the rigging destroyed," Captain Horner said.

"We should be up and running within the day," Lieutenant Curnow said.

"Did you feel the ship list just then?" Captain Horner asked. He then held his flagon of wine to stop it sliding across the table.

"Yes, this part of the sea is prone to storms this time of year," Lieutenant Curnow replied as the knock on the door of the cabin was heard.

"Enter!"

As Captain Kerry and Ironman Slim with their hands in iron chains were led into the captain's quarters by three burly marines the ship began to list from one side then the other. The pirates had to be held up by the marines as the ship listed from side to side. The noise of the sea outside could be heard by all inside the captain's quarters as giant waves crashed over the ship and the timber masts could be heard creaking.

"Take a seat," Captain Horner stated to Captain Kerry and Ironman Slim as the captain gestured with his hand to the pirates to take a seat at the table.

"Now, would you like some food and wine?" Captain Horner asked the pirates sat opposite him.

"Yes, why not?"

"Lieutenant, get these men some food and wine," Captain Horner demanded.

"Yes, captain," Lieutenant Curnow replied. He then ordered one of the marines standing guard in the cabin down to the galley with a request for food and wine.

"I have a problem that you can help me with. I understand from Lieutenant Curnow that you have not been truthful with us, Captain Kerry. We believe that you have more treasure hidden somewhere. Now, would you like to make a deal with me? You tell us and lead us to your hidden treasure and we won't have to torture you," Captain Horner said to Captain Kerry.

"What sort of deal had you in mind, captain?" Captain Kerry asked.

As Captain Horner was about to lay out his deal with the pirates a knock at the door was heard.

"Enter!"

Yuki entered the captain's quarters with a tray of food and the cook brought in some bottles of wine as requested. Yuki laid out the dishes of food on the table as the captain continued his conversation with the pirates.

"I have decided to release your men at the port of Zanzibar, but for now you and your second in command will stay until we have a share of your treasure," Captain Horner said.

"You were not satisfied with the treasure you already have?" Captain Kerry asked as he paused and spit out onto the floor some more blood from the injury he sustained in the battle for his ship.

When Yuki and the cook were ushered out of the cabin by the captain, she wondered where the pirates had hidden more treasure and hoped Nathaniel would have a share.

"The deal is you and Ironman Slim get to avoid the gibbet and get a captain's share if you lead us to your treasure and avoid being tortured," Captain Horner said as he took a large gulp of wine from his flagon.

"Have some wine and food, Captain Kerry," Lieutenant Curnow stated.

"You too, Ironman Slim," Captain Horner said as he watched both pirates tuck into the food like people that hadn't eaten for days. They ate like vultures and drank like drunkards without any time for pleasantries.

"That you won't renege on the deal what I can be sure of?" Captain Kerry asked as he washed down his food with a large swig of wine straight from the bottle.

Lieutenant Curnow looked on in disgust and secretly hoped the pirates wouldn't play ball. The lieutenant still wanted revenge on the pirate for his cousin's finger that the pirates cut off.

"Listen, you have my word," Captain Horner said. He wasn't in the mood to be challenged by these pirates, he said to himself.

"Hold his right hand onto the table," Lieutenant Curnow stated to the two marines guarding the pirates.

As the marines struggled with Captain Kerry to hold his hand flat on the table, Lieutenant Curnow held a pistol at the head of Ironman Slim and told him to take a knife and cut off a finger.

"Now, cut off a finger or you're dead," Lieutenant Curnow stated to Ironman Slim as he held the pistol to his head.

As Ironman Slim held the knife over Captain Kerry's finger he felt the sweat trickle down his face and for a moment wondered who would break first, his friend or him.

"Now do it!"

Ironman Slim felt the knife penetrate Captain Kerry's skin as the pressure brought the first sign of blood as if it was his own finger.

"Do it!"

Captain Kerry felt no pain as the knife cut into flesh and bone of his little finger. From a child he knew he could sustain an injury and feel no pain, it was something he had told nobody about. Ironman Slim felt the pain as if it was his own finger being cut off.

"Now you have four fingers," Lieutenant Curnow stated. He had watched Captain Kerry for any signs of pain but had seen none, but felt he had revenged his cousin's loss of a finger and was satisfied.

"Perhaps, we should try Ironman. Hold Ironman's hand to table," Captain Horner ordered the two marines guarding the pirates.

"Hold his right hand firm to the table. We will see if he talks or not," Lieutenant Curnow said to the marines.

As the marines struggled with Ironman Slim they heard a knock at the door of the cabin.

"Enter!"

"What is it, Lieutenant Hawkes?" Captain Horner asked in an angry voice. He was angry at being interrupted just as the proceedings were getting interesting, he thought.

"The Portobello has been sighted... just off our port side, captain," Lieutenant Hawkes said, his voice quivering as he reported the news.

"Is the ship showing any signs of distress?" Captain Horner asked. He wondered why the ship had been sighted.

"No, captain it looks like the ship is trying to catch up with us," Lieutenant Hawkes replied.

"Okay, send a signal and report back with its reply," Captain Horner stated. He didn't feel the need to leave the cabin at that moment.

As Lieutenant Hawkes exited the captain's quarters and made his way to the quarter deck he heard the shout from the sailor in the crows' nest.

"Their flying a flag of distress," the sailor shouted from the crows' nest.

As Lieutenant Hawkes entered the captain's quarters with the news that the Portobello was flying a flag of distress the captain immediately ordered the lieutenant to trim the sails and wait for the Portobello to catch up.

"It looks like the Portobello is in distress of some kind; we'll have to continue our interrogation later. Take the pirates back to the cells and see to it Captain Kerry sees the doctor," Captain Horner stated to the marines.

"I wonder what the problem is with the Portobello," Lieutenant Curnow said to Captain Horner as they made their way to the quarter deck.

As Lieutenant Curnow viewed the Portobello through his telescope he noticed their rowing boat being loaded into the sea with Black Eye and his woman and several men attempting to cast off from the Portobello in the rough seas.

"They must be mad to attempt to row in this weather," Captain Horner said as he viewed them rowing towards his ship.

"Yes, captain completely mad."

"It must be important to risk the journey," Captain Horner said, who was intrigued by what he saw.

As Black Eye and his party climbed aboard HMS Antelope they immediately made their way to the quarter deck where they saw Captain Horner and Lieutenant Curnow waiting for them.

"What so important you risk your lives in this weather to get here?" Captain Horner asked, as he watched Black Eye and Maisha climb the steps to the quarter deck.

"There are two Dutch ships looking for you and on your tail," Black Eye said panting, who was nearly out of breath from the excursion in the rowing boat.

"Yes, the Dutch are not far behind us," Maisha reiterated.

"How do you know this?" Captain Horner asked.

"From a Portuguese ship's captain who told us," Black Eye replied.

"Are you sure this information is true?" Lieutenant Curnow asked in a sceptical voice.

"Yes, Lieutenant Curnow."

"Well, we thank you. Let's retire to my quarters and plan our escape, what, what," Captain Horner said.

"Lieutenant Hawes make hast to Zanzibar all speed!" Captain Horner said in a bad-tempered voice as all four of them made their way down to the captain's quarters.

As Captain Horner was first to sit at the table, he invited the three of them to take a seat and offered each some wine. He enquired if they would like some food while they discussed their plans and ordered the marine guarding the door to the cabin down to the galley to ask the cook and Yuki to bring some more food.

"Oh, where is Lord Trethowan, what, what?"

"He is unwell and decided stay aboard the Portobello," Black Eye replied as he poured some wine into his flagon.

"Eh, perhaps he has the sickness that many of my crew have," Captain Horner said in a matter of fact voice before continuing. "Would you like me to send the ship's doctor to tend to his needs?"

"No, that's okay, he's in fine hands with our doctor," Black Eye replied.

"Our doctor has plenty of experience, he should be fine in his care," Maisha said assertively.

"Okay, let's discuss our plans against the Dutch," Captain Horner said in a commanding voice.

"We're three days away from Zanzibar with fair winds," Lieutenant Curnow interjected before continuing and stressing the point. "But we're still making repairs to our rigging and sails, which could be a problem if we were attacked by the Dutch now. We would be at a disadvantage in any battle."

"I understand your concerns, lieutenant. But, we shall overcome any disadvantage through our ability as better sailors," Captain Horner said in a condescending manner, who knew more about the abilities of HMS Antelope than the lieutenant did.

"What about if we risk the Portobello in any battles, by letting her defend our rear allowing us to escape?"

"You're asking a lot," Black Eye replied in an angry tone of voice.

"Yes, a fucking lot," Maisha said angrily.

"Listen, hold your tongues. It's only a suggestion at present but it may come to this. We don't have the men fit enough to outgun the Dutch ships. It's as simple as that, what, what," Captain Horner said, smiling and as cavalier as a jester at court.

"I think, you should use the pirates as gunners," Black Eye said with conciliatory tone of voice.

"Yes, there must be men amongst those pirates who can handle the cannons in battle," Maisha said, who was eager to back up her man.

"What do you think, lieutenant?" Captain Horner asked briskly. He was eager hear what the lieutenant thought.

"It would solve our problem if we could trust them, if they were under the command of Captain Kerry and Ironman Slim and told of their release. They would more likely fight for their lives if they knew they were to be released at Zanzibar. Better they fight than rot in those cells below," Lieutenant Curnow said as he tried to calm the situation with a lucid response to the captain and to agree with Black Eye and Maisha.

"Okay, I will consider it, while we talk," Captain Horner said whose voice had softened and wondered if the proposal was safe to have pirates manning the cannons on the ship. It sounded like a rational proposal, but the lieutenant didn't always consider the downside, he said to himself.

"You intend to release all the pirates at Zanzibar then?" Black Eye asked as took a long gulp of wine from his flagon.

"Yes, I believe the sickness we have on board this ship is from the pirates, and I cannot risk this ship from disaster, so I intend to release all the pirates except Captain Kerry and Ironman Slim," Captain Horner replied sharply, stating that he was in command and knew what he was doing, but realised as soon as he had said it that he had let the cat out of the bag.

"Why keep just the two?" Maisha asked in an inquisitive tone of voice which showed her precocious manner in plain view.

Hearing a knock at the door the cook and Yuki entered with trays of food and heard what was said next as they laid the food on the table.

"I guess you will find out soon enough. We believe there is more treasure and before you arrived we were trying to get the information from the two pirates," Captain Horner replied.

"More treasure!" Maisha said. She had hoped she had seen the last of gold fever.

As Yuki and the cook exited the cabin, she could hear the voice of Maisha and the word 'treasure' and hoped again that somehow Nathaniel would gain a share of any treasure.

"Well, this deserves a drink to celebrate our agreement, which we all agreed before about the sharing of any treasure," Black Eye said as he raised his flagon of wine in the air to toast their agreement with the prospect of more treasure to come.

"Yes, let's agree to share any treasure again amongst ourselves and the crew of both ships," Lieutenant Curnow said agreeably.

"Yes, what, what," Captain Horner agreed as his tone of voice echoed the lieutenant's words like a servant to his master.

"I guess, we are in agreement then...gold fever here we come," Maisha said like a school girl repeating her teacher's wishes.

"Lieutenant, ask the guards outside the door to fetch Captain Kerry and Ironman Slim for further interrogation," the captain said.

"Perhaps, we should get the pirates to agree to our plans against any Dutch attack first before we go torturing them," Lieutenant Curnow said with a doubtful manner usually only reserved when he felt he could among friends. It was said in a tone of voice and manner that was rhetorical something he would never usually use in front of the captain.

"How do you propose we do that?" Maisha asked cheekily, and was not expecting an intelligent answer.

"Bring Captain Kerry and Ironman Slim from the cells here and see to it that more wine is brought from the galley," Lieutenant Curnow ordered the marines standing outside the cabin.

"I propose that we torture the pirates first and then worry about our plans for them later when they've had time to recover. Besides the pirates that can handle cannon need to be organized and trained to our means," Lieutenant Curnow said calmly.

"Yes, what, what…you could be right, lieutenant. That's what we will do, there is no time to waste, before these pirates get sick and die on us before we get the information we require," Captain Horner said. He was as eager to get to the treasure like a man dying of thirst.

"I knew gold fever would raise its ugly head before time," Maisha said looking straight at Black Eye with eyes like a teacher ready to scold a pupil.

"Whatever we do, Maisha its better this way," Black Eye said as he smiled back at Maisha, with the knowledge that he too was bitten with gold fever like a man possessed of the devil.

"What do you mean?" Maisha asked.

"Well, the devil you know than the devil you don't know," Black Eye replied.

As the knock at the cabin door was heard by all, the marines entered the cabin with Captain Kerry and Ironman Slim chained as before. Captain Kerry's right hand was now bandaged as he stood with his second in command before the table with two marines guarding them.

"Where is the treasure?" Captain Horner asked the pirates.

"Hold down the right hand of Ironman Slim fast to the table," Captain Horner ordered the marines.

"Cut his little finger off," Captain Horner ordered.

"As the marine slowly cut into the flesh of Ironman's little finger blood oozed out like a fountain of water spraying the table with blood as Ironman cried out with pain. Captain Kerry knew he could not see his friend suffer.

"Wait!" Captain Kerry shouted at the marine holding the knife.

"Are you willing to talk now?" Captain Horner asked with his voice crisp with anger, and that he was just starting to enjoy the spectacle unfolding.

"Yes."

"Good, then start talking, captain," Captain Horner said whose patience was wearing thinner by the antics of the pirates.

"There is more treasure hidden in India, but first we make a deal for our lives and a share of the treasure," Captain Kerry said with a commanding tone of voice. He knew Ironman Slim could undoubtedly endure the torture as he was a former fighter in his youth, he remembered, but that was then, and he was older now. And Captain Horner had the upper hand for the moment, he said to himself.

"You are in no position to bargain, captain," Captain Horner said sharply.

"I'm only asking for a captain's share for myself and my friend Ironman," Captain Kerry said in a conciliatory tone of voice, hoping Captain Horner would make a deal.

"Whereabouts in India?" Captain Horner asked as a knock at the door was heard and Yuki and the cook entered with more wine. Captain Horner then remembered his promise to return Yuki to her homeland.

"Bombay," Captain Kerry replied.

"Yuki…would Bombay in India be a good place to return you with enough money to get home to Siam?" Captain Horner asked.

"Yes, captain that would be good," Yuki replied with a brimming smile.

"Good, then that's settled, Yuki. You may go now," Captain Horner said as Yuki bowed and exited the cabin with the cook.

"Okay, Captain Kerry we have a deal. You and Ironman shall have your freedom once we have the treasure and you shall have a captain's share of the treasure. But, remember if you cross us then you shall hang on the gibbet where you belong," Captain Horner said assertively.

"Yes, captain," Captain Kerry said, who knew for now the captain held all the cards.

"There is another problem, which we need your cooperation, captain," Captain Horner said in an appeasing manner as he watched the reaction of the pirates.

"We are being followed by two Dutch war ships that are out to sink us, and we need your help with your crew, to man the cannons that currently we cannot man. Are you willing to help organise and command your men in any battle we may have with the Dutch?" Captain Horner asked.

"Yes, we are, but we would like our freedom aboard this ship and food and drink for my men. Is that possible?" Captain Kerry asked. He knew now that he held the cards. If the ship was attacked it would be his men that would save the day.

"Yes, that sounds reasonable, but I have to have your word that you or your men will not try anything that warrants a noose around your necks," Captain Horner said as he watched Lieutenant Curnow, Black Eye and Maisha look on with doubt expressed on their faces like they had all seen a ghost.

"Is this wise, captain?" Black Eye asked with a strained tone of voice, as he remembered back to his first encounter all those years before with Captain Kerry and his pirates. He hadn't forgotten how they had sneaked up upon the ship he was working on with a false flag, and proceeded to kill everyone on board and steal its treasures. He had escaped by the skin of his teeth by being blasted into the sea by cannon fire and saw from a far what happened to any survivors. It was still as vivid in his memory as the day it happened, he said to himself.

"We have no choice Captain Black Eye, but to sail with the devil," Captain Horner replied, who knew his ship was at peril if attacked by the Dutch with so many of his crew stricken by the mystery sickness and unable to man enough cannon.

"The sooner we make Zanzibar the better," Maisha said gleefully. She knew how her man felt about trusting the pirates.

"Lieutenant, how say you on this matter?" Captain Horner asked. He was intrigued to know what his subordinate thought.

"Better we ride with the devil than go down with the devil," Lieutenant Curnow said with a courteous tone of voice towards his captain's plan knowing that any deviation would bring a reprimand from his superior.

"Good! Lieutenant, what, what…" Captain Horner stated, in his quizzical style to the lieutenant.

"Take Ironman to the doctor and free the chains on both and see to it they have food from the galley," Captain Horner ordered the two marines guarding the pirates.

When Ironman Slim and Captain Kerry were set free from their chains and allowed the freedom of the ship they first made their way to doctor, and then onto the galley for some much needed food and drink.

"Lieutenant how many men have we free from the sickness currently fit for duty?" Captain Horner asked. He was eager to know his strength and weaknesses on board the ship. In his mind, he was preparing for battle with the Dutch. He knew he had a deal with the pirates, but he too didn't trust them.

"We have one hundred and twenty men fit and about the same with the sickness," replied Lieutenant Curnow.

"We could transfer some men from my ship to make up the numbers," Black Eye offered.

"No, don't do that, we need your ship to cover our ass," Captain Horner said.

"Besides, we will need our men to cover our ass," Maisha said in her casual way.

"It sounds like you need all the help you can muster," Black Eye said.

"Lieutenant, start as soon as you can with weather in mind to organise Captain Kerry and his crew to specific cannon and have marines placed to cover their ass. We will not leave anything to chance," Captain Horner said.

"Yes, captain."

"Good, we shall be prepared for any eventuality should the Dutch attack us before we reach Zanzibar," Captain Horner said.

"Sounds like a plan," Maisha muttered.

"Yes, I agree," Black Eye agreed.

As the storm came and went, HMS Antelope and the Portobello sailed on towards the port of Zanzibar without sight or sound of the Dutch warships that were pursuing them. The crews of both ships had time to practice their cannon routines and make ready for any future battle with the help of Captain Kerry and Ironman Slim and many of the pirates that were fit enough for duty. Captain Horner was pleased with the conduct of the pirates and felt HMS Antelope was ready and waiting for the Dutch to appear.

Standing on the quarter deck was Captain Horner and Lieutenant Curnow with Black Eye and Maisha enjoying the cool breeze as HMS Antelope headed towards Zanzibar under the relentless heat of the sun.

"It's good to be out here, today...what, what?" Captain Horner asked happily to his lieutenant.

"Yes, captain."

Chapter 16

"We are making good speed with this wind?" Black Eye said as he surveyed the horizon with his telescope watching for any sign of ships.

"Yes, Captain Black Eye," Captain Horner replied. He always addressed Black Eye with the title captain even though Black Eye felt he didn't need to.

"Ship ahoy on the starboard side," the sailor shouted from the crows' nest.

"Can you make out its flag?" Captain Horner asked as he reached for the lieutenant's telescope to view the ship for himself.

"Too far away," Black Eye replied.

"Another ship ahoy!" the sailor shouted from crows' nest.

"Its two frigates flying the Dutch flags," Black Eye said.

"Sound the bell," Captain Horner shouted.

"Action stations!" Lieutenant Curnow shouted.

"Signal to the Portobello to turn to port," Captain Horner said as he readied his thoughts to the coming engagement with the Dutch warships.

"Yes, captain," Lieutenant Curnow replied as he watched the Dutch warships position to fire their cannons.

"Turn starboard now!" Captain Horner shouted to Lieutenant Curnow.

"Turn to starboard," Lieutenant Curnow ordered the bosun at the wheel house as a volley of chain shot just missed most of the rigging and sails of the ship.

"Fire!" Captain Horner shouted at his men waiting by their cannons to fire back at the Dutch ships.

As HMS Antelope turned into the wind and fired at the Dutch warships an explosion was heard as the ship was hit broadside on and instantly killing many of the crew manning their cannons on the upper deck with splinters of wood crusading from every direction. The cannon ball had blasted a large hole through the upper rail of the ship and disabling several cannon crews. Captain Kerry and Ironman were below the upper deck firing their cannons at the ships as they crossed on their broadside enabling the pirates to get most of their cannon to hit the Dutch ships as they passed by before turning to attack again.

"Get ready to fire again," Lieutenant Curnow shouted from top of the quarter deck down to the men below manning the cannons as chain shot hit HMS Antelope square on leaving the sails with holes and some of the rigging cut from their housing.

"Quick, take cover!" Black Eye shouted to Maisha as another round of chain shot hit the ship lower down across the upper deck sending splinters of wood in all directions.

"Are you all right?" Lieutenant Curnow asked Maisha as she recovered to see the devastation on the upper deck where the brunt of the chain shot had hit the ship and killing and injuring many of Captain Horner's men.

"Get ready to fire again!" Captain Horner shouted as he waited for HMS Antelope to manoeuvre into firing position along the broadside of one of the Dutch war ships.

"It looks like the Portobello has taken too much cannon and is struggling to position itself to respond in kind," Lieutenant Curnow said as he watched the Portobello continuing to move out of the way of the Dutch cannon fire.

"The Portobello is signalling for help," Black Eye shouted as he saw his ship being blasted by cannon ball and chain shot with wood flying in every direction without an effective reply from her gun crew. It looked to him as though it was in desperate trouble and not much he could do about it but watch as the ship was torn apart by the Dutch warships, which had too many cannon for the Portobello to handle. It looked to him as a lost cause, he thought.

"There launching their rowing boats on the lee side away from the cannon fire," Maisha said. She wondered if Two Coin was still alive and able to get to HMS Antelope without being blow out of the water by the Dutch.

"Turn to port," Captain Horner shouted as he tried to avoid the Dutch cannon fire and provide some protection for the rowing boats as he watched the scramble of men trying to get into the boats without being blown to bits by the Dutch cannon fire.

"Get ready to fire again!" Lieutenant Curnow shouted to the gun crews on the three decks all working in unison through a series of relayed commands from the quarter deck.

"Fire!" Captain Horner shouted with a husky voice from the smoke of burning timber as the rowing boats desperately tried to move closer to the ship and climb aboard the ship, with some men being helped aboard the ship as the ship was about to turn to avoid a broadside target.

"Get those injured men down below," Lieutenant Curnow shouted as he watched the Portobello take a direct hit below the water line and begin to sink. He hoped all that could be saved had got away because it was now too late to save anyone else from its fate with the sea.

"Get those sails in order and make hast," Captain Horner shouted as the ship started to sail into the wind creating a distance the Dutch ships could not counter. It was time to retreat and fight another day or lose the ship in folly. The Dutch had had the day but the battle was not over that would come another day when HMS Antelope was fully repaired, and ready to fight another battle, he said to himself.

Black Eye and Maisha watched as the masts of the Portobello sunk beneath the waves and to its watery grave. Maisha had a few tears to wipe away as the ship finally met its grave and Black Eye wondered if he would ever captain another ship, he had spent many a moon on its decks and the ship had been a good companion over the years in good times and bad. Now, Black Eye considered the fate of his men and principally his good friend Two Coin. Had Two Coin made it to the safety of HMS Antelope or had he been killed along with many of his crew on the Portobello, he said to himself.

"I wonder if Two Coin made it." Maisha said to Black Eye. He was thinking more or less the same while watching the battle from the quarter deck with Maisha.

"I think I caught a glimpse of Lord Trethowan as he climbed aboard the ship with the help of two of our crew," Black Eye replied.

"It's easy to see a fat man in a crowd...they stick out like a sore thumb," Maisha said with laughter in her voice.

"Yes, you're right. We could make it down below now that we're far enough from the Dutch," Black Eye said as he and Maisha made their way down to the belly of the ship, to the doctor's space where they were amongst men with all sorts of injuries, and stepping over many that were already dead.

". ...over there!" Maisha shouted as she pointed out with her arm to the unmistakable figure of the man who was propped up against the wooden beam amongst other men with terrible injuries from the battle. Blood was everywhere. His huge gait was the giveaway and what flesh could be seen were covered in tattoos, it was Two Coin, she said to herself.

As Black Eye and Maisha clambered over men waiting their turn to be seen by the doctor their caught sight of Yuki and Nathaniel who were assisting the doctor in his endeavours to save the lives of men with appalling injuries. The moans and groans of men were like a chorus of death that lingered throughout the belly of the ship.

"Two Coin you made it!"

"Only just," Two Coin replied. His out stretched arm pointed to his right leg, which had been severed below the knee and had been wrapped in cloth to stop the bleeding.

"Doctor, this man needs attention," Black Eye shouted with urgency at the doctor.

Black Eye and Maisha carefully took hold of Two Coin on either side of the huge man and managed to make it to the makeshift table, which was now covered in blood. They could see the many parts of legs and arms that lay casually in a pile in the corner of the space.

"Lay him on the table," the doctor said.

"He's already lost a lot of blood," Maisha said anxiously as she hoped the doctor could save the man she counted as a good friend.

"Hold him down both sides and his leg, while I try to stop the bleeding," the doctor said as Yuki passed a hot iron sword from the wood fire that had been erected to cortisol wounds of injured men.

"Argh, argh, argh!"

The groan from Two Coin was mild compared to some of the screams Black Eye and Maisha had heard that day from men that had lost a leg or an arm. Two Coin was used to pain, he had fought many battles in his time and sustained many injuries over the years, but this was the worst so far, Black Eye thought.

***

The following day, Two Coin sought the ship's carpenter who was busy making temporary crude legs for the many men that had had their legs amputated by the doctor. Two Coin wanted the carpenter to fashion a wooden leg that would last his years rather than the crude wooden legs that the carpenter had made for some of the crew.

"Make me a leg with a secret part where I could stash a weapon if I wanted to," Two Coin stated to the carpenter.

"Why?" the carpenter asked.

"Look here is some silver for your time and just make like I say," Two Coin replied with a commanding tone of voice as he balanced on two wooden crutches.

"Okay, so be it," the carpenter said as Two Coin slowly hobbled away and up to the quarter deck where Black Eye and

Maisha stood admiring the scene as HMS Antelope sailed along the coast towards the port of Zanzibar.

"Good day."

"Is it?" Two Coin asked. He was in no mood to be pleasant having had the experience of losing a leg.

"Are we near to Zanzibar?" Two Coin asked Lieutenant Curnow, who was on watch.

"Yes, most likely tonight," Lieutenant Curnow replied tersely, who had watched Two Coin struggle with his crutches to reach the quarter deck.

"Why do you ask?" Black Eye asked Two Coin. He still looked pale in the face from the loss of blood and his leg.

"I would like to go ashore and buy myself some pleasure," Two Coin replied, who was lying, he had other intentions that he intended to keep secret even from his friend and captain. Maisha and Lieutenant Curnow both smiled at what Two Coin had said, and believed that he meant buying the pleasure of a female.

"You do understand that we'll not be docked at Zanzibar for long, but long enough to find what you want," Lieutenant Curnow said as a broad smile crept along his face like a baby with too much wind.

"Why are you in so much of a hurry don't you need to make repairs to the rigging and buy fresh supplies?" Two Coin asked the lieutenant incredulously, but he already knew why they were in a hurry to leave Zanzibar without waiting to make repairs to the ship.

"I guess you don't know, we are on another treasure hunt before we lose the pirates to sickness," Lieutenant Curnow replied with a mask of disbelief in his voice that Two Coin didn't know about the treasure from Black Eye or Maisha. Surely he thought, they would have told him before now, he said to himself as he watched the expressions on the faces of Black Eye and Maisha.

"No, I didn't," Two Coin replied as he too watched the expressions on the faces of his captain and Maisha.

"We were going to tell you when you got well again. The pirates Captain Kerry and Ironman Slim have more treasure hidden at Bombay in India, and we sail as soon as we can leave Zanzibar with fresh supplies," Black Eye said happily, with a broad smile to Two Coin.

"No need to brood Two Coin there is enough treasure to go around," Maisha said, who was trying to lift the spirits of her friend.

Chapter 17

It was early the following day that HMS Antelope entered the port of Zanzibar rather than the night before because the wind had dropped in its intensity. The port was a hive of activity, with many ships docked or anchored in the bay, with many people busily going about their business. Captain Horner and Lieutenant Curnow were stood on the quarter deck overseeing the docking of the ship. After HMS Antelope was secured to the dock, Captain Horner gave the order to release the pirates in to the busy port.

"Is that all the pirates released except for Captain Kerry and Ironman Slim?" Captain Horner asked Lieutenant Curnow as he heard the familiar sounds of people mulling about the port with the sounds of seagulls squawking relentlessly for attention. At times, the captain wondered, how the pirates released would fare among the population of the port. He had no choice; he said to himself, it would be a complete disaster for his crew and his ship if he continued to hold the pirates in the cells. He could not inform the local population of the sickness that had stricken his ship for fear of being barred from docking at the port.

"Yes all have been released," Lieutenant Curnow replied, who also worried what would become of the population, but it was orders he could not challenge, and he knew the risk to the ship was the main concern.

"Make hast with fresh supplies, before someone finds out we have released a sickness into their town," Captain Horner said to Lieutenant Curnow. Lieutenant Curnow had already listed the supplies needed for Lieutenant Hawkes as he watched through his telescope. Hawkes had made his way with six sailors and four marines to gather the supplies from the port traders.

"I have already sent Hawkes with crew and marines to gather the supplies we need," Lieutenant Curnow replied with a commanding tone of voice.

"Good man, what, what," Captain Horner said as he watched Two Coin hobble down the plank into the port.

"Where's Two Coin going?" Captain Horner asked curiously.

"I understand he needs the comfort of a woman," Lieutenant Curnow replied pertly.

Both the captain and the lieutenant laughed at the thought of what Two Coin was about to do, but neither knew Two Coin's true intentions, which had been kept a secret from Black Eye and Maisha as well.

Two Coin made his way along the port docks struggling to keep his balance on his new wooden leg with the aid of a wooden crutch when he saw the Inn he was looking for. It had been many years since he had last saw the Inn and the person he hoped to visit.

The 'Pirates' Inn' as it was called was as old as the town, which had been a pirates' haven when the town was first used as a safe port for pirate ships raiding shipping along the east coast of Africa, before the European countries made colonies of much of the continent. Back then pirates traded everything from slaves to gold and the town became well known for its slave market from where black slaves were transported around the world.

Two Coin stepped inside the Inn, and he was greeted with the noise of a busy place where patrons of all kinds from sailors to merchants were enjoying their ale amongst the female company. Some of the patrons were sat at tables playing cards and others just too interested in the women of the night that were gracefully employed to encourage the patrons to spend their money in the Inn.

There sat at one of the tables with only his flagon of ale sat the man Two Coin had come to see. He was much older than he last remembered him, but he still looked every inch a pirate. Perched on the pirate's right shoulder was a canary bird. The man still had the hat he remembered him wearing, it was a Spanish officer's hat, which Two Coin never remembered him wearing anything else. His beard was now longer and grey and dressed, and twirled into a point as before when it was black as tar. As Two Coin got closer to the man he noticed the unmistakable scar that ran from his right ear to his mouth. Dressed in a white shirt and pantaloons it was 'Harry the hat' for sure, he said to himself.

"Harry, it's me," Two Coin said as he stood in front of the table as Harry looked up from his sleep.

"Harry, it's me," the canary bird repeated in a squawking tone of voice.

"Two Coin is it really you, it's been a long time," Harry the hat said still half asleep from too much ale and time on his hands.

"Would you like some ale, sir?" the woman said.

"Yes, fetch some ale for us both," Two Coin replied as he pressed some coin into the woman's hand.

"What are you doing here?" Harry the hat asked with a mystified expression across his face like he had seen a ghost.

"Well, that's a long story and one I will tell you when we are alone," Two Coin replied as the woman came with two flagons of ale and placed them on the table and asked if he needed anything more, meaning the comfort of a woman, which is all the Inn offered was ale and the company of a woman and a room. Two Coin declined the offer, and continued his conversation with Harry when the woman had gone.

"Listen, I have gold and more treasure to come," Two Coin said as he whispered his words to Harry so none in the Inn could hear him speak and especially the bird.

"Treasure, you say from where?" Harry the hat asked with a voice so quiet his canary could not hear above the raucous patrons in the Inn.

"It's the treasure of Captain Kerry," Two Coin replied in a whisper.

"That rogue owes me," Harry the hat said as he remembered, the day Captain Kerry had drawn his cutlass across his face and left him for dead in a feud about gold in the local Inn.

"That rogue owes me," the canary squawked out loud to the patrons in the Inn.

"We need to move to a quiet place where we can talk," Two Coin said in a whisper again.

"Finish your ale, I have a place at the back of the bakers," Harry the hat said as he gobbled his ale in one long session, and waited for Two Coin to finish his ale.

As Two Coin hobbled out of the Inn and followed Harry to his place, Harry noticed that Two Coin had lost a leg and was struggling to keep up with him at his pace.

The walk along the docks towards the bakers wasn't far for Harry but Two Coin felt every step, because he still hadn't got used to having a wooden leg and relying on a crutch to keep his balance.

The room behind the local bakers wasn't much to write home about, but it was enough space to live and occasionally receive free bread from the baker. With just a bed and a small table and a couple of chairs and an outside toilet Harry felt lucky to have a stable home, he said to himself.

"Take a seat. I have some wine I've been saving for such an occasion," Harry the hat said as he watched his friend struggle to sit down.

"I have lots to speak about, but first you must leave this place as soon as possible," Two Coin said quietly as the canary bird was placed in a small cupboard by Harry.

"Hopefully, the bird will hear nothing," Harry the hat said, who was now worried at what Two Coin had said before.

"The captain of our ship has released many pirates that have a sickness, which we don't know what it is. Many on our ship fell ill with sickness and there have been several deaths. The sickness could sweep across the town like an ill wind," Two Coin said, who spoke in a whisper still fearing the threat of the canary bird repeating some of his words.

"You fear a plague then?" Harry the hat asked as he too spoke in a whisper.

"Yes, it looks like it. I suggest you move out somewhere into the country away from people and the sickness before it strikes you," Two Coin replied in a whisper as he watched the worried face of Harry appear to light up like the light from the moon.

"Is this the reason you came to see me?" Harry the hat asked as again he spoke in a whisper.

"Yes and no. I came to repay the debt I owe you for saving my life all those years ago," Two Coin replied as he pulled a small cloth bag tucked inside his shirt and placed it onto the table.

"What this?"

"It's yours for saving my life."

When Harry opened the bag and emptied the contents onto the table the gold doubloons shone like a ship's lantern in the dark. The gold glistened against the sun's rays of light through the only window to the room. Harry hadn't seen gold doubloons since his days with the pirate Captain Kerry. On the table there was enough gold to see out his days, he said to himself.

"All this gold for me," Harry the hat said out loud and momentarily forgetting his canary bird. His dark brown eyes lit up like candles flickering in the darkness.

"Shush! Yes, it's all yours."

In the bakers premises, stood the plump baker, looking on through a small knot hole in the wooden partition that separated the bakers from Harry's room. The baker had noticed the man with a wooden leg struggling to keep up with Harry as they made their way to the back of the building. The baker knew most of the gossip around town from his patrons that visited his shop and they told him everything, so it was natural in his nature to spy on his tenant when he knew he never had any visitors before this day. Everyone knew the baker as Barry the baker and the candlestick maker. There was a time when he did make candles from the excess fat produced during the preparation of his meat pies. However, he had stopped making candles to sell, but the nickname had stuck like honey to a beehive.

"Now, get you from this place as soon as possible. And speak to no one else or you may catch the sickness, Harry," Two Coin said. He hoped his friend would heed the warning before the town ran riot with the plague.

"Are you sure it's a plague?" Harry the hat asked in a whisper.

"Yes, it will strike at the weak and may kill them. Take your gold and flee into the countryside without stopping and wait there until you hear it's safe to return," Two Coin said with a hand shake as he prepared to leave his friend.

"Will I see you again?" Harry the hat asked as he watched his friend struggle to rise from his chair and balance himself again on his crutch to exit the room.

"Who knows but God," Two Coin replied as he waved his hand before exiting the back of the building and back to HMS Antelope.

Barry the baker had heard enough of the conversation between the two men to warrant the concern on his face. His plumb cheeks had turned reddish from the worry of what he had overheard and decided to take immediate action and saddle the horse and cart for the journey away from town with his wife and young son into the countryside.

***

Meanwhile, Yuki and Nathaniel were busy in the galley of HMS Antelope preparing food with the cook for the crew and the officers.

"Yuki, would you like to go into town with me?" Nathaniel asked. He was eager to explore whenever he got the chance and hadn't thought about the sickness that had ravaged the ship's crew like an ill wind that sweeps into your bones and leaves a chill.

"No, we are about to depart for India and I don't want to miss leaving this place. Don't you know why the pirates were released into town?" Yuki asked incredulously, that Nathaniel hadn't considered why the ship was docked at the port. Yuki hadn't seen love between a man and a woman and hadn't considered how much Nathaniel was now in love with her. Nathaniel was so smitten with her that he had only seen her and forgotten everything else, but his love for her.

"Two peas in a pod," the Chinese cook said, who had watched the lovers begin their romance from the start.

"Yes, we are," Yuki said as she smiled back at him with the innocence of a child at play.

"You are right, we don't want to miss the chance to sail to India and from there who knows," Nathaniel said happily that he had finally found his calling in life.

As Two Coin struggled up the plank and onto the deck of the ship, he was greeted by a raft of laughter and cheers from the crew and the officers on duty. He assumed they thought he had spent his time and money with a woman of the night, which he gleefully continued with the deceit.

"Two Coin have you had a good time my friend?" Black Eye asked shouting from the quarter deck.

"We sail soon as the crew have finished loading our fresh supplies," Lieutenant Curnow said, who was standing next to Black Eye and Maisha on the quarter deck.

"Not soon enough for me," Two Coin replied loudly and ready to play the game. If only they knew his true intentions, he said to himself as he made his way below deck.

**

As HMS Antelope upped anchor and began its journey out of the bay of Zanzibar towards its destination of Bombay, India the officers and the crew of the ship all in their own way wondered what fate laid ahead. Yuki and Nathaniel were standing on the quarter deck with Captain Horner who had given permission to them to witness the departure from Zanzibar with him. The captain wanted to be sure that Yuki understood his plans to drop her off at Bombay and from there he would find safe passage for her to her homeland of Siam. He had made a promise to her and he hoped this would suffice.

"I plan to drop you off at Bombay, India and find safe passage with another ship for you and Nathaniel to your homeland," Captain Horner said in a soft tone of voice.

"I thank you very much," Yuki said to the captain, who smiled back at the young girl's gratitude.

"And you Nathaniel, I suppose you want to stay with Yuki and visit her homeland?" the captain asked in his usual commanding manner.

"Yes, captain we are in love and I want to see Yuki's parents and ask for their permission to marry Yuki," Nathaniel replied is his upbeat manner, not thinking about anything else, but the love he had for Yuki.

"What about your parents Nathaniel won't they worry about you?" Captain Horner asked. He had witnessed the young lovers' romance from the very beginning, and it reminded him of his own days courting and the woman he married.

"I have told my cousin Jack… I mean Lieutenant Curnow to find the time to visit my parents and tell them about my plans to marry Yuki, and perhaps return to England one day," Nathaniel replied as he smiled at Yuki, and conveyed his thoughts and plans to the captain.

"Okay, its settled then, I will retire to my cabin and I expect you two to bring me a fine meal and some wine to toast our plans as soon as you can," Captain Horner said as he made his way down the stairs to his cabin.

"Yes, captain," Yuki and Nathaniel said, at the same time, as they too followed the captain down towards the galley to prepare some food for the captain.

Lieutenant Hawkes, who had been standing by the wheel house with the bosun had heard every word and wondered why the captain was so smitten with the two young lovers, and was jealous of his attentions and his lack of noticing his actions in the recent battle.

"We are making good sail with this wind," the bosun said.

"Just keep to your course, Serril," Lieutenant Hawkes said in an irritable tone of voice, which the bosun immediately noticed and wondered what had annoyed the lieutenant, because the crew and officers had wealth now, and could if they so wished retire in comfort from the gold that had been handed out. So what was it that the lieutenant was annoyed about, he said to himself.

Chapter 18

Meanwhile, two Dutch war ships had docked at the port of Zanzibar requiring fresh supplies and information from the Portuguese port authority. The Dutch commander sent out some officers and sailors with the task of finding out if any English ships had recently docked at the port. From the information gathered from a local man who had witnessed the departure of HMS Antelope, and heard from one of the pirates released that the ship was sailing towards Zinjibar, Yemen before heading for Bombay, India. The Dutch also witnessed the effects of the plague that had stricken the town soon after the English ship had released a number of pirates, and had set sail for its destination. The Portuguese port authority were angry with the English navy for releasing the pirates with the sickness they carried, and offered the Dutch as much help as they wanted. The two Dutch ships knew exactly what day the English navy had departed and what condition the ship was in before they too departed in earnest.

***

It had been several weeks since HMS Antelope's departure from Zanzibar as Captain Horner and Lieutenant Curnow sat at the table in the captain's quarters discussing their plans and the course to take to India when there was a knock at the door. It was Yuki and Nathaniel with food and wine for the table as the marine guarding the door allowed them into the cabin.

"Argh!"

"It's our food…something special I hope," the captain said as he smiled with satisfaction at the lingering pleasant smell of the food.

"It smells great!" Lieutenant Curnow said praising the thought of hot food with an empty belly.

"What is it?" the captain asked.

"It's a dish we call 'We Chong' in Siam. I asked the cook to seek out fresh fish at the port. I hope you enjoy," Yuki said, smiling at the captain and the lieutenant.

"I will miss your cooking when you leave us," the captain said, smiling, and happy in his mind that he would be fulfilling his promise to the girl.

"There is a favour I ask of you, captain?" Nathaniel asked as he stood proud before Captain Horner.

"And, what is that, what, what?" the captain asked.

"Yuki and I would like for you to marry us. I understand you have the authority to do so," Nathaniel said, hoping the captain would oblige the honor.

"Yes, of course it would be an honor. When do you expect this to take place?" the captain asked. He was also wondering when he would see his wife again.

"Tomorrow, midday if that is alright with you," Nathaniel replied as he gently took hold of Yuki's hand.

"Yes, we will hold the ceremony then. Now, go and make yourselves ready for tomorrow," the captain said as he watched the young lovers exit the cabin hand in hand.

"Your cousin has found his calling," the captain said as he ate his meal with thoughts of his younger days in his mind and the woman he married.

"Yes, I believe he has," the lieutenant said.

"Now, if we take the ship north towards Yemen along the coast of Africa we can then catch the trade winds to India, and sail south along their coast towards Bombay. What do you think of my plan?" Captain Horner asked as he took another gulp of wine from his flagon as he waited for the lieutenant to reply.

"Yes, precisely what I would have chosen rather than try to go against the winds and sail across the sea from here. We should also consider what the Dutch will do if they find out we are heading for India," Lieutenant Curnow replied. He knew it was wise and prudent not to disagree with the captain, but to always put a different scenario forward if there was one he could respect.

***

The following day, Captain Horner assembled the officers and crew on the upper deck of HMS Antelope, and on the quarter deck where he stood with Lieutenant Curnow, Yuki and Nathaniel under the midday sun and a calm sea, with only a fresh breeze from the east, he began the wedding proceedings.

"We are gathered here, today to wed Nathaniel Curnow and Yuki Tong under God's will and sacrifice."

"Do you take this woman Yuki Tong to love and forsake all others in sickness and wellness?"

"I do," Nathaniel replied.

"Do you take this man Nathaniel Curnow to love and forsake all others in sickness and wellness?"

"I do," Yuki replied.

Lieutenant Curnow now gave Nathaniel the only ring he possessed and placed it on the tiny finger of Yuki's left hand.

Lieutenant Curnow had the ship's blacksmith during the previous night make the ring small enough to fit Yuki's finger without it falling off.

"Place this ring on Yuki's finger and then you may kiss," Captain Horner said.

Nathaniel placed the ring on Yuki's finger like it fitted for all time and gently kissed Yuki on her lips.

"You two are now married under the law that is given to me by the Crown," Captain Horner said as he watched their embrace to raucous cheer and clapping from the officers and crew.

"Some rum for all," Captain Horner stated to Lieutenant Curnow as the lieutenant repeated the order to the assembled crowd.

"We shall retire to my quarters and celebrate with the young couple," Captain Horner said to Lieutenant Curnow as they made their way down to the captain's quarters where food and wine had been previously delivered by the cook for the celebration. On the table was an array of fresh fish and meat with bottles of wine for the occasion.

"Thank you, Captain Horner," Yuki said in a soft tone of voice with a smile so wide that it filled her face from cheek to cheek.

"Yes, thank you for all that you have done for us," Nathaniel said with an unassuming manner with genuine gratitude for what the captain had done for him and Yuki.

"I need to get Black Eye to the altar someday," Maisha said, who was then laughing at her own words.

"I will, I will," Black Eye said as he downed a large gulp of wine.

"Best wishes to you both," Lord Trethowan said. He had now recovered from his sickness and was now happy at the thought of more gold. Even Captain Flynn was looking forward to some treasure hunting before returning to England.

"All the best," Two Coin said to the young lovers as he tried to maintain his balance as the ship started to lurch from one side to the other, which didn't bother anyone else, only his reliance on his crutch and a wooden leg made it difficult for him.

"I will tell your parents what became of you and your plans with Yuki and of course your marriage when we finally return to England," Lieutenant Curnow said to Nathaniel as he watched the precarious antics of Two Coin trying to maintain his balance as the ship moved between the highs and lows of the ocean waves.

"Yes, and tell them not to worry, for Yuki and I will make it to England at some point in the future," Nathaniel replied as he too saw the plight of Two Coin, but everyone else wasn't bothered by the ship's movements.

***

It was over a week more before HMS Antelope reached the bay of the port town of Zinjibar, Yemen, which was well known for its slave market. Captain Horner hoped to send out a search party for any of the captives the pirates may have sold in the thriving slave market, and at the same time procure hemp rope so that the last of the rigging, which was destroyed in the previous battle with the Dutch, could be repaired. Without the hemp rope to repair the rigging the journey across the ocean between Yemen and India would be a fool's endeavour, and one the captain was eager to avoid without the necessary repairs to his ship.

As HMS Antelope made anchor in the bay, rather than at the docks of the port, because the captain felt it prudent to stay away from the docks, just in case he needed to escape the clutches of any unfriendly forces the Dutch may have induced to attack his ship. So, instead he chose to launch the rowing boat with several marines and sailors and Lieutenant Hawkes to organise and procure fresh supplies and enough hemp rope to finish repairing the rigging to the ship.

"So, Lieutenant Hawkes you have your orders and make hast and you Lieutenant Jones," Captain Horner said as he watched his men climb into their rowing boats.

"Yes, captain," Lieutenant Hawkes replied before he made his way to climb over the railing and down into the waiting rowing boat. Finally, he said to himself, the captain has the trust in him for this mission. It was now up to him to successfully carry out the mission for the captain.

"Lieutenant Jones, your mission is to check out the local slave market and retrieve any captives."

"Yes, captain."

Lieutenant Curnow watched the view through his telescope as Lieutenant Hawkes and Lieutenant Jones and their men made it to the port docks, and secured their boats to the docks. He could see Lieutenant Hawkes talking to a local man before him and his men continued towards one of the many warehouses that fronted the dock area. And he watched as Lieutenant Jones and his marines made their way into the town.

"Can you see Hawkes?"

"Yes, captain. He has entered a warehouse," Lieutenant Curnow replied.

"Well good, we just have to wait, what, what." the captain said in his usual abrupt manner.

"I hope he can cope with the responsibility," Lieutenant Curnow said sullenly.

"Well, I told him to make haste. He should know we're being followed most likely by the Dutch who could arrive at our anchor at any time."

"Without the hemp rope, we have little chance of making it across the ocean with the damage to our rigging," Lieutenant Curnow said.

"Yes, lieutenant I'm quite aware of that," Captain Horner said angrily at the thought of the lieutenant repeating his thoughts on the ship's capacity to handle the ocean between Zinjibar and India.

"Hopefully, he brings back what we need, otherwise, we are stuck here until we have the rope, like a fish out of the water," Lieutenant Curnow said.

"Yes, lieutenant we are indeed. What about the slave market? Has Lieutenant Jones been seen?" Captain Horner asked.

"Not yet."

"I hope we are not too late, if the pirates have off loaded any captives here," Captain Horner said.

The sound of wood being sawn and nailed kept the ship's carpenter and the crew busy trying to make the ship fully fit, but without the hemp rope to repair the rigging of the sails the voyage across the ocean wasn't a prospect the captain relished, so he hoped that Lieutenant Hawkes would soon return with supplies and rope, so that they could continue their journey, before the Dutch warships arrived on the scene.

Meanwhile, Lieutenant Hawkes and his men were busy securing fresh supplies from a warehouse near the docks. The warehouse was full of everything a ship's crew would want. The merchant trader even offered to deliver the goods to the docks for the lieutenant. After buying enough hemp rope, which was crucial to repair the rigging of HMS Antelope before it could sail to India, Lieutenant Hawkes thanked the Arab trader, and watched as the goods were loaded onto a horse drawn cart.

"Thanks for the cart," Lieutenant Hawkes said to the Arab merchant.

"You are welcome anytime," the Arab merchant replied as he watched the lieutenant and his men follow the horse and cart out of the warehouse towards the docks.

The Arab merchant was pleased with his sales, but was most pleased to learn of the lieutenant's plans. One of the lieutenant's men had said where their ship was heading for and this information was more valuable to the Arab then the sales to the lieutenant.

"I can see Lieutenant Hawkes with his men unloading the supplies into the boat," Lieutenant Curnow said as he stood on the quarter deck with Captain Horner, Black Eye and Maisha.

"Launch the other rowing boat to bring back the men," Captain Horner said as the order was repeated by Lieutenant Curnow down the ranks until the rowing boat was being man handled into the water.

Unbeknown to him was an Arab man called Sadiq Ahmed a local Inn keeper who was watching every move the lieutenant and his men were making. Sadiq Ahmed had seen the English frigate arrive in the bay and wondered where it was heading. Now, the Arab knew the English had procured fresh supplies from a local Arab merchant who he was friends with, and wondered what the merchant would have to say.

"I understand you sold supplies to the English this morning and what information did you find out?" Sadiq Ahmed asked. He knew the Arab merchant would have gleaned some information from the English.

"This information is worth coin," the Arab trader replied briskly, and not willing to give the information freely without payment.

"You can have the pick of my girls at the Inn and some ale if your information is good," Sadiq Ahmed said, who knew the Arab would not be able to resist the offer and feel like a king for the night.

"They are heading for India for treasure," the Arab trader said, who saw Sadiq Ahmed's eyes light up like a fire on a dark night.

"Yes good but where?" Sadiq Ahmed asked.

"Bombay."

"Here is some coin to keep your mouth shut and not to tell anyone what you have told me or you may find the point of a knife in your belly for payment," Sadiq Ahmed said intently, which made the Arab trader think twice not to cross him or else.

Sadiq Ahmed immediately made his way to the port authority to send a message to his business partner Sheik Abu Ben Ali, who was in Bombay securing deals with the local Indians.

***

Meanwhile, the crew of HMS Antelope had begun the task of repairing the ship's rigging from the hemp rope brought back by Lieutenant Hawkes. Captain Horner and Lieutenant Curnow stood on the quarter deck beside Black Eye and Maisha watching the frenetic activity of the crew trying to make repairs to the rigging at speed, following the urgency to set sail as soon as possible were the orders that came from the captain. In the meantime, Lieutenant Jones had returned without any captives having been told the pirates had sold their captives several weeks before HMS Antelope arrived in the port.

"How long before we can safely set sail?" Captain Horner asked Lieutenant Curnow in a husky voice as if he had a cold or something similar.

"Perhaps, by midday," Lieutenant Curnow replied as if he really knew the speed, at which the necessary repairs to the rigging could be made without risking the lives of any of the crew.

"Good, what, what," Captain Horner said as he surveyed the upper decks and saw how his men were working at speed to ready the ship for the open seas.

"The sooner we are away from here the better. I don't like the thought of us anchored in this bay, like a floating target for the Dutch," Black Eye said, who was only speaking his mind, and wondered if anyone else around him felt the same as he did.

"Captain Black Eye, you are not alone in your thoughts, because I feel the same as you do. That's why I have urged my crew that we make repairs as fast as possible, otherwise, we could end up a sitting target for the Dutch cannons.

"What happens if they arrive on the scene now, what would we do?" Maisha asked expecting a reply from the captain.

"Well, we could surrender or try and make a run for it even if the rigging is not fully repaired," Captain Horner replied.

"We still don't have enough men to man all our cannons, so I have organised the men to take control of both sides of the ship with the help of everyone aboard this ship. This means we're not wasting men on one side of the ship when not needed allowing us to fire cannons without serious delays," Lieutenant Curnow said as he watched the captain's reaction to his plans for action.

"This you did this without my orders, lieutenant?" Captain Horner asked intently. He wanted to know the reasoning behind the lieutenant's strategy.

"Yes, captain but with the knowledge that you would approve of my strategy should we wish to fight the Dutch with a good chance of success," Lieutenant Curnow replied intensely.

"Good, you are starting to think ahead of things, which I like in an officer under my command," Captain Horner said. He was well aware the lieutenant liked to make orders, but sometimes disliked taking orders.

"Thank you, captain."

"It's a good thing someone got his head on his shoulders, otherwise, we could end up at the bottom of the sea in a flash of light like lightning," Maisha said eloquently for just such an occasion.

***

It's was midday, as Lieutenant Curnow had predicted, when finally the repairs to the rigging were complete and HMS Antelope could set sail for India using the trade winds that allowed shipping to cross the vast ocean from west to east at that time of the year.

"With good weather and God willing, we shall see the coast of India within the cycle of the moon," Lieutenant Curnow said to the bosun at the wheel house on the quarter deck, as he stood on duty watching for any change in the weather, which could hamper the ship's progress to India. He had specific orders from the captain to maintain taut canvass at all times unless a storm was upon the horizon. From his telescope as he viewed the horizon he could see what looked like a formation of dark cumulus clouds, and heard the faint sound of thunder in the distance. It would be his decision to make but one he had to make before it was too late and the ship was suddenly forced into a storm without taking the right precautions.

"Storm approaching," the sailor shouted from the crows' nest.

Lieutenant Curnow didn't need another warning before he was issuing orders to slacken the canvass and have some of the rigging of sails rolled in. Within minutes, the ship was in almost in complete darkness as the ship entered the eye of the storm and the ship started to list from side to side like a piece of flotsam being tossed around without a care in the world. Suddenly, waves as tall as the smallest mast on the ship crashed over the ship and swept everything not fixed down out to sea with some of the crew hanging on to whatever they could to avoid being swept out to sea. Lieutenant Curnow hung onto the wheel house with the bosun as the huge waves crashed onto the quarter deck.

"Make hatches water tight," Lieutenant Curnow shouted to the crew on the upper deck who were hanging on for their lives as the waves crashed over them.

Lieutenant Curnow could see one of the upper deck hatches was wide open and allowing the sea to flood the decks below, and if allowed open for much longer risked the ship capsizing. Most of the crew, he could see, were hanging on for their lives and none seemed willing to get to the hatch and close it, There was only one option, he would have to close the hatch himself. As he crawled down the stairs and along the deck of the upper deck he was hit by a huge wave and pushed up against the railing of the ship. Lieutenant Curnow felt the grab of someone's hand in the darkness of the storm preventing him from being swept through the ship's railing and into the sea, and for a moment, he thought, it was the hand of God saving his life.

Turning around he saw it was Black Eye who had saved his life. If Black Eye hadn't grabbed his body, he felt sure he would have been swept into the sea and died.

"It's you...thank God you saved my life," Lieutenant Curnow said panting. He hadn't had time to think before Black Eye had crawled towards the hatch and was closing the hatch when another huge wave crashed over the upper deck and the two of them. Within seconds, the wave had gone and both men could see each other in what light there was under the dark clouds of the storm.

"There no time to waste...thanking me, we have to get below, and dry off before we get a fever," Black Eye said to Lieutenant Curnow hurriedly.

"Yes, of course you're right," Lieutenant Curnow replied, who was already starting to tremble.

"Follow me, and hold on to my shirt," Black Eye stated to Lieutenant Curnow as both men crawled towards the door to the lower decks below the quarter deck. Black Eye crawled like a large crocodile with each movement clinging to the deck like a man possessed while Lieutenant Curnow clung to his body and matched every movement forward with the same determination to hold on for his life as waves continued to crash across the upper deck and them. Black Eye saw the door and he reached up and flung it open and crawled inside with the lieutenant holding on as waves continued to hit the ship. Finally, both men were inside and able to breathe a sigh of relief that they had made it to safety.

"Now, we have to get you to the galley and get some dry clothes before you get a fever," Black Eye said hurriedly to Lieutenant Curnow knowing that the worst was over, and that they had been lucky to survive not being swept out to sea.

"Some wine will do as well," Lieutenant Curnow said as Black Eye strung his arm under the lieutenant's body and helped him down the stairs to the galley.

Both men were greeted by Yuki and Nathaniel trying to prepare hot food while the cooking fire was safely providing a warm place for many of the crew to sit and wait out the storm.

"Nathaniel your cousin needs hot food and some warm clothes for both of us...can you see to it?" Black Eye asked Nathaniel as one of the crew offered to help.

"Here...start to eat this," Yuki said to both men as they sat down at the table nearest the fire.

Yuki looked worried as she watched Black Eye and Lieutenant Curnow shivering from the cold and the wet clothes they were still dressed in. She steadied her balance every time the ship violently listed from one side to the other and wondered if the ship would withstand the storm outside. Nathaniel held her hand for comfort and reassurance, but he felt the same about the prospects of the ship not sinking, and wondered if he and Yuki would ever make it to her homeland safely.

"Here take these dry clothes and get warm!" the sailor said as he returned from below deck with a dry uniform for the lieutenant and clothes for Black Eye.

It wasn't long before Lieutenant Curnow and Black Eye started to recover from their ordeal outside, but both men had caught a chill and it showed in their speech.

"Are you feeling alright Jack?" Nathaniel asked Lieutenant Curnow as he noticed the sweat streaming down the lieutenant's face as was the same with Black Eye.

"You better take them to the doctor," Yuki said to Nathaniel as she worried that both men now had a fever. She had witnessed the signs of fever before and hoped it wasn't the sickness the pirates had brought to the ship. With the help of several sailors Nathaniel led Black Eye and Lieutenant Curnow down the stairs from the galley to the doctor's quarters, which wasn't much more than a makeshift room beside the ship's supplies.

"Doctor, these men have a fever can you help them?" Nathaniel asked as Black Eye and Lieutenant Curnow were laid down on two makeshift beds.

"What happened to these men?" the doctor asked. He immediately noticed the signs of the sickness, which had struck the crew of the ship like a plague, and was worried the plague was back.

"They were outside in the storm and got wet and cold and now have started to sweat," Nathaniel said to the doctor, who started to examine the men under their clothes for any signs of the plague that had befallen the ship only weeks before.

"Is it the sickness, we had from the pirates?" Nathaniel asked. He was worried if he and Yuki would catch the same sickness.

"No, it's not the sickness we had from the pirates…they just have a fever that will pass with rest and time…God willing," the doctor replied, who hoped he was right, otherwise, the sickness we passed on at Zanzibar would return and there wouldn't be anything he could do except pray, he said to himself.

"Thank God for that, you had me worried for a moment," Nathaniel said as he watched both Black Eye and his cousin Jack drift into sleep, which was the best remedy his mother would say to him when he got ill. Rest and sleep she would say was the best for most ills and he believed in her wisdom. He suddenly thought about his parents and hoped they were alright on the farm and hoped his cousin Jack when he returned to England would tell them of his marriage to Yuki and their plans for the future.

"They'll be alright here, you can get back to Yuki and help feed the hungry crew," said the doctor briskly, who wanted to be alone with Black Eye and Lieutenant Curnow, and find out some information from them when they awoke from their sleep.

***

It was several days, before the storm had fully dissipated, and the crew of HMS Antelope could get the ship back to normal. The rigging of the sails had been pulled taut to allow the ship to maintain a good speed with the trade winds, this allowed HMS Antelope to make up for lost time during the storm. Black Eye and Lieutenant Curnow had fully recovered, and were now standing on the quarter deck with the captain and Maisha viewing the activity of the crew as they practiced readiness with their cannons on the upper deck, with the below deck crews relying on a system of relayed orders from Captain Horner from the quarter deck.

"Fire!" Captain Horner shouted as the order was further relayed to each deck below by a series of junior officers shouting the order to fire their cannons. The practice of the cannon crews was needed because of the lack of enough men to man the cannons on both sides of the ship, so each crew on their respective deck was duly responsible for each side of the ship, which required each gun crew to be well organized and readied to fire at any moment.

"Ship ahoy," the sailor shouted posted in the crows' nest as Lieutenant Curnow looked up to the crows' nest for more information.

"Where?" Lieutenant Curnow asked the sailor in the crows' nest.

"On our port side," the sailor replied in the crows' nest.

Lieutenant Curnow quickly turned and began viewing the port side for the sight of the ship, when he noticed, the unmistakeable presence of a ship flying a Dutch flag, and the ship was heading straight for HMS Antelope at great speed.

Without thinking, he ordered the bosun to turn to starboard, so that HMS Antelope would not be caught broadside to the Dutch ship as it approached at speed.

"What was that?" Captain Horner asked in a commanding tone of voice, and not pleased with the lieutenant for superseding his authority while on the quarter deck.

"Ship ahoy," the sailor shouted from the crows' nest.

"Sorry, captain…it won't happen again," Lieutenant Curnow said as he quickly apologised for his actions.

"Full speed and turn to port," the captain shouted to the bosun as a volley of chain shot flew over the ship like a flock of birds in a formation of numbers.

"Fire!" Captain Horner shouted to the cannon crew on the upper deck, as he took cover behind the wheel house with Black Eye and Maisha, and with Lieutenant Curnow running down the stairs towards the cannon crew on the upper deck.

"Load the cannon with pellets," Lieutenant Curnow ordered to the gun crew as he waited for the order to fire from Captain Horner.

"Fire!" Captain Horner shouted just as another volley of chain shot just missed HMS Antelope.

"Fire!" Lieutenant Curnow shouted repeating the order from Captain Horner, who was now injured from stray pellets hitting the quarter deck like a downpour of relentless rain drops. Blood now covered the quarter deck as Captain Horner struggled to save himself from the barrage of cannon fire now hitting the ship from two Dutch war ships. Black Eye held the captain in his giant hands and felt the life of the captain slip away as Maisha tried to stop the blood from the captain's injuries, but it was too late the captain had died.

Lieutenant Curnow quickly took charge of HMS Antelope and ordered the bosun to turn to port to outflank the two opposing Dutch warships, which were bearing down on HMS Antelope like lions stoking their prey ready to pounce at any time they got the chance.

"Fire!" Lieutenant Curnow shouted at the gun crews as HMS Antelope fired back at the Dutch warships with a mix of cannon and shot to disable the Dutch ships, without fear of being fired upon because HMS Antelope had confused the Dutch officers as to the true intentions of the English ship's movement.

"Fire!" Lieutenant Curnow shouted again as HMS Antelope hit the Dutch warships with several volleys of chain shot, which cut the Dutch ships rigging to pieces and effectually ending their ability to counter manoeuvre.

"Load hot cannon and fire," Lieutenant Curnow shouted the order at his gun crews as HMS Antelope now had the upper hand in the battle.

When the hot cannon balls hit the Dutch warships they caught fire and started a panic aboard the Dutch ships as they started to burn from all directions. Men and boys were seen jumping into the sea to escape the inferno.

"Load the rowing boats and rescue those men," Lieutenant Curnow shouted to Lieutenant Hawkes as he ordered his men to search for survivors. Lieutenant Curnow respected the law of battle even if they were the enemy and hoped to save as many as he could.

"Get the captain's body down to his quarters," Lieutenant Curnow ordered the bosun, who immediately repeated the order to two of the crew who carried the captain's body down to his cabin.

"It looks like the Dutch are finished," Black Eye said as he viewed the Dutch ships through his telescope. Both of the Dutch ships were now in flames and there wasn't anything anyone could do to save the ships.

Lieutenant Curnow could also see through his telescope the destruction of the Dutch warships, and ordered his gun crews to stop firing as the fires aboard the Dutch ships would consume them within minutes. There was no point in trying to capture a burning ship for a prize, he said to himself.

"That's it then," Maisha said, who had witnessed the battle, and had wondered if they would come out on the winning side.

"Yes, we have survived and can continue on our journey to India without fear," Lieutenant Curnow said, who was willing to speak his mind, now that the captain had died, and he was now the acting captain of HMS Antelope. He had wanted to be captain of a ship at some future date, but not at the expense of losing a captain to battle and one that he had grown to respect. He would have to visit the dead captain's wife and tell her how her husband had served the navy with honor and respect from his officers and crew under his command.

***

The following day, Lieutenant Curnow conducted the funeral service for Captain Horner and the other members of the crew who had died in battle and now their bodies would be consumed by the sea. Lieutenant Curnow explained to those stood to attention on the upper deck of HMS Antelope how the captain had bravely served the navy in times of peace and war. He promised the crew that he hoped to live up to the standards of Captain Horner as the acting captain.

"We give up their bodies to the sea. Amen," Lieutenant Curnow said as he gave the signal for the bodies to be released into the sea.

When the crew of HMS Antelope were dismissed, Lord Trethowan and Captain Flynn joined Lieutenant Curnow on the quarter deck to view the activity of the crew rigging the sails for the journey across the Indian Ocean to India. Some of the crew were now made up from the survivors from the Dutch warships and as such were entitled to better food rations rather than the meagre rations issued to prisoners in HMS Antelope's prison cells.

"Can we trust these Dutch sailors to perform their duties?" Black Eye asked Lieutenant Curnow, who was now the acting captain of the ship, but still insisted that he be addressed as Lieutenant Curnow rather than captain.

"Yes, they have everything to lose and it's their choice to work or starve," Lieutenant Curnow replied, who knew what was at stake. The ship needed the help of the Dutch sailors to function correctly without over working the existing number of English sailors who were fit and well to carry out their duties. Lieutenant Curnow knew it was a risk to use prisoners of war as replacements for English sailors who had died in battle or succumbed to the sickness. It was a risk he felt he had to take so that the voyage to India could be made without hampering the efficiency of the ship.

"I hope you are right," Maisha said, who wasn't about to follow protocol, and it allowed her thoughts to be clearly spoken even if it upset the status quo.

"You haven't changed," Lieutenant Curnow said with a smile and a soft tone of voice as he looked at Maisha and Black Eye, as he continued his perusal of the crew going about their duties.

"How long before we reach India?" Lord Trethowan asked in his autocratic manner? He was eager to find the treasure and get back to England as soon as possible with his estate manager Captain Flynn.

"It all depends on the winds. If we have the wind we should reach the coast of India by the full moon, then, we have to sail down to Bombay, which could take some time," Lieutenant Curnow replied curtly. He was irritated by the question because it all depended on the mercy of God and the weather, he said to himself.

***

It was another week, before HMS Antelope arrived at the coast of India, and according to Lieutenant Curnow's calculations they were still hundreds of miles from Bombay in the south of India. Looking at his sea charts in the captain's quarters, where he now resided, and slept in, his visual location was north of Bombay, and still many miles tracking the coast down towards Bombay. As he stood, at the chart table, he heard a knock at the door guarded by two marines.

"Come in!"

"Oh, it's you, Black Eye and Maisha," Lieutenant Curnow said as he raised his head from surveying the sea charts.

"What can I do for you?" Lieutenant Curnow asked in an uninterested manner.

"When are we likely to reach Bombay?" Black Eye asked. He was now impatient to get to the treasure.

"You and everyone on this ship would like to know, but unfortunately I don't have that information," Lieutenant Curnow replied curtly.

"But, you must have an idea when we are likely to arrive at Bombay," Maisha interjected in her precocious manner, not wanting to be ignored from the conversation.

"If I guess then by full moon it all depends on the weather, and of course God willing," Lieutenant Curnow said, who was silent about the possible time, because he feared trouble amongst the officers and crew, whom he had noticed had started to have gold fever. He had already had to discipline a junior rank officer over an argument about treasure. He had already banned the playing of cards, because some of the crew were gambling their share of treasure and losing, which created a lot of resentment amongst the crew and officers.

"Okay, but I hope it's soon because I see a lot of frustration amongst the crew," Black Eye said, who already had gold fever as did many of the crew.

"Yes, I have noticed this. I will be giving a speech to all officers, marines and crew later, today. I hope to dispel any worries and arguments that may occur on our adventure to retrieve the treasure," Lieutenant Curnow said gloomily, to show Black Eye and Maisha that he was in control of the situation presented to him.

Suddenly, they all heard the sound of pistol fire as the door opened to the cabin and the marine said, "A marine has just shot one of the crew."

As Lieutenant Curnow, Black Eye and Maisha rushed to the stairs and up to the quarter deck to view what had happened they were met by the doctor who was already waiting on the quarter deck and covered in blood.

"What's happened, doctor?" Lieutenant Curnow asked anxiously.

"It's Lord Trethowan, he's seriously injured. He's been shot by one of your marines by accident," the doctor said nervously that worried Lieutenant Curnow and those that heard it.

"How did it happen?" Lieutenant Curnow asked in a concerned manner, even though he was no friend of Lord Trethowan, and he considered the man had no regard for his fellow man.

"Apparently, the marine was trying to hit an albatross and the gun shot hit the iron clasp on the main mast and was then directed towards Lord Trethowan, who was walking along the upper deck," the doctor replied.

"So just an unfortunate accident."

"Yes, an unfortunate accident."

In Lieutenant Curnow's mind, he had the feeling, that the crew and officers were getting restless, and the prospect of more treasure had raised the hopes and dreams of his men under his command, and it was time to calm the situation, before anything else happened aboard the ship.

"Lieutenant Hawkes, call the crew and officers on deck for roll call," Lieutenant Curnow said.

"Roll call," Lieutenant Hawkes shouted as a marine with a horn blew the sound for roll call on deck.

As the crew and junior ranks took their places for roll call, Lieutenant Curnow thought about what he was about to say to his men. He knew he had to calm the feelings of his men towards the prospect of more treasure, and the aspirations that they had.

As Black Eye, Maisha and Captain Flynn stood behind Lieutenant Curnow on the quarter deck, wondering, what the Lieutenant would have to say to his men. Yuki and Nathaniel stood below the quarter deck with the crew and officers wondering also what the acting captain would have to say. Everyone on the upper deck eyes were drawn to the acting captain, and waited patiently, for Lieutenant Curnow to speak. Dressed immaculately in his uniform and wearing the captain's sword, which glistened from the sun's rays reflecting off the sword.

"Today, Lord Trethowan was accidently shot. Later, we continue towards Bombay. Until, we reach Bombay, all guns and pistols will be locked away, and the marines will continue with their duties without any arms or swords. At battle stations call, all arms will be allowed. Any person caught gambling will forfeit their share of any treasure. All these orders are for your benefit, so any person caught fighting will also lose their share of any treasure. Anyone, breaking these orders will also face the lash. Any officer caught breaking the orders will be court marshalled under the rules of the navy under Crown rule. Dismissed," Lieutenant Curnow ordered as he watched his men get back to their duties.

***

"Your cousin Jack Curnow is now the captain and doing well," Yuki said to Nathaniel as she looked up to him.

"Yes, he makes me proud to be a Curnow and will honor the promise Captain Horner made to you," Nathaniel replied, smiling.

"Let's get back to the galley and to work," Yuki said, who was planning to cook a special meal for Lieutenant Curnow.

***

As Yuki and Nathaniel prepared food with the cook they wondered how long it would be before they would be on their own. The plan had been to find passage with another ship going to Siam and from the coast of Siam make their way back to Yuki's parents' home.

"I can't wait to see my parents and tell them of our marriage," Yuki said with a beaming smile from cheek to cheek as she talked to Nathaniel.

"It won't be long now. Jack told me within days we will arrive at Bombay, and he told me, everyone on board the ship will receive a share of any treasure found. Whatever happens, he has promised me enough coin to get back to Siam from his pocket if need be. Did you feel that, the ship has started to list, we must be in rough waters," Nathaniel said worriedly, as he remembered the last storm where the ship nearly sank.

"It's not a storm...the ship is turning," the cook said.

"Turning?" Nathaniel asked.

"Yes, it's turning to catch the wind," the cook replied.

"Yuki and I will take this food to the captain if you don't mind?" Nathaniel asked.

"Yes, go ahead you two, and take some wine," the cook replied.

***

As the knock at the door was heard by Lieutenant Curnow, Black Eye and Maisha they could already smell the aroma of hot food.

"Enter!"

The door to the captain's quarters was opened by one of the marines guarding the door. Yuki and Nathaniel saw Lieutenant Curnow, Black Eye and Maisha sat at the captain's table waiting to eat and drink.

"Eh, food!"

"What smells so good?" Lieutenant Curnow asked.

"It's a special dish; we call 'Tong Wong' in Siam. Its fresh fish with spices and rice," Yuki replied with a smile beaming across her face from cheek to cheek.

"I have also brought some wine for you and your guests," Nathaniel said.

"Yuki, you will be glad to know that within a few days you and Nathaniel can depart our ship and find passage to Siam," Lieutenant Curnow said.

"What about the treasure? We would like to share in any treasure, Jack sorry Lieutenant Curnow," Nathaniel said.

"Yes, you too will share as all aboard our ship will share in any treasure," Lieutenant Curnow replied.

"Don't worry, you may now leave us be," Lieutenant Curnow said.

As the door to the cabin shut, Lieutenant Curnow, Black Eye and Maisha continued with their conversation while tucking in with their food and wine.

"I will miss, Yuki's cooking...hopefully, our cook has picked up some useful tips from Yuki," Lieutenant Curnow said as all three of them laughed.

"Seriously, you have made a lot of promises to your men," Black Eye said curiously.

"Yes, some will be disappointed if no treasure is found," Maisha said, snappily, who was worried about gold fever aboard the ship.

"None more than our late captain, who I intend to honor," Lieutenant Curnow replied optimistically, like a man with gold fever on his mind.

Chapter 19

It was several days later, when HMS Antelope arrived at the bay of Bombay in calm waters ready for the final treasure quest. Lieutenant Curnow, Black Eye, Captain Flynn and Maisha stood on the quarter deck as the ship was positioned towards the docks and ready to lay anchor.

When HMS Antelope laid anchor at the Bombay docks, there was real excitement among all the crew and officers at the prospect of more treasure. Most of the crew and officers already had gold fever, and had been dreaming of how they would spend their share of the treasure to be found. Lieutenant Curnow had given orders for everyone aboard to not mention a word about treasure, fearing the worst that the local population would attack their party or the ship for treasure.

"Lieutenant Jones, I leave you in command."

"Yes, Lieutenant Curnow, I will follow your orders."

"Good, are you ready Captain Kerry and Ironman Slim?" Lieutenant Curnow asked briskly.

"Yes, we will need horse and cart to get there," Captain Kerry replied.

"Yes, that's in hand. I have sent men ahead to find such and supplies for the journey," Lieutenant Curnow said.

"How far is the treasure?" Black Eye asked. He was as eager as any man aboard HMS Antelope.

"A couple of days," Slim interjected, his huge gait stood out like a cat amongst birds.

"I hope you're right or we will be feeding you to the birds," Maisha interjected as everyone on the quarter deck laughed except for Captain Kerry and Ironman Slim.

Lieutenant Curnow noticed the docks were as busy as any docks he had visited before but there was a smell of excrement that floated in the waters around the ship. He was impatient for his men to return with the horse and cart with supplies before his party could go on their journey for the treasure. Looking through his telescope he saw the melee of people and carts transporting goods from ships to warehouses close to the docks.

There was no wind to blow away the smells that lingered like a winter cold in the heat of the early morning sun that day. Lieutenant Curnow had arranged for four marines and two sailors and Captain Kerry, Ironman Slim, Black Eye, Maisha, Captain Flynn, Nathaniel and Yuki to accompany him on the treasure quest. Yuki was brought along because Captain Kerry had said someone small was needed to retrieve the treasure from where it was hidden and Nathaniel came along because he didn't want to be away from his wife.

"I can see your men with horse and cart," Black Eye said.

"Good, I'm eager to get going," Lieutenant Curnow said.

As Lieutenant Curnow and his party made their way with horse and cart towards the outskirts of Bombay, and into the uncharted jungle with enough supplies to last several days, Lieutenant Curnow wondered, how long this treasure quest would last. He had the two pirates Captain Kerry and Ironman Slim chained with iron believing they may try to escape.

"I don't trust the pirates," Maisha said as she rode with Lieutenant Curnow and Black Eye in the cart.

"Nor do I, we have a deal with the pirates, but you never know if you can trust them to honor it," Lieutenant Curnow said sceptically.

The party followed the path led by the pirates, which had to be cleared by sailors with machetes. Lieutenant Curnow saw that daylight was fading, and wondered, what animals came out at night to feed on their prey. He had heard stories about the tigers that roamed these jungles, and how they could strike without warning, and wondered if just a fire burning all night would keep the animals away.

"It's getting darker…it soon will be night," Black Eye said.

"Yes, will make camp soon," Lieutenant Curnow said as he surveyed the surroundings for a suitable location to make camp for the night.

"Nathaniel, tell your cousin to look for a place away from the path," Yuki said in a concerned manner.

"Why, Yuki?" Nathaniel asked. He didn't understand the reasons behind Yuki's logic.

"Because the tiger will walk along the path and not travel through the jungle if it can. That is why," Yuki replied.

"Jack did you hear that?" Nathaniel asked.

"Yes, I did. It makes sense and I will do what Yuki suggests Nathaniel," Lieutenant Curnow said as he heard the different chorus of sounds from animals making them known. He could hear the sound of monkeys calling out through the jungle, and a cacophony of birds singing their tunes, and wondered, if a tiger was nearby, and hoped it would pass them by, he said to himself.

"Stop, over there…there's an outcrop of boulders. We will camp there for the night," Lieutenant Curnow shouted to his men leading the way.

"We will use the rocks for protection and form a barrier with prickly vines and twigs around our camp," Lieutenant Curnow said as he ordered his men to find suitable vegetation to form a barrier against any predators.

That night was spooky for many of the men as they had not experienced sleeping in a jungle before, and an unknown sound that came from the jungle made several men fear the worst. Some of the men had heard tales told about the tigers that roamed the jungle, and there were a few men that could not sleep for fear of being taken by a tiger.

"Look at the stars it's a clear night," Maisha said to Black Eye as they lay together trying to get to sleep without tents for cover.

"Did you hear that?" Black Eye asked. He wasn't frightened, but was curious of the many sounds that came from the jungle.

"You're not scared are you?" Maisha asked curiously, and knew the giant she lay with wasn't afraid, and that she was just having fun with him.

"No, just curious…it's at night when the sounds of the jungle are louder. It looks like Yuki and Nathaniel are already asleep," Black Eye said, as he surveyed his surroundings.

"No, it's because during the day the sounds are masked by the sound of us travelling with horse and cart…that's all," Maisha said.

"Yes, I guess you're right…as always," Black Eye said as he closed his eyes for the night.

It was early before the sun had risen for the day when the two marines on guard heard the sound like the sound of someone gurgling in the distant and paid no attention to it. The two marines heard not a sound when a giant tiger caught one of the marines by the neck and began to drag him into the jungle. The other marine was so in shock that he didn't immediately react and fire his flintlock at the animal.

"Quick fire!" Lieutenant Curnow shouted at the marine. Lieutenant Curnow, who had heard the commotion, was ready to fire his pistol when Black Eye lunged at the tiger with his cutlass and cut the tiger's head nearly from its torso. It was too late for the marine the tiger had already severed the man's spine in the vice like grip it had on the man's neck.

"We will have to bury both, otherwise, we will encourage other animals to stalk us," Lieutenant Curnow said as he gave orders to his men to bury the marine and the tiger.

"Why did the tiger attack us?" Maisha asked Yuki.

"Most likely the locals have killed most of the prey the tigers hunt. Tigers have a keen sense of smell and can smell food from a long distance away. They have no choice but to kill man," Yuki replied, who remembered the times when tigers would attack people from her village in Siam because the local lord had killed most of the prey in the area the tigers liked to hunt.

"Hopefully, we have seen the last of any tigers," Nathaniel said, who was worried for the safety of Yuki and himself.

"Why don't you get the pirates to dig the graves for the marine and the tiger?" Black Eye asked Lieutenant Curnow.

"We would have to unchain the pirates and I consider it too much of a risk. They could escape or kill one or two of my men. Then we would have come all this way without reward for our troubles. Now, do you see my logic?" Lieutenant Curnow asked. He wasn't about to risk anything at that stage of the treasure hunt.

"Yes, you're right…in this jungle we would never find them," Black Eye replied, who was eager to get moving and on towards the treasure without thinking ahead. It was early morning, and sweat had already started to pour from his head from the heat of the jungle, and he wasn't thinking clearly, he said to himself.

"He's too eager to get to the gold," Captain Flynn interjected, who had taken the place of Lord Trethowan to make sure he received his share of any treasure forthcoming.

"Yes, you're right…he's got gold fever," Maisha said, who knew everyone had gold fever except herself.

Lieutenant Curnow had few words to say at the burial service and just wanted to get to the treasure and get back to his ship as soon as possible. He would make sure the dead marine's family would receive his share of any treasure and would explain that the marine died in battle rather than the jaws of a tiger, he said to himself.

***

"Eh, Captain Kerry how long now?" Lieutenant Curnow shouted at Captain Kerry, who was just behind the sailors cutting the path way.

"Not long now, tomorrow morning," Captain Kerry replied loudly.

"Why so far?" Black Eye asked curiously.

"That's easy…because it's an old copper mine. And we wanted to be sure we were not followed by anyone from Bombay," Captain Kerry replied.

"Yes, because there are many bandits and thieves that operate around Bombay," Ironman Slim interjected.

"That's like calling a magpie a thief," Maisha interjected in her precocious manner.

"There's no love among thieves," Captain Kerry said, as he laughed at what he had said.

"I just hope it will be worth it," Lieutenant Curnow said to Captain Flynn as Nathaniel and Yuki who were sitting in the back of the cart heard what was said, and they both wondered, what if any would be their share, and would it be enough to start a new life in Siam.

That night as the party of treasure hunters gathered around the fire Lieutenant Curnow started to gather his thoughts for the following day. He had doubts about what the pirates had told him about the treasure, but he had travelled too far and risked so much not to continue onward and hoped for the best.

"Captain Kerry, you say we will arrive at the treasure, tomorrow…is that true?" Lieutenant Curnow asked. He was eager to interrogate the pirate for the truth.

"Yes, lieutenant as I said before," Captain Kerry replied.

"We will need Yuki to get into the small opening to get at the treasure," Ironman Slim said.

"Will you honor your side of the bargain?" Captain Kerry asked curiously.

"Yes, of course I will honor my side of the deal if you honor your side of the deal," Lieutenant Curnow replied curtly.

"That means a captain's share for Slim and I and freedom for both of us. That was the deal," Captain Kerry said in a commanding tone of voice, as he tried to commit Lieutenant Curnow to the deal with many witnesses hearing the terms.

"Yes, you two will have your share and freedom," Lieutenant Curnow said authoritatively, and that he planned to honor the agreement made by the late Captain Horner.

"Did you hear that noise?" Black Eye asked. He was worried another tiger was on the prowl.

"Is not a tiger…it's a monkey calling," Yuki said, who remembered the sound heard around her village at night when the monkeys would call their mates between their tree dwellings.

"I hope you're right, Yuki," Maisha said, who was worried another attack by a tiger was imminent.

"Well, we shall put more thorny branches and twigs around our camp just in case," Lieutenant Curnow said. He hoped this would calm any fears the group had that night.

***

The following morning, the group went on their way, and by the midday sun they came across the old mining caves that Captain Kerry had said was where the treasure was hidden. Most of the cave openings were now over grown with trees and vegetation after many years of being not in use.

"So, where is the treasure hidden?" Lieutenant Curnow asked Captain Kerry, who wished to get going as fast as possible.

"There…over there near that large outcrop of boulders is a small opening only a child can enter…in there is the treasure," Captain Kerry replied.

"Okay, I see it. Yuki are you ready to go into the opening?" Lieutenant Curnow asked. He was eager to get started.

"Yes, Lieutenant I'm ready," Yuki replied, as two sailors with machetes cleared the vegetation from the surrounding opening before Yuki saw how small the opening was. The opening was indeed small even for her child like gait. It would be a tight fit, but she concluded she would be able to manage the opening, she said to herself.

"Captain Kerry, how far inside is the treasure?" Lieutenant Curnow asked. He was concerned for Yuki's safety even though he had gold fever and was eager to see the treasure.

"Crawl in the length of a man and you will see the treasure plied high as the opening becomes larger. Yuki will see the treasure and have to pass it out somehow. You will have to make something for Yuki to pass the treasure out to us," Captain Kerry replied.

"Right, tie some rope to my hat and make a hole for the rope to go through and this will be our means to retrieve the treasure. We will use a long straight tree branch to push the hat to Yuki and she can call out when the hat needs to be pulled. Do you understand what we are going to do, Yuki?" Lieutenant Curnow asked.

"Yes, I understand, lieutenant, but first we have to make sure there are no snakes or other animals in the opening before I go in," Yuki said.

"Yes, of course."

"You men...light a fire and use that long tree branch to force out any animals in the opening," Lieutenant Curnow ordered his men.

After the smoke had cleared from the opening Yuki gingerly approached the opening with trepidation, as she squeezed herself through the narrow opening, hoping that there were no surprises from any animals that may have been still inside the opening, she said to herself.

"How is it inside?" Lieutenant Curnow called out has he arched over the front of the opening hoping to hear good news from Yuki.

"I have found the treasure...there is much?" Yuki replied, as she struggled to move her body into position to move the treasure.

"Push the hat into me," Yuki called out.

The treasure was all mingled together with one large chest. As Yuki opened the chest she saw the glint of gold and silver. She immediately knew the contents of the chest contained gold doubloons because she had seen the same coins before on Madagascar. Each time the hat was pushed into the opening Yuki placed as much as she could into the hat and called out for it to be retrieved.

"Lieutenant, there is a large chest here that will need to be pulled out with rope. Pass some rope into the opening," Yuki called out, wondering how the pirates were able to get this chest into the opening without a struggle.

Yuki tied the rope around the chest the best she could and called out for the rope to pull as she tried to guide the chest through the narrow opening. But the chest was stuck against the sides of the rock opening because of the rope around it. As much has she tried to move the chest it wouldn't budge.

"Cut the rope!" Lieutenant Curnow ordered his men.

"Now, try and push the chest Yuki," Lieutenant Curnow shouted.

Slowly, Yuki pushed the chest with all her strength and the chest gradually appeared at the front of the opening and the lieutenant's men took hold and pulled the chest clear of the opening. Yuki followed the chest and squeezed out of the hole to a roar of gratitude from everyone with a kiss and an embrace from Nathaniel, who now also had gold fever.

Lieutenant Curnow opened the chest to see the glint of gold and silver, as did Yuki before in the opening, and he was mesmerized by the sight of so much gold shinning in the daylight, that for few seconds, he was motionless like a statue. Everyone gathered around the chest to see how much gold the chest contained. Each gold doubloon was worth more than a sailor would earn in a year, and so the sailors and marines knew that their share of the treasure would be more than plenty to retire somewhere and live a comfortable life.

"To everyone here and those that have died will have their share that I swear on my honor," Lieutenant Curnow said as he spoke to everyone gathered around the chest. He was keen to dampen down everyone's excitement before anyone started to argue on the matter.

"We better load the cart and make hast," Black Eye said to Lieutenant Curnow in a courteous tone of voice.

"Yes, Black Eye."

"Load the gold and the chest and cover it well," Lieutenant Curnow ordered his men.

The return journey went quicker because the path was already cleared of vegetation and the party continued until it was too dark to travel. Lieutenant Curnow hoped there would be only the need for one night's camp before they made it back to Bombay. That night the party camped and made a huge fire to deter any animals especially tigers from coming near their camp. Most could not sleep but think about what they would do with their new found wealth, but some still feared an attack by a tiger.

"Lieutenant Curnow, when will you free us, and give us our share?" Captain Kerry asked. He watched the lieutenant's face like a hawk stalking its prey for any signs of betrayal.

"When we are aboard HMS Antelope and the treasure has been valued. Then you and Slim will have your share and be free to go. Can you wait until then?" Lieutenant Curnow asked. He intended to honor his and the late Captain Horner's bargain with the pirates.

"Yes, of course. I just wanted to know what your plans were with us. Did you hear that sound? It sounded like the growl of a tiger in the distance. Get your men to make lots of noise…because it'll scare the tiger away," Captain Kerry said.

"I heard it," Ironman Slim repeated.

"Yes, I heard it as well," Lieutenant Curnow repeated as he made orders for his men to make as much noise as possible.

"We all heard it…its best someone fires a pistol," Yuki said, who knew from previous experience that gun fire was an effective deterrent to the tiger coming any closer.

"Jack, fire your pistol…before that tiger comes our way," Nathaniel said to his cousin, who withdrew his pistol from his holster and aimed into the air and fired one shot.

"No need to fire your pistol, Captain Flynn," Maisha said, who noticed the captain was ready to fire his pistol as well.

"It won't hurt to fire off another shot to scare away the tiger," Captain Flynn replied with a conciliatory tone of voice, as he fired his pistol into the air. At that moment, the jungle came alive with all kinds of sounds, but mostly the sounds of monkey and bird calls.

The next morning, the treasure hunters broke camp early; Lieutenant Curnow hoped to reach HMS Antelope by the first signs of the evening. He hadn't had much sleep, as was his party, who were woken by any sound from the jungle. No one wanted to be taken by a tiger in their sleep. Most in the party of treasure hunters were still under the spell of gold fever, with their thoughts consumed by the dreams of what they would do with their new found fortune, only Maisha, managed to sleep through the night.

As the party headed towards Bombay with few stops they eventually started to smell the odour of human colonization. Most of the sewage eventually ended up in the rivers and in the end the sea. It was no surprise to the party they could smell the foul stenches that often lingered on the incoming wind.

"Can you smell that?" Captain Flynn asked out loud, as he walked beside the horse and cart that was weighted down with the treasure they had retrieved from the pirate's hideaway.

"Yes, it's unmistakeable, shit is shit," Lieutenant Curnow replied.

"Were not far from Bombay, that's for sure," Maisha interjected as she sat beside her man in the cart. "It's the same in London…the place sinks of shit."

"They need to engineer a means of dealing with the waste, otherwise, it will always stink like a pig's farm," Captain Flynn said has he thought about his future.

"What about you and Yuki?" Black Eye asked Nathaniel has he walked beside the cart with Yuki sat inside the cart with Maisha.

"We plan to return to Siam and find Yuki's parents, and then we will see what happens from there," Nathaniel replied has he smiled into the eyes of Yuki, who returned the smile from her child like face.

"Yuki, do you agree?" Maisha asked.

"Yes, that's what we have planned…from there, it's always in God's hands," Yuki replied, who explained what they had decided to do, that they had made no plans from the coin they had been promised from Lieutenant Curnow.

Soon they would see the scattered villages that bordered the out skirts of Bombay, and within a few hours, they would be at the docks in Bombay. As Lieutenant Curnow climbed a tree in the jungle for a better view of the surroundings, he saw the first signs of life.

"I can see the thatch roofs in the distance and farther, the buildings of Bombay," Lieutenant Curnow shouted.

"Good, we have no time to waste," Maisha said, who was eager to get back to the ship and back to normal with her man.

"Remember, we are due our freedom," Captain Kerry interjected as he directed his words towards the ears of Lieutenant Curnow as he climbed down from the tree.

"Let's move on with haste and with God's speed we will arrive before dark," Lieutenant Curnow said, who was worried about being attacked during the long walk through the back streets of Bombay where every thief and bagger-bond could lay waiting, especially at night.

"Yes…it's best not to think too far ahead…fate always has a way of finding its direction," Maisha said.

"Hopefully, we don't see the Dutch warships again," Captain Flynn said.

"Do you think we could encounter the Dutch again?" Lieutenant Curnow asked. He was intrigued to know what the captain thought.

"Yes, there's a good chance…they haven't given up…it all depends on their intelligence," Captain Flynn replied.

"The sooner we get back the sooner we can sail back to England," Lieutenant Curnow replied.

As the party reached the out skirts of Bombay, they had no knowledge that a rumour had been circulating for days within the local population that English men were on a treasure hunt. A local Arab had heard the rumour and knew the rumour to be true and had scouts out looking for the English and their return.

***

"Remember, they must be no survivors," Sheik Abu Ben Ali said, who had been paid before by the Dutch to attack the village of Trethowan in England, and now, had an even bigger reason to attack the English sailors.

Sheik Abu Ben Ali had men positioned along a narrow street, which the English would have to cross to get to the Bombay docks. His men each had pistols loaded and cutlass ready to cut the English to pieces and retrieve the gold for the sheik. As the English party came into view, one of the sheik's men opened fire and missed his target, allowing the English party to take cover behind their cart.

"Who's firing?" Black Eye asked anxiously.

"We are trapped here like ducks in a pond," Lieutenant Curnow replied, as he ordered his marines not to fire back, unless, they had a target to shoot at.

"I count at least five and perhaps more," Nathaniel said as he and Yuki took cover under the cart.

"We need to reach that wall over there," Yuki said has she pointed to the wall, which was perfect cover from the pistol fire.

"We will give you cover," Lieutenant Curnow said, has he ordered his men to open fire at their targets, while the rest of the party ran across the street to the cover of the wall.

"I've been hit," Nathaniel said has he rolled into the wall with great speed and held his leg in severe pain.

"Let me see it!" Maisha said.

"It's okay you will live," Maisha said to Nathaniel and Yuki, as Black Eye looked on with his pistol ready to fire.

"I've counted at least five," Captain Flynn said to Lieutenant Curnow worriedly.

Within seconds, more than twice that had been firing at the party rushed out from their hiding places and stormed Lieutenant Curnow and his men with cutlass and Arab scrabels blazing above their heads. Lieutenant Curnow, ordered his men to fire in unison, and four of the thieves fell to the ground dead or dying. The numbers were more even now, Lieutenant Curnow thought, as he had drawn his cutlass for the melee.

Captain Flynn drew his cutlass and rushed in like a man possessed, and cut down two of the thieves with two choice swipes, cutting the men so badly they lay bleeding to death.

With the party embraced in a man to man fight with swords and knifes, within minutes Lieutenant Curnow's men had saved the day with only the loss of one marine.

"Fetch that man here," Lieutenant Curnow shouted, who was almost out of breath as the sheik tried to get away without being seen.

"Bring him here."

"What's your name," Lieutenant Curnow asked has he pointed his cutlass at the man's neck.

"I know him…it's Sheik Abu Ben Ali," Captain Flynn said, who was surprised to see the Arab again.

"You know him?" Lieutenant Curnow asked Captain Flynn.

"Yes, he's a thief and works for the Dutch," Captain Flynn replied.

"Speak…you runt."

"Yes, I work for the Dutch. I was told to look out for your arrival and try to stop your departure," the sheik said with a croaky tone of voice with the point of the lieutenant's cutlass still pointing into his throat restricting his voice.

"How were you to stop our departure?" Lieutenant Curnow asked.

"Get the Indians to hold your ship at the docks claiming you had stolen treasure from the Indian government," the sheik replied.

"Have you told the Indians anything of our stay at the docks?" Lieutenant Curnow asked, eager to know exactly what the sheik had planned for HMS Antelope and his crew.

"No, I haven't told them anything."

"Well, you have to come with us, until, I decide what to do with you," Lieutenant Curnow said, as he withdrew his cutlass from the sheik's neck.

"Leave the bodies and let's make haste before we find an audience we don't want," Lieutenant Curnow said, as he mounted the cart and took the reins to move onwards.

***

It was later that day that the party arrived at the docks, and found HMS Antelope in good order. After loading the gold into the captain's quarters for safe keeping with two marines guarding the room Lieutenant Curnow spoke to his officers and crew and informed them of their good fortune and promised the gold would be shared by all aboard, and that included Captain Kerry and Ironman Slim.

"I have counted the gold and value and your share as agreed is on the table, Captain Kerry," Lieutenant Curnow said happily, and now he could conclude the deal with the pirates.

"Are we free to go?" Captain Kerry asked.

"Yes, you and Slim may go your way, but don't continue in your previous ways or you will see the rope at the end of gibbet," Lieutenant Curnow replied.

"I thank you, for keeping your promise to us. We will now be on our way," Captain Kerry said.

"Yes, thank you, Lieutenant Curnow," Ironman Slim interjected, as he and Captain Kerry made their way out of the cabin.

***

"The doctor says you will recover in a few days, Nathaniel. We will be on our way back to England within a short time. Here is your share and Yuki's share for your help in the treasure's recovery. I will tell your parents of your plans, and perhaps, see you again in England," Lieutenant Curnow said.

"We plan to stay in Bombay until my leg is healed, and then find passage to Siam," Nathaniel said.

"Yes, we will find passage to Siam to see my parents," Yuki said with tears in her eyes has she spoke the words. "Thank you, lieutenant for the coin, which will help us start a new life in Siam. Until the days we come back to England, I thank you for all that you have done for us."

Nathaniel and Yuki said goodbye to all their friends on HMS Antelope, and watched on the docks as the ship waved anchor and raised its sails and slowly sailed out of the harbor.

"I will see my cousin Jack again someday," Nathaniel said as he held Yuki's hand and walked away to find lodgings for the night.

"Make haste and steer a course south," Lieutenant Curnow said to the bosun at the wheelhouse on the quarter deck.

"Tonight, Lieutenant Jones, we will share the treasure between officers and crew," Lieutenant Curnow said, and then ordered his crew to make haste for England.

Nathaniel and Yuki, several days later, had secured passage on an Indian sloop with a cargo of spices heading for

Siam. Within weeks, Nathaniel and Yuki were in Siam, and walking into the village where Yuki's parents had almost given up hope of ever seeing their daughter again. Their parents surprise at seeing Yuki again was matched by their happiness, at knowing, she had found love with a man that loved her, and was willing to go where she wanted to go. It was several years later, that Nathaniel and Yuki took the long passage to England to start a new life to the village where it all started the village of Trethowan. Neither of them knew what lay ahead of them, but both Nathaniel and Yuki were still in love and that's all that mattered to them.